P9-CEI-816

SOPHIA KNEW SHE SHOULD LISTEN TO REASON

Sophia knew it was utter folly to pine after the unattainable Lord John Stokes when so many eligible gentlemen were pursuing her.

There was Lord John's best friend, the eminently attractive and appealing Sir Frederick Hawksworth, whom every other young lady in London society adored. There was Sophia's cousin, the dashing and magnetic Prince Misha Kirov, who used all his strength, wit, and wiles to urge her to abandon the England of her father and return with him to Mother Russia. And there was the sophisticated Comte d'Chaleur, as dangerously attractive as only a Frenchman could be.

Sophia knew she should listen to reason—but how could she when every time she saw Sir John, all she could hear was the wild beating of her heart . . . ?

Dear Reader:

As you know, Signet is proud to keep bringing you the best in romance and now we're happy to announce that we are now presenting you with even more of what you love!

The Regency has long been one of the most popular settings for romances and it's easy to see why. It was an age of elegance and opulence, of wickedness and wit. It was also a time of tumultuous change, the beginning of the modern age and the end of illusion, when money began to mean as much as birth, but still an age when manners often meant more than morality.

Now Signet has commissioned some of its finest authors to write some bigger romances—longer, lusher, more exquisitely sensuous than ever before—wonderful love stories that encompass even more of the flavor of this glittering and flamboyant age. We are calling them "Super Regencies" because they have been liberated from category conventions and have the room to take the Regency novel even further—to the limits of the Regency itself.

Because we want to bring you only the very best, we are publishing these books only on an occasional basis, only when we feel that we can bring you something special. The first of the Super Regencies, *Love in Disguise* by Edith Layton, was published in August to rave reviews and has won two awards. It was followed by two other outstanding titles, *The Guarded Heart* by Barbara Hazard, published in October and *Indigo Moon* by Patricia Rice, published in February. Watch for future Signet Super Regencies in upcoming months in your favorite bookstore.

Sincerely,

Hilary Ross
Associate Executive Editor

Lord John's Lady
Gayle Buck

A SIGNET BOOK

NEW AMERICAN LIBRARY

NAL BOOKS ARE AVAILABLE AT QUANTITY DISCOUNTS WHEN USED TO
PROMOTE PRODUCTS OR SERVICES. FOR INFORMATION PLEASE WRITE TO
PREMIUM MARKETING DIVISION, NEW AMERICAN LIBRARY,
1633 BROADWAY, NEW YORK, NEW YORK 10019.

Copyright © 1988 by Gayle Buck

All rights reserved

SIGNET TRADEMARK U.S.REG. PAT. OFF. AND FOREIGN COUNTRIES
REGISTERED TRADEMARK—MARCA REGISTRADA
HECHO EN CHICAGO, U.S.A.

SIGNET, SIGNET CLASSIC, MENTOR, ONYX, PLUME,
MERIDIAN and NAL BOOKS are published by
NAL PENGUIN INC., 1633 Broadway, New York, New York 10019.

First Printing, March, 1988

1 2 3 4 5 6 7 8 9

PRINTED IN THE UNITED STATES OF AMERICA

1

LORD JOHN Anthony Peter Stokes stood on the
fringe of the glittering crowd. A faint smile touched his lips
and he nodded to those acquaintances who chanced to
catch sight of him in the shadow of a heavy marble
column. He had deliberately chosen his post beside the
column for its semi-seclusion from the heavy press of the
restless company.

In his capacity as undersecretary to the British
ambassador to St. Petersburg, Lord John had assiduously
attended to his diplomatic duties. He had made the rounds
of the ballroom to leisurely chat with his Russian
acquaintances and to bow with negligent ease to their
magnificently bejeweled ladies. His pleasant countenance
reflected interest only in his elegant surroundings and his
companions. None of those whom he conversed with so
pleasantly guessed that Lord John would have preferred
not to have attended the ball that evening.

Lord John suffered from boredom and readily admitted
it to himself. He had attended twenty-seven social functions that same week, and the allure and novelty of the
sumptuous gatherings had long since palled. Hence he had
suspended his diplomatic duties long enough to enjoy the
few moments of privacy his vantage point gave him.

Lord John idly watched the constantly shifting crowd
and the graceful couples twirling around the polished
mirrorlike ballroom floor. Gradually he became conscious
of voices engaged in conversation on the other side of the
wide column upon which he leaned. Lord John started to
step away before he became an eavesdropper, but the
young woman's next words, spoken in prettily accented
English, riveted him.

"But I do not wish to marry Prince Tarkovich. How dare you contract my hand without my consent!"

The other woman answered with a hint of sharpness. "You have been told to speak your mother tongue, Sophia."

"Indeed, my mother's native tongue was Russian. But my father's tongue was English and I am equally proud of my English heritage," said the young woman.

Lord John's curiosity was thoroughly aroused. He moved slightly so that he could glance between the marble column and the velvet, brocaded window draperies. The young woman was petite and blond and utterly charming in profile. The older woman was also of small stature and handsome, but she was overly adorned with several bracelets and a massive diamond necklace.

"You are extremely foolish, Sophia. What means your English blood here in this, the most glorious capital of the world? You would do well instead to remember that your destiny is Russian. You will live and die a Russian," the older woman said empthatically.

"If by that you mean that I shall marry Prince Tarkovich, Aunt, you are mistaken. You cannot force me to the altar when my heart is not engaged," said Sophia.

Her companion snorted in disdain. "Your heart! What has that to do with a marriage of convenience?"

"That is precisely my point," said Sophia. "I do not intend to wed without love, Aunt. I have seen too many husbands and wives made unhappy because they married without love. I do not wish to be one of their number."

"The ones you have seen unhappy are those who have not yet taken a lover," said the older woman matter-of-factly. "I speak from experience, Sophia. I myself have enjoyed several lovers through the years."

Color rose in Sophia's face at her aunt's unexpected crudity even though she had long ago become accustomed to the Russian penchant for frank speech on delicate topics.

The older woman's dark slanted eyes mocked her niece. She nodded at Sophia's blush. "I see you are truly your father's daughter, Sophia. The cold English and their prudish ways! I am somehow disappointed in my late sister.''

Sophia threw up her head and stared coldly at her aunt. Her embarrassment was forgotten. "You shall not speak of my mother, madame.''

"In truth, your mother is of the past, and we do not speak of her tonight. Sophia, this evening you shall give Prince Tarkovich encouragement,'' said the older woman.

"And if I do not?'' asked Sophia, her eyes narrowing.

The older woman shrugged. "I shall regret very much the necessity of sending you to the summer dacha, naturally.'' She paused to watch the effect of her words, but her niece's gaze did not falter. "And afterward, if you continue to defy me, you will fulfill your destiny in a nunnery.'' With satisfaction she took note of the shudder that ran through her niece's slender form. She smiled gently. "But I know you to be a sensible girl, Sophia. Come, Prince Tarkovich must not be kept waiting. It is for a few moments only. And then you may dance to your heart's content.''

Much subdued, Sophia followed her aunt across the crowded ballroom. Her thoughts were in turmoil. She dared not publicly defy her aunt, for she knew that Princess Elizaveta Kirov's threats were not idle. But perhaps later, when she had time to think, some options would present themselves to her. In the meantime she could only hope that Prince Tarkovich would take an instant dislike to her.

Unnoticed, Lord John watched the ladies go. His blue eyes had darkened to gray with anger by the conversation he had overheard. He thought it was unspeakable that a young woman of proud spirit and beauty should be brow-beaten in such a fashion. His sense of boredom gone, he crossed the ballroom, keeping the two unknown women in sight.

The ladies approached a small knot of Russian noble-men, who greeted them courteously. Lord Stokes sauntered closer for a better view of the gentlemen in the group, wondering which of them could be Prince Tarko-vich. He recalled the name, but to his knowledge he had never met the gentleman at any of the countless social functions he had attended during his two years of service in St. Petersburg. However, that was not unusual because there were numerous minor provincial princes who made but rare trips to the capital.

Sophia covertly eyed the tall silver-haired nobleman to whom her aunt was speaking. After the initial greeting she did not pay attention to what they were saying, but studied the Russian. The gentleman was well-set. Ribbons and orders decorated his broad chest. His eyes were deep-set and clever and she liked the warmth in his gaze when their glances met. Perhaps her aunt's choice for her was not so unreasonable as she had supposed. Sophia thought that given time she might develop a fondness for such a man. The gentleman was much older than she, but many such marriages managed very well.

Then the Russian took Sophia's hand and gently turned her toward a nobleman seated behind them in a heavy ornate chair. Sophia's immediate feeling was shock that a living being could be so grotesquely fat. The nobleman was a mound of flesh upholstered in rich brocade. His massively jowled face was pudding-white and his small eyes peered forth like black currants pressed into dough.

The nobleman beside her spoke. "My prince, allow me to present your affiancéd bride, Miss Sophia Wyndham."

A nightmarish feeling enveloped Sophia as she stared at the huge nobleman. Her brain could barely grasp that this gargantuan was Prince Tarkovich. The nobleman gave her hand to the prince and stepped back. Sophia felt her hand engulfed by the prince's soft, hot palm. She felt as though she would faint, but her social training had been rigorous. Still in shock, Sophia managed to curtsy, her head bowed.

Prince Tarkovich made no effort to rise from his chair. He stared Sophia up and down, and his wide red mouth turned down. "She's a pretty-enough piece, I suppose. Does she have an appetite?"

The tall Russian nobleman quirked a brow toward

Princess Kirov, who blinked at the abrupt question before she answered. "Indeed, your highness. My little Sophia has a healthy appetite at the table, I assure you."

The prince at last released Sophia's hand. He transferred his hard gaze to Princess Kirov. "Then fatten her up at once, madame. The contract does not obligate me to bed a broomstick."

Princess Kirov bowed, still somewhat taken aback but recovering. "Of course, my prince. I promise you that you shall hardly recognize your bride as this same underfed young lady."

"You have two months, madame," Prince Tarkovich said with finality. From the box on his knees he brought a bonbon up to his eyes and inspected it greedily before he popped it into his mouth. A rivulet of chocolate drooled down his quivering chins.

There was a short silence as the ladies stared at the man. Princess Kirov recalled herself. "Rest assured that my dear Sophia will receive the nourishment and attention that her position as your prospective bride demands," said Princess Kirov, throwing a steely glance at her niece's unnaturally white face.

Prince Tarkovich appeared to lose interest in the conversation. He lifted another bonbon.

The tall nobleman cleared his throat. "Prince Tarkovich will be in contact with you, Princess Kirov." He graciously separated the ladies from the circle of hangers-on around Prince Tarkovich. He bowed to Princess Kirov with correct courtesy, but lingered over Sophia's hand as he shrewdly inspected her pale face. He gave her fingers a reassuring squeeze. "You may count on myself as your most devout friend and servant, mademoiselle," he said, his voice deep with meaning.

Sophia did not respond. Her shock was too great. The nobleman smiled faintly. He bowed and went back to his prince.

Princess Kirov watched him go with satisfaction. "It went very well. You are to be congratulated, Sophia. You have successfully gotten yourself a wealthy bridegroom

whose family is well-connected at court. And unless I am
mistaken, you have also attracted a most suitable nobleman to become your first lover."

Her aunt's words penetrated the hard frozen shell about
Sophia. Her mind whirled and she perceptively swayed.
Princess Kirov took her arm in an unexpectedly gentle
grip. "You are overcome, Sophia, and no wonder! It is too
much for a young woman to take in such good fortune all
at once."

Sophia shook off her aunt's hand. "You mean to marry
me to that—that monstrosity!" She choked hoarsely.

"Prince Tarkovich's family is powerful, Sophia. It will
be advantageous for the Kirovs to be linked with them."
Princess Kirov shrugged. "The prince is not handsome,
no. But he will soon eat himself into the grave and then
you will be very comfortable, Sophia. Remember that,
niece, and smile. Now, come and be seated by that window
where it is cooler. I do not wish you to faint. You have
your dance card, of course. And I see that it is nearly full.
Very good. Prince Tarkovich will see the grace of the jewel
that he acquires. When he overhears the admiration your
dancing evokes, perhaps then he will not want you so very
fat."

Sophia shuddered. She felt herself suffocating, but she
could think of nothing that could extricate her from the
grip of her nightmare. Numbly she allowed her aunt to
lead her off.

Lord John stood rooted as he watched the young woman
follow in the wake of her imperious aunt. The drifting of
the crowd had carried him near enough to overhear
snatches of the ladies' last conversation, and he was
appalled and repulsed.

A hand clasped Lord John's shoulder. His diplomatic
training asserted itself and his expression was properly
bland when he turned. He was relieved to see his closest
friend, Sir Frederick Hawkesworth. "Lord, Freddy, you
gave me a start."

"Had your eye on a beauty, did you? Well, if you hope
to dance with her this evening mark her card posthaste."

Sir Frederick good naturedly glanced around. "A devilish squeeze, ain't it? I think every titled nonentity in the country has come to this one."

"Indeed," said Lord John absently, his eyes again seeking out the young blond woman, Sophia. His friend's casual words had given him an idea.

Sir Fredrick laughed, sensing his distraction. "One can see that your thoughts are still with some fair goddess. I wish you good hunting, Stokes. Only make certain that her husband is not the jealous sort."

Lord John smiled. "You may be sure of that, Freddy." His friend went off. It was but the work of a moment to discover from an acquaintance the young woman's identity. Lord John sauntered over to write his name on Miss Sophia Wyndham's dance card.

Sophia hardly noticed Lord John's approach and her replies to his civilities were mechanical. Lord John saw with a glance at the dance card that there were several ahead of him. After a few more words to Princess Kirov, Lord John bowed to the ladies and retreated.

"Sophia, you must do better. That is the third gentleman you have snubbed. Even though he is English, he is handsome and deserves your respect," said Princess Kirov with asperity. Her niece turned on her such a glance of indifference that she was taken aback. Thereafter Princess Kirov held her tongue and Sophia was grateful for it.

Sophia went through the motions as each partner claimed her, but even her deep distraction could not completely hinder her natural grace on the dance floor.

Lord John, who had observed her even as he conversed with several acquaintances, was filled with admiration for the young lady's tight control. His chivalric instincts had been aroused by her plight, and it was gratifying to him to see that she was made of stern stuff.

Eventually Lord John presented himself to Miss Wyndham. He bowed politely to her aunt, who graciously dignified him with a nod, before he led out his partner.

Sophia had long since resigned herself to the farce of pretending enjoyment in the evening. She pinned on a polite smile and gathered herself to pursue the typical banal conversation with her new partner. It came as a shock to be addressed in a conspiratorial whisper.

"Mademoiselle, forgive my presumption, but the destiny outlined for you with Prince Tarkovich is preposterous."

2

Startled, Sophia looked up. Her partner's expression was distantly polite and she thought she had been mistaken in hearing such an incredible statement from him. Then her gaze focused on Lord John's eyes, which were alive with warmth and mirth.

Lord John smiled down at her reassuringly. "I am not a clairvoyant, mademoiselle. Alas, embarrassing as it is to admit, I am but a humble eavesdropper. And I hope that I may be of some service to you."

Swift color warmed Sophia's face, but her gaze remained steady. "You interest me profoundly, sir. Who are you?"

"Lord John Stokes, Undersecretary to his Excellency the British Ambassador to St. Petersburg," said Lord John. "And you are Mademoiselle Sophia Wyndham, betrothed against your will to a certain prince. I have seen the gentleman. He is unworthy of you, mademoiselle."

There was a dry note in his voice that made Sophia laugh. She eyed him with a great deal of interest. "Indeed, sir, so I believe. However, my aunt thinks otherwise. But then you must know that if you overheard so much." She tried to recall when he could have been so near and yet gone unnoticed by herself or her aunt.

Lord John read her mind and grinned. "The window recess and its marble column provided me with ample cover to satisfy my lamentable curiosity, mademoiselle."

Sophia nodded, satisfied. She arched her brows. "Surely such all-consuming curiosity is a detriment to your career, my lord."

"On the contrary. Curiosity and the ability to skulk in odd corners are prime qualities for a diplomat," said Lord

John swiftly, the twinkle in his eye belying the gravity of
his expression.

Sophia giggled, delighted, and shook her head. "I am
indebted to you, my lord. I had quite thought that I had
lost the capacity to laugh."

"We English are known for our ability to smile even
when under fire," said Lord John evenly. "I salute your
spirit, my lady. I did understand correctly that your father
was an Englishman?"

Sophia was once again startled. "You did indeed hear
much, my lord," she said quietly. She began to wonder at
the depth of the gentleman's interest in her. Her manner
was perceptibly cooler when she again met his gaze.
"What is your concern with me, my lord?"

Lord John immediately sensed her withdrawal and
appreciated the reason behind her belated wariness. "I
mentioned at the outset that I wished to be of service to
you if I possibly could, mademoiselle. Every sensibility
must revolt at the manner in which you are being treated."

Sophia shook her head somberly, and the pall that had
lifted so briefly once more settled over her spirits. "You
are kind, my lord, but there is nothing anyone can do. My
aunt is a determined woman who usually manages to gain
her way. I shall fight her, of course, but . . ."

Lord John did not need her to complete her thought. He
thought he understood fairly well the predicament that she
found herself in. A spirited young lady would naturally be
appalled at the thought of being incarcerated in a nunnery.
"Do you have relatives in England, Miss Wyndham?" he
asked gently.

Sophia nodded and flashed him a smile of gratitude for
his tact in changing the subject. "My uncle and aunt live in
London. My mother encouraged me to correspond with
them after we returned to Russia. She often expressed the
desire to one day accept their entreaties to return to
England and live near them. I think that, even though my
mother was Russian, she became increasingly homesick for
the land that held so many good memories for her. But her
health was never strong and she could not travel far.

Toward the last she urged me to go alone to England, to my uncle and aunt."

"But you would not leave her alone," said Lord John softly.

Sophia shook her head and gave him a tremulous smile. "I am at times a very stubborn creature, my lord."

"Do you still correspond with your uncle?" asked Lord John.

Sophia nodded. "Quite often, though my Russian aunt, Princess Elizaveta Kirov, disapproves. She wishes me to forget my English blood. In his last letter my uncle asked me once more to come to London and I wished very much to go now that Mama is gone. But Princess Kirov will not hear of it."

The waltz ended. Lord John and Sophia parted, but he retained hold of her hand and drew her fingers through his crooked elbow. "I would like an ice and I will count it an honor if you would accompany me, Miss Wyndham."

Sophia was not particularly anxious to return to her aunt's side and she enjoyed Lord John's company, so she readily agreed. They crossed to a refreshment table and then leisurely began to make their way back through the crowd. Lord John kept up an amusing commentary and Sophia surprised herself by giving way to laughter more than once. She knew that she would regret saying good-bye to Lord John when he had returned her to Princess Kirov's chaperonage.

For his part, Lord John scanned the company alertly, his expression betraying none of the determination within him. At last he spotted the gentleman he wished to see and blessed his good fortune that the gentleman had chosen that moment to discreetly retire alone to a window embrasure for a cigar.

With seeming casualness Lord Stokes led Sophia over to the gentleman and pleasantly addressed him.

The gentleman turned and his pensive face lighted up. "Glad to see you, John. I've another pretty puzzle for you to handle. The bureaucracy has fouled once more."

Lord John sighed with mock resignation. "Of course, my lord. I am delighted to be of service."

His lordship laughed heartily. "Indeed, and I know it." Still with the twinkle in his eye, he looked at Sophia, and said in Russian, "And who might this charming lady be?"

"My lord, allow me to present a fellow countrywoman, Miss Sophia Wyndham," said Lord John. He smiled down into Sophia's startled blue eyes. "This gentleman is my employer, Lord Cathcart, His Excellency the British Ambassador to St. Petersburg."

Lord Cathcart's expression was momentarily startled, but he quickly recovered. He took Sophia's hand and held it between both of his. "My dear Miss Wyndham, I am delighted to make your acquaintance. I had not heard of your arrival in St. Petersburg."

Lord John interjected. "Miss Wyndham has resided with her Russian aunt since her widowed mother's death last year, my lord. She hopes to permanently join her uncle and aunt in London in the near future."

"Indeed, then I must wish you a comfortable journey, my dear. The distance is daunting, but the thought of breathing England's sweet air again is reward enough for any of us, heh?" said Lord Carthcart genially.

His pleasantries seemed to strike a false note, for instead of responding in kind, Miss Wyndham's face fell. Lord Cathcart was appalled when tears formed in her extraordinary blue-gray eyes. "Forgive me, my lord. I had not intended . . ." She ended on a shaky laugh.

Lord Cathcart had enjoyed a long and distinguished career in diplomacy. Seldom had he felt himself at a loss for words, but the experience had always been a peculiarly unpleasant one. He felt just such a sensation in that moment and he looked to his undersecretary for assistance.

Lord John smoothly entered the breech. "Miss Wyndham's aunt has refused to allow her to leave Russia, possibly because she has contracted the lady's unwilling hand in marriage to a certain minor prince."

Lord Cathcart glowered at his undersecretary, understanding in an instant how finely he had been trapped. Part of his mind acknowledged that Lord John had exhibited a finesse worthy of a born diplomat. The boy could go far, he thought with grudging admiration. But his uppermost feeling was of outrage that Lord John knew his sensibilities so well and could play them with such uncanny accuracy. Matters were not helped by the lady's obvious unhappiness. She was attempting to put a brave front on it, and was dabbing at her eyes with a scrap of lace that had appeared from nowhere that he could see. She was so like his own little Elizabeth, who before her recent marriage had turned to him whenever she was troubled. Lord Cathcart steeled his melting resolve. He glanced at Lord John and his voice took on a firm tone. "I apologize for unwittingly upsetting you, Miss Wyndham. I fear that I must be unpleasantly frank with you, however. Lord John has led you to believe that I may be of help to you in fleeing from Russia, but—"

"But he never said a word!" exclaimed Sophia. She turned suddenly shining eyes on Lord John. "Oh, sir! You have been so kind. I would not ever have thought of appealing to the British embassy, but of course I can, for I was born in England."

Lord Cathcart was taken aback. With a lowering feeling of having stepped into quicksand, he glared at Lord John. He was outraged by his undersecretary's bland expression. With difficulty he maintained a polite expression for Miss Wyndham's benefit when his impulse was to let forth a resounding curse. "You are a British subject, then, Miss Wyndham? That of course changes the complexion of matters somewhat. It is possible for me to register a formal request with the czar on your behalf. I am certain in a few months' time . . ."

Sophia's soaring hopes plummeted once more. She shook her head. "It must come sooner, my lord. In a few months' time I will be a stuffed goose."

"I beg pardon?" asked Lord Carthcart, startled.

"Miss Wyndham's intended has stated that he prefers a wife with a most . . . well-rounded figure. He expressed the wish that Miss Wyndham apply herself dutifully to the table," said Lord John blandly.

"My dear miss," exclaimed Lord Cathcart, revolted and yet fascinated.

"It is true. And my aunt, Princess Elizaveta Kirov, is determined that I shall prescribe to the very letter of Prince Tarkovich's wishes," said Sophia. She placed an entreating hand on Lord Cathcart's sleeve. "I beg you, my lord . . ."

"Did you say Tarkovich?" Lord Cathcart asked.

"That is the gentleman's name, yes," said Lord John. "Have you met him, sir?"

Various emotions chased across Lord Cathcart's face, before his expression finally settled into determination. "I have indeed met Prince Tarkovich. My dear Miss Wyndham, I shall do all in my power to serve you. But it will take a little time to arrange. Have you someone you can trust, that I may send a message through?"

Sophia thought a moment. "I often visit with Mistress Wheeler. She was a dear friend of my mother's when we stilled lived in Papa's house in St. Petersburg."

"Excellent! Nothing could be better. The Quakers are high in the czar's favor at this time," exclaimed Lord Cathcart. "It is fortunate, my dear, that you have existing ties to the English colony. Already I am beginning to see how we may turn it to the purpose. When will you next see Mistress Wheeler?"

"Why, I visit with her every week," said Sophia, her heart beginning to pound. She could hardly believe her good fortune in meeting Lord John, who must surely be the instrument of a merciful God. She would at last be going home to England.

"Then I shall arrange a message to be left for you with Mistress Wheeler," said Lord Cathcart. "I make no promises, Miss Wyndham, but I hope that you shall be returning to England sooner than you expected."

"Oh, thank you, sir," Sophia said, her eyes shining.

"Not at all, my dear child," said Lord Cathcart. He glanced at Lord John. "Now, sir, I suggest that we have spoken long enough. Miss Wyndham's aunt may be wondering about her absence."

"Of course, sir. I shall escort Miss Wyndham back immediately," said Lord John. A grin tugged at his mobile lips. "Rest assured that I shall attend to your newest puzzle with all due speed, my lord."

"Tit for tat, my boy?" said Lord Cathcart softly as he walked past.

Lord John laughed and turned to Sophia to offer his arm to her once more. "Allow me, Miss Wyndham."

Sophia placed her fingertips on his forearm and looked up at him, saying with warm sincerity, "I must again thank you, my lord. You have made all the difference between dark and light for me."

"I am honored to have been of service," said Lord John. He turned the subject, and by the time he had returned Sophia to her aunt, they had chatted amiably on a great many facets of Russian life.

Princess Kirov stiffly acknowledged Lord John's bow. When he had left, she turned to Sophia with a frown. "You were a long time with the Englishman."

"He was very interested in Russian life. I told him of the Winter Palace and its beauty. He was suitably impressed, of course," said Sophia, half-fearing that her aunt could sense the new lightness of her spirit.

Princess Kirov smiled, pleased. "I am happy to know that your Russian blood speaks so strongly to you, Sophia."

"I have never denied the heritage to which I was born," said Sophia quietly.

"Good, good." Princess Kirov was enormously pleased, interpreting Sophia's docility as resignation to the destiny that had been chosen for her as Prince Tarkovich's bride. "I have decided that you shall remain in St. Petersburg with me, Sophia, for I wish to treat you to much amusement before you are wed. We will preside over such feasts as you could never imagine."

"Yes, Aunt," said Sophia, at once relieved and dismayed. She was happy that she would not after all be exiled from St. Petersburg to the summer dacha, where she could not have hoped to continue her visits to Mistress Wheeler. But the promised feasts for her edification horrified her. She hoped that escape was to be soon, for she had the most lowering feeling that she would soon become too indolent to care.

3

AFTER LORD John had taken leave of Miss Sophia Wyndham and her aunt, he had felt that his responsibility in the matter was at an end. In the following days he did occasionally wonder with a mild interest if Lord Cathcart had been true to his word and was making arrangements for Miss Wyndham's succor, but the incident at the ball was never mentioned. However, there was an uncharacteristic twinkle in his excellency's eyes when he briefed his undersecretary on his latest "puzzle." "You'll detest this one, John. The bureaucrat in question is an idiot of proportions. But I have all the confidence in the world in you," said Lord Cathcart cheerfully.

"Thank you, sir," said Lord John dryly. His excellency gave him a knowing smile. Lord John thought himself dismissed and started to leave the room.

"Oh, John, I had almost forgotten," said Lord Cathcart. He casually flipped a sealed missive across the mahogany desk to Lord John. "I wish you to pay a call on Master Wheeler, the Quaker gentleman who is overseeing the czar's land-drainage project. This wresting of farmland from a swamp is an extraordinary undertaking. And it is certainly worthy of recognition from myself in my capacity as ambassador since Master Wheeler is essentially furthering good relations between Russia and England. Wouldn't you agree, John?"

"Indeed, my lord," Lord John said, now alerted that his superior was not yet done with him. He picked up the sealed envelope.

Lord Cathcart did not disappoint him. From his pocket he withdrew a small twist of paper and handed it to Lord John. "Pray feel free to inquire of Master and Mistress

Wheeler regarding their acquaintances. I feel certain that some must be mutually known between us and I will be curious to hear their names."

Lord John had difficulty suppressing a grin as he secreted the twist of paper in his coat pocket. Lord Cathcart was deliberately imbuing his mission as messenger with a decided air of drama, but he was willing to play along with the older man. "Of course, my lord. I shall see to it immediately."

"See that you do, John." Lord Cathcart's tone was careless, almost absentminded, but there was steel in his glance. Lord John was taken aback. Surely this was no more than an ordinary errand, he thought as he bowed.

When Lord John opened the door, he almost trod on a Russian clerk. The clerk busied himself with shuffling the papers in his hands and looked up as though just then noticing Lord John. He bowed low. Lord John nodded and his brows creased as he strode away. It was odd that the clerk should chance to be just outside the door when Lord Cathcart was instructing him in so mysterious a manner about contacting Miss Wyndham. Lord John dismissed the incident as a coincidence, but it left him with a vague feeling of unease.

Sophia glanced up as the sleigh started away, wondering if anyone suspected her plans or the purpose of her visit to Mistress Wheeler that day. But she saw no one looking out from the several windows in her aunt's three-storied residence. As she gazed at the building, the oddest feeling settled on her. She felt that she would not again have the opportunity to see her aunt's home like this, and Sophia deliberately studied it with new eyes to entrench it firmly in her memory.

The House of Kirov was built of light-colored stone. A half-circle of stone steps led up to a recessed porch through the middle archway. Three archways supported the dome that covered the porch and connected the separate wings of the residence. Stone carvings glazed with ice stared blindly from between the windows.

Sophia tilted back her head. The metal roof, painted black, could be seen only dimly through the sheet of slick ice that covered it. Huge icicles hung like teeth from the eaves, and the snow on the ground was packed hard about the structure. Even as the sleigh entered the street Sophia could still glimpse the residence through the trees because the grounds were surrounded only by an iron spike fence. The Kirovs were as proud as any of the other Russian nobility of their magnificent home and did not hide it behind a stone fence.

Sophia turned her back on the swiftly disappearing residence, at once sad and exhilarated. She had spent many years under that proud roof, but it was now time to let go of her familiar life. She felt a growing anticipation for the future that would surely open to her in a very short time, beginning with her visit to Mistress Wheeler.

Sophia had anticipated this particular weekly visit to Mistress Wheeler's with barely concealed impatience. But the morning she meant to go, Princess Kirov commanded her presence at a tea. Sophia thought the very world was crumbling under her feet. Sophia sent a hurriedly scrawled message to Mistress Wheeler that she would come the following week instead. She lived thereafter in dread that when next she had an opportunity to drive to Mistress Wheeler's home, she would again be prevented from doing so by her aunt's wishes. Her overwhelming fear was that she would receive Lord Cathcart's message too late to act upon it. Sophia even questioned whether Lord Cathcart would keep his word. What if he never sent a message at all and had no intention of helping her? In her blackest moments she was convinced that she was doomed to the regimen of frequent sweets that Princess Kirov plied her with. But she had only to conjure up Lord John's handsome face and the interested, vital light in his eyes to take courage. Lord John would not disappoint her. He would not forget. Somehow she would hear from him even if it were bad news. Through the tense days and nights, Sophia held on to her trust in Lord John like a comforting beacon.

St. Petersburg in winter presented a frozen, but bustling

scene. Humble sleighs and the flamboyant troikas of
princes skimmed in every direction over the streets of ice.
The horses blew frost on the air and their traces jangled
with the speed of their passage. The drivers shouted
greetings to one another and cracked whips to urge on their
teams.

Sophia had no eyes for the sleighs flashing by on either
side, nor for the busy market on the frozen Neva River.
Usually she would have signaled her driver to slow so that
she could gaze on the crowds wrapped warmly in sable and
bear coats and wearing fur caps and heavy boots. The
shoppers strolled among the pyramids of frozen carcasses.
When they had chosen their purchases, a waiting peasant
would take out his hatchet to chop off the specified
amount of iron-hard beef or lamb, and the frozen chips
showered the air like wood splinters. The market was a
spectacle that had never lost its fascination for Sophia in
the five years she had lived in St. Petersburg, but this day
she waved the driver on. She was impatient to reach Peterhof, the English merchants' colony, with its English
cottages and dormant gardens.

When the sleigh drew up before the Wheeler cottage,
Sophia jumped down and hurried up the hard-packed
path. The door was opened by Mistress Wheeler herself.
"Pray thee come in, and quickly. Thee must not stand
about in the cold, Mistress Sophia." She drew Sophia
inside with a quick glance at the sleigh's driver before
shutting the door.

In moments Sophia was divested of her fur cap, gloves,
and heavy sable coat. She was encouraged to take the plain
wooden-backed chair that was closest to the fire, and a cup
of steaming broth was pressed into her hands.

"Thank you, Mistress Wheeler. I am always certain of a
fine welcome with you," said Sophia, gratefully sipping at
the broth. The welcome warmth spread within her.

"Thee is always most welcome, and well thou know it,
Mistress Sophia." Mistress Wheeler seated herself in a
chair farther from the hearth. She marveled that her young
visitor did not appear uncomfortable so close to the fire's

heat, but Sophia once explained to her that the homes of most Russians were kept heated at a much higher temperature than the Quakers thought necessary. Sophia had remarked that she was now more Russian than English because she had become accustomed to the warmer rooms. Mistress Wheeler's fingers nimbly plied a darning needle to the man's shirt that she had drawn out of the mending basket that always stood beside her chair. "Sophia, thou are like a daughter to me. Thee may speak thy trouble openly," said Mistress Wheeler.

Sophia looked at her in startlement. "My dear ma'am, how did you know?"

Mistress Wheeler smiled and shook her head. "Come, Sophia, do I not know thee well?"

Sophia gently ran her fingers along the rim of her cup. "My aunt wishes me to marry someone not of my choosing. She threatens to incarcerate me in a nunnery if I refuse to abide by her wishes."

"Duty is hard at times, but can thee not learn to respect this man, Sophia?" asked Mistress Wheeler.

Sophia shuddered. "You have not seen him, Mistress Wheeler. The prince is crude and grotesque. He is forever shoving bonbons into his mouth. My aunt only desires the marriage because the prince's family has influence with the court." She looked up with grave eyes. "I will die if I am forced to marry the prince, Mistress Wheeler, I know it. I cannot bear the thought of living intimately with such a man."

Mistress Wheeler's face pinkened. She was well aware that Sophia had in certain matters been reared in the Russian manner. The Russian women that Mistress Wheeler had encountered were much freer in their discussions of childbirth and marital relations. She had once gently scolded Sophia's mother for explaining such things to the young girl, but Elena had said that since Sophia was both English and Russian, then she should be taught those things that would enable her to be at ease in either society. Sophia was raised to recognize the differences between her English and Russian heritage, and as a consequence,

Mistress Wheeler considered her to be an unusually self-possessed young woman. Sophia was correct in her manners and her speech, but always there was the hint of something warmer in her eyes and her voice. Mistress Wheeler fancied that Sophia's shared inheritance gave her an almost feline nature, fusing English reserve to Russian passion, calm to turbulence. Oh, Sophia was a delight, mused Mistress Wheeler. But even the sweetest, most amiable kitten had claws. "Thou wait here," she said, rising.

Sophia looked up in surprise as her hostess left the room.

Almost immediately Mistress Wheeler returned accompanied by a tall gentleman that Sophia recognized. "My lord!"

Lord John smiled and took her hand. "Forgive me for giving you a start, Miss Wyndham. Mistress Wheeler thought it best that I wait in another room until she was certain of her visitor's identity."

Sophia glanced at her friend, whose face expressed a trace of guilt. She laughed, knowing that Mistress Wheeler had wanted not so much to learn who her visitor was but to gently probe Sophia on her predicament, for Sophia had no doubt that Lord John had been cajoled into revealing what he knew of Prince Tarkovich. "How very glad I am to see you again, Lord John," she said easily.

Lord John was surprised and yet pleased by Miss Wyndham's frank pleasure at his appearance. "And I am fortunate to have found you calling on Mistress Wheeler. Lord Carthcart requested that I bring a message for you, Miss Wyndham." As he spoke he drew the twist of paper out of his pocket and gave it to her.

Sophia smoothed out the sheet. She read the brief note and looked up with shining eyes. "I am to go home to England in only two weeks!"

"Thou are happy, Sophia?" asked Mistress Wheeler, still a little uneasy over the part she was playing in the secret rendezvous.

Sophia flung her arms about her friend and hugged her fiercely. "Oh, I cannot describe how happy I am!"

"Then I am happy for thee," said Mistress Wheeler.

Sophia released her and turned to hold out her hand to Lord John. "Thank you, my lord. I shall always remember what you have done for me."

"It was little enough, Miss Wyndham," said Lord John. He smiled down at her animated face and released her hand. "Forgive my haste, but I must be going. In the event I do not see you again, Miss Wyndham, I wish you all the best."

Sophia smiled at him. "I shall undoubtedly see you again, Lord John, as his excellency has written that his messenger will contact me when it is time."

Lord John appeared momentarily surprised, then his expression smoothed. Lord Cathcart had not mentioned any such role to him, but the notion would certainly appeal to his excellency's sense of humor. Lord John bowed to each of the ladies. "Miss Wyndham, Mistress Wheeler, your servant."

After he had taken final leave of the ladies and instructed his sleigh driver to return to the city, he thoughtfully contemplated the consequences of his chivalric actions at the ball. Lord Cathcart had apparently taken it for granted that he would act as the girl's nursemaid. Lord John decided it was past time to speak to his superior. He had no desire to add nursemaiding to his diplomatic experience, and he would make that very clear.

4

A FEW days after Lord John made his report to Lord Cathcart, he and another attaché to the British embassy received word to present themselves to Lord Cathcart.

Sir Frederick Hawkesworth looked at Lord John with a brow raised in exaggerated question. "Any notion as to what it is all about?"

"I've no inkling, Freddy," said Lord John.

They were not long left in ignorance. Lord Cathcart nodded to them as they entered the office, and when they were seated, he said, "Gentlemen, I have news for you both. Lord John, you are being posted back to London. Your time with us in St. Petersburg is at an end. You will be leaving us in a week's time."

"But, sir . . ."

Lord Cathcart held up a quelling hand. "Sir Frederick, you too are returning to England. I have word that your mother is gravely ill and desires to see her son."

Sir Frederick stared at him in astonishment. "My mother, sir? There is a mistake."

Lord Cathcart glowered at him. "Perhaps I did not make myself clear, Sir Frederick. Your mother is gravely ill. You will naturally take an extended leave to join your family."

"Of course I shall, if you say so, sir," said Sir Frederick woodenly. He caught Lord John's eyes and shrugged.

"My lord, I am compelled to protest. I have no desire to leave foreign service just yet," said Lord John.

"I have decided that it will do you good to see how the Home Office runs things. Then, if you desire it, there will be a new foreign appointment for you. Gentlemen, there is no room for discussion." Lord Cathcart stood up, signaling an end to the interview, and both men reluctantly rose. They were surprised when he came around the desk and clasped each of their shoulders. "I shall miss you both. But some matters require sacrifice, and losing two good men is mine." Lord Cathcart lowered his voice. "John, you will understand better when I say this involves a lady's honor."

Lord John realized that his superior referred to Miss Wyndham. He thought he could guess the rest. His jaw firmed and his pleasant blue eyes hardened. "My lord, I stated before that the role of nursemaid was not to my liking."

"Nursemaid? Why, that is exactly what Freddy here will be, heh?" Lord Cathcart laughed and half-turned them to the door. Lord John saw that the door was cracked open and he caught a glimpse of the same Russian clerk he had previously caught too near Lord Cathcart's door.

Lord Cathcart felt the instinctive tensing in his subordinate and his fingers tightened warningly on Lord John's shoulder. He said softly, "Leave it alone, John. I know about him and I occasionally find him useful." Lord Cathcart raised his voice as though responding to a continued conversation. "How well I know it, gentlemen. I shall miss your cheerful faces, of course. But you shall have a splendid time rediscovering our own dear London. Sir Frederick, pray give my deepest regards to your dear mother. I hope she recovers quickly."

Sir Frederick bowed. He said gravely, "Thank you, sir. I anticipate that she shall, but one never knows with these unexpected illnesses." Making certain he was in profile to the Russian clerk he allowed himself an exaggerated wink.

"Yes, well, I wish you Godspeed," said Lord Cathcart hastily. He waved both men out and closed the door.

Lord John and Sir Frederick sauntered past the Russian clerk, who watched them surreptitiously. "Awfully sorry about your mother, Freddy," said Lord John.

Sir Frederick heaved a huge melancholy sigh. "Indeed, John. She's a damn splendid woman. I find it difficult to imagine her laid down in her bed."

Lord John had a sudden coughing fit. When they were out of the clerk's earshot, he said mildly, "Damn your eyes, Freddy. You nearly overset me right there."

Sir Frederick grinned at him. "I couldn't resist it. Imagine my long-departed mother sending me a message to visit! The old man's behavior is damned peculiar over that clerk fellow, don't you think? I half-believe that the fellow is actually a spy from the czar's Okhrana."

"He may be, Freddy. I've caught him before with his ear practically wedded to his lordship's keyhole," said Lord John, frowning.

"The devil you say!" Sir Frederick reflected for a moment on their recent interview and then glanced shrewdly at his silent companion. "The old man was uncharacteristically low-voiced when he made mention of a certain lady's honor. Have you by chance gotten yourself tangled up with a petticoat you shouldn't have, John?"

Lord John grinned. "In a manner of speaking, Freddy. Do you recall what I told you about a young woman I met at the princess's ball last week?"

"Miss Wyndham? Of course I do," said Sir Frederick. His companion gestured quickly and he saw that they were not alone in the hall. A servantman walked past, too slowly. Sir Frederick stared at the man fixedly until the servant rounded a corner into another hall. He said in a low voice, "I pride myself on my quick understanding, John. The Banbury tale about my mother on her deathbed and your reappointment have to do with this young lady."

Lord John nodded. "So I believe, Freddy. We have apparently been chosen to act as her gallant knights."

"I see. Is she beautiful?"

"What?"

"In the old tales, the damsel in distress is always beautiful," said Sir Frederick.

Lord John had a quick vision of Sophia Wyndham's gleaming blond hair and her almond-shaped blue-gray eyes, her eyes that had been so warm in expression when last he saw her. "The lady is not a typical English beauty. But she is very attractive in an exotic way," said Lord John slowly.

"I shan't mind playing knight-errant, then. An attractive woman can make even the most pointless exercise seem plausible," said Sir Frederick ingenuously.

Lord John burst out laughing. Together the gentlemen walked away.

The servantman who had rounded the corner into the next hallway had strained for the last few moments to hear their conversation. His knowledge of English was imperfect, but he understood enough to know that the taller English lord was having an affair with a young woman with powerful friends. "Miss Wyndham," he said softly, and nodded with satisfaction at his pronounciation. He peered around the corner to be certain that the English milords were truly gone, and then slipped back the way he had come. It was time to take information to the clerk who had sent him so quickly to follow the English lords. He thought that this time he would surely earn more than two or three kopecks.

The information given to the clerk who hovered near his excellency's office was duly passed on to his superior, who knew a vast number of people. This man recognized the name of Wyndham and his brows rose. Not long after, Princess Elizaveta Kirov received a visit from an old knowledgeable friend. When her friend, who was a mousy man easily passed over in a crowd, had left, Princess Kirov sat immobile for a few moments in deep thought. She came to a decision and called for a manservant. She directed him to inform Sophia that she desired her company at once.

Sophia was mystified by the abrupt summons. She hurried to her aunt's sitting room, wondering what could be so urgent. When she entered, she seated herself in the chair that her aunt indicated with an imperious wave of the hand.

"So, niece, you have a lover," said Princess Kirov without preamble, her eyes narrowed on Sophia's expression.

Sophia was staggered. "What?"

"We should have no secrets between us, you and I. This is why I speak to you now, Sophia. I know of the English lord who is your lover," said Princess Kirov.

Sophia was at once angry and frightened. What did Princess Kirov know of any English lord? Flushed, she said heatedly, "I do not know what you are talking about. I have no lover, English or otherwise."

Princess Kirov put up her brows. "No? Then why is there fear in your eyes, Sophia?" Her niece stared at her with open disdain. She laughed hugely. "Niece, I admire your defiant spirit, but your eyes have already betrayed you. I think this Englishman was at the princess's ball. Lord John Stokes, was it not? The one who so admired Russian life."

Sophia's mouth dried. Her heart bumped painfully in her breast. "Lord John was but an amusing companion met by chance, Aunt."

"And you met him again, by chance?"

Sophia flushed, then paled. She wondered wildly how her aunt had known about her meeting with Lord John at Mistress Wheeler's cottage. She was undone. Princess Kirov knew too much. She would never again be allowed to leave the house without escort. She would never be able to escape to England. Sophia was surprised when Princess Kirov reached out to take her tense fingers in a firm grasp.

"Sophia, I do not condemn you for taking a lover. It is understandable that a young and beautiful girl would want to do so, especially when she is to be married to one such as Tarkovich." She felt Sophia shudder and said in a kind tone, "You think me unfeeling, niece. I am not. Therefore, I do not insist that you end the affair with this English lord."

Sophia's eyes flew to Princess Kirov's calm face. She could hardly believe what she had heard. "Thank you, Aunt," she said faintly.

Princess Kirov released her fingers. "You have been discreet, Sophia. Remain so, and I have nothing to complain of. And if you become with child . . ." She paused, watching Sophia's face flame. She shrugged. "It will be good for you if you do. Tarkovich marries only to get an heir, but his family is notorious for impotence. Provide him at once with a boy and you will be free to choose a new lover. The child's parentage will never be questioned since Lord John returns to England so soon." Sophia sucked in her breath sharply. Princess Kirov smiled with a shade of malice. "Did he not tell you, Sophia? Your English lover has been ordered back to London. He is to leave this week."

"So soon," whispered Sophia under her breath, hardly aware of what construction her aunt would put on her words. She was busy wondering how he would send word to her and what she should pack.

Princess Kirov laughed heartily. "You are angry with him. But be kind to your English lord while you have him, Sophia. Then you will have only a good memory of your first love affair. I once thought you cold like all the English ladies. I am happy to discover that you have the heart of a Russian, Sophia." She rose from her chair. Her dark eyes were bright but unreadable. "Josef the deaf-mute will be your driver this week."

Sophia's face flamed once more as she caught her aunt's meaning. Her eyes dropped. Princess Kirov smiled again and left the sitting room. Sophia covered her hot cheeks with her hands. She could hardly believe what had happened in the past few minutes. She gave a little laugh. It was ironic that her aunt approved of her taking a lover and so much so that Sophia had virtually been given permission to meet with him. It made things at once easier and yet more dangerous. She would have to maintain the fiction that Lord John was her lover, perhaps even allow Josef to observe an intimate gesture. Sophia was no fool. She knew that Josef was her aunt's personal serf and would somehow communicate what he observed to his mistress. Sophia only hoped that Lord John would not be too shocked when she greeted him with unladylike enthusiasm. His expression could betray them both to the ever-observant Josef. But she would manage it somehow.

5

THE DOOR opened and a young man attired in military togs walked in. His ice-blue eyes immediately took in Sophia's still-flushed face. She had risen at his entrance and her movements were somewhat nervous as she curtsied. "Good afternoon, cousin."

Prince Mikhail Kirov ignored Sophia's formal greeting and swooped across the room to catch her up from the carpet in an affectionate bear hug. "Cousin Sophia! You are extremely handsome today." As he looked down into her clear, smiling eyes, he thought regretfully, as he had ever more recently, that it was a pity that Sophia Wyndham was his poor little first cousin. If Sophia were an heiress, or if she at least had powerful connections, he would seriously consider her for a wife. But as it was, he planned to marry well and to his advantage. A pretty face and figure were not all that a marriage should bring to a man, he thought.

"Misha, put me down this instant," said Sophia breathlessly.

He did so. Then he pinched her cheek and said teasingly, "I see the bloom of spring in your face, little Sophia. Or is it a lover who brings out the English rose?" He was astonished when Sophia colored hotly, but he quickly masked his surprise. "I thought to find my mother here in the sitting room."

"Aunt Elizaveta was with me but a moment ago. I suppose she has returned to her apartment," said Sophia, glad that her cousin had not commented on her furious blush. Her relief was short-lived.

"What did my mother speak to you about?" asked Misha, throwing himself in an ornate armchair. Immediately a dwarf appeared beside him to hold out a gold snuffbox. With hardly a glance for his servant Prince Kirov took a pinch of snuff and delicately sniffed it.

"She spoke of Prince Tarkovich," said Sophia shortly. Her gaze was challenging.

Prince Kirov grinned. "You do not display happiness over your nuptials, Sophia."

"Should I? I have told you before what I feel, Misha," said Sophia. She shuddered. "Each time I think of Prince Tarkovich and what he wants to make of me, I feel ill."

Her cousin's grin faded. "True, you should not be fattened like a cow to slaughter. I shall speak to my mother."

"I wish instead that you could persuade her to nullify the marriage agreement," said Sophia wistfully, quickly.

Prince Kirov rose to his feet, laughing. "You wish for the moon, Sophia. Each of us has a duty to perform for the family. Your duty is to establish for us an alliance with the Tarkovich family. If I were to hinder what has been pledged, it would sully our family honor. And I do not regard my honor lightly, Sophia."

"Then truly I have no choice," said Sophia quietly, thinking of Lord John and her anticipated departure from Russia.

"I am happy that you understand, little Sophia. Now I will go speak with my mother." Prince Kirov raised Sophia's hand to his lips before leaving the room, followed by his faithful dwarf.

Sophia made a quick decision and imperiously called for a manservant. When the manservant answered her summons, she requested that a sleigh be readied for her. Sophia had not been to her father's house on the Peterhof road since the day her mother died, when she had come to live with her aunt. But it was time now to make plans for her future and she could not think of a more suitable place to do so than the house where there were so many poignant memories of the past. And afterward she would visit Mistress Wheeler.

* * *

Prince Kirov found his mother playing her favorite air on the pianoforte. He paused a moment to listen. The music was forceful and hard-driven, but mixed with soft rippling runs. He smiled because the piece illustrated exactly his mother's personality. Princess Kirov was at once forceful and ambitious, but she had her vulnerabilities and her son was well aware that he was one of them. He bent to kiss his mother on the top of her head.

Immediately Princess Kirov turned to hold her hands out to him. "Misha, my dear one. I am always happy to see you."

Prince Kirov hooked a chair by the leg and dragged it to him, waving aside the dwarf's assistance. "Thank you, Fedor. You may go now. I speak privately with my mother."

As the dwarf bowed and left, Princess Kirov looked at her son with her head tilted to one side like a curious bird. "So you wish to be private even from loyal Fedor? Dear Misha, what is it?"

"It is little Sophia, my cousin. She is unhappy with the marriage contract arranged for her," said Prince Kirov.

His mother shrugged carelessly, but her eyes were suddenly hard. "Sophia is young and does not understand the demands of duty. Tarkovich will teach her that."

Prince Kirov smiled and said mildly, "I do not speak against the marriage, Mama. Sophia will bring us a powerful alliance at court through the Tarkovich family. it is this overfeeding of her that I dislike. She is already more plump than when I was last in St. Petersburg."

"Good. Prince Tarkovich wants a plump wife, and the fatter the better," said Princess Kirov with a quick smile.

Prince Kirov contemplated his nails. "Prince Tarkovich could die suddenly of his obesity and leave Sophia a very wealthy widow, still young and in need of guidance. I would not wish Sophia to leave this house with unhappy memories, memories that would cloud her judgment in choosing who to turn to in her bereavement."

There was a short silence. "You are wise, my Misha. Sophia is not yet a Tarkovich. She still answers to me and I am a loving aunt. Sophia will remember my leniency with gratitude," said Princess Kirov. She laughed suddenly. "Your little cousin now has two reasons to be grateful to me today. And so does her lover."

Prince Kirov was startled. "Sophia? She has a lover?"

"Why so surprised, Misha? You thought perhaps that Sophia was a cold English miss?"

Prince Kirov stared at his mother. He remembered Sophia's fiery blush when he had teased her about having a lover. His ice-blue eyes brightened with anger. "I am surprised at you, Mama. How can you know and yet allow her to bring dishonor on her head?"

"I allow it because Sophia weds Tarkovich, that monster of flesh. I understand a girl's dreams even if you do not, Misha. She will remember her first lover with gratitude and sighs, and then she will uphold her duty," said Princess Kirov sharply.

"I shall kill him," said Prince Kirov softly. "I will have his name from Sophia, and then he will die."

"You will do nothing," said Princess Elizaveta flatly.

Prince Kirov thrust back his chair and paced a furious circle. "It is our family honor, Mama. And what if Tarkovich hears of it? What shall you say, then, Mama?"

"Sophia is surprisingly discreet. I do not think Tarkovich will know. Besides, the affair ends soon. The English lord leaves Russia in only a few days," said Princess Kirov.

"An English lord . . . And you know his name, don't you?" said Prince Kirov slowly.

His mother shrugged. "Of course. I approve Sophia's taste. Lord John Stokes is very fair, very handsome." She narrowed her eyes when her son muttered an explosive oath and slammed a fist into his palm. "I think you feel too much over this, Misha. Did you perhaps wish more of little Sophia than the affection of a cousin?"

Prince Kirov controlled his expression, masking the rage seething within him. "I apologize for interrupting your practice for so long, Mama. I will leave you now." He bowed and strode from the music room. His mother watched him go with a faint smile.

Prince Kirov was aware that his mother had told him the English lord's name only because she knew that he would obey her. He would do nothing about Sophia's lover. But when he thought of Sophia with this Englishman, his blood boiled. Sophia safely wedded was one thing, but to imagine her seduced—and by an Englishman—was something altogether different. He found himself striding down the hall toward Sophia's rooms and abruptly stopped. What did he mean to do, beat such foolishness out of her? he thought with a snort of disgust. Prince Kirov turned on his heel. He was forbidden to kill Sophia's lover and he would not beat her. So he would do the next best thing. "Fedor," he bellowed. He stomped back the way he had come. The dwarf appeared instantly. "Come, Fedor. We are going to get drunk," he said.

"Yes, lord," said the dwarf, hurrying after his master.

The tavern was a meeting place for merchants, but several noblemen chose to patronize it. The tavern mistress, dressed in gold embroidery and diamonds, sat at the head of the table. Her face, neck, and plump arms were painted red and white in the national manner and her teeth were stained black. "She's a rare one," said Sir Frederick, staring at the hostess with fascinated eyes as he nudged his companion. Lord John agreed and glanced around at their surroundings.

Pungent smoke hung over the noisy crowd. Over a hundred dishes had been served at the table by bearded men attired in yellow or purple shirts, and drink was lavishly provided. After coffee was served, a troupe of gypsies was brought in to dance with spectacular frenzy and grace.

Near the two Englishmen a tall Russian in military dress set up a folk song of profound sadness and the familiar words were instantly taken up by the crowd. The young Russian broke off in midnote and demanded that his tankard be refilled. A stout dwarf silently poured another drink for his master. Lord John's eyes narrowed thoughtfully and he studied the Russian with greater curiosity.

While in St. Petersburg he had seen several noblemen accompanied by dwarfs for companions, but this particular gentleman was not familiar to him.

Sir Frederick leaned close to him and pitched his voice to carry over the singing. "I'll remember this night all my life, Stokes. It's a fitting end to our stay in St. Petersburg."

The young Russian's head whipped around. He waved aside the dwarf's soft query, suddenly intensely interested in the Englishmen.

"I shall remember it, too, Freddy. But I think it time that we take ourselves off," said Lord John.

Neither Lord John nor Sir Frederick noticed the Russian's attentive bloodshot eyes on them. They rose to pay their bill and walked outside. A manservant tramped away to summon their sleigh while they waited in the circle of light thrown from the tavern window.

Lord John watched his breath frost on the cold night air. Overhead the stars sparkled with breathtaking clarity against the dark velvet sky. It was a beautiful night. "It has been a rare evening, Freddy." He laid a gloved hand on his friend's fur-clad shoulder and pressed it. "Thank you. I was brooding overmuch over my reappointment."

Sir Frederick nodded. "I know. I, too, will miss this odd cold land of expansive hospitality. But we will adjust quickly to London, John. Imagine an English spring when the ladies drive in the park and bow and nod like so many graceful daisies."

"You should watch yourself, Freddy. One could take you for a Byronic romantic," said Lord John in mock seriousness.

Sir Frederick was revolted. "I do not in the least resemble Lord Byron," he said empthatically.

"Oh, I don't know. You've already the dark looks that the ladies sigh over. You need only to affect an interesting limp," said Lord John.

"Damn your eyes, John. I can't stomach that flashy fellow, and well you know it!" said Sir Frederick, nettled.

Lord John burst out laughing.

"Stokes!"

Lord John and Sir Frederick turned in surprise at the furious shout. The young Russian in military togs stood nearby, slightly weaving. The dwarf was beside his master. His face was expressionless except for the lively wariness of his gaze.

"I am Stokes," said Lord John calmly, curiously studying the Russian, who towered a full head over him. The man was perhaps twenty-five, a bear of solid muscle, he thought.

"I am Kirov." The stranger's voice was arrogant. "I should kill you now in the snow, Stokes."

"What the devil!" exclaimed Sir Frederick, taking a hasty step forward.

Unobtrusively the dwarf slid a dagger free of its sheath. Lord John shot out his arm to block his friend. He recognized the name "Kirov." Surely Miss Wyndham had mentioned an aunt by that name. Then he realized that the stranger's gloved fingers were clenched on the hilt of the dress sword on his hip. Lord John stiffened. He shot a quick glance up at the young Russian's shadowed face. "Kill me, Kirov? I assume that you have sufficient reason."

"You have insulted my family. That is reason enough," said Prince Kirov furiously, weaving slightly as he stood.

"I do not intentionally insult anyone, Kirov," said Lord John, carefully feeling his way.

"Then you deny that you seduced her?" demanded Prince Kirov.

"I have never seduced a lady against her will, Kirov," said Lord John. Beside him, he heard Sir Frederick's heavy breathing and he could feel his own heart pumping. His instinct told him that he stood on the borderline of life and possible death. He was unarmed. If Kirov lunged for him with the saber . . .

There was a pregnant silence. "Not against her will," repeated Prince Kirov. His aggressive stance slowly relaxed. He stared at Lord John. "No, I shall not split you open now. I will wait until the time is right. But know that you will not escape Kirov justice forever.'' He brushed past Sir Frederick and Lord John. "Come, Fedor!"

"Yes, lord." The dwarf slid his dagger back in its sheath and hurried after his master. Lord John and Sir Frederick turned to watch them go. The dark swiftly swallowed them up.

"Who was that?"

"I haven't the faintest notion," said Lord John, breathing easier. He did not think it worth while to explain that Miss Wyndham was related to a Kirov family. "Do you know, Freddy, for a moment I thought he meant to run me through!"

"The fellow was mad," Sir Frederick said with conviction.

"He was drowned in his cups, certainly," said Lord John.

Their sleigh arrived. Sir Frederick clapped his companion on the shoulder. "We've all the luck, John. How many others would top off their evening with an encounter with a drunken madman and his fierce dwarf?"

"Not anyone with sense," retorted Lord John as they settled back in the sleigh and pulled the fur rug over their knees.

Sir Frederick glanced across at him as the sleigh picked up speed. "Not my business, of course. But have you dallied with someone you shouldn't have, John?"

Lord John stared at him with a faint smile. "You have the most damnable cheek, Freddy."

Sir Frederick nodded, satisfied. "I thought not. But all the same, it's best that you are leaving St. Petersburg. We can't have you skewered by a Russian madman, you know."

Lord John made an ironic half-bow to his friend. "Thank you for your concern, Sir Frederick."

"Always happy to oblige, my lord," said Sir Frederick blandly.

The following morning Lord Cathcart informed his two undersecretaries that travel arrangements had been made for them and that they would be taking separate routes. Sir

Frederick would take passage on a merchant ship that was to set sail from the docks near the Peterhof road where the English merchants had established a community of stately homes. Lord John would travel cross-country by sleigh until he reached Poland, where he would be able to hire a carriage in Warsaw for the remainder of his journey across Europe. The Russian clerk who always hovered near Lord Cathcart's office passed on the information he had heard. He did not see the note passed from Lord Cathcart to Lord John, who read it and then passed it to Sir Frederick. Lord Cathcart then lit a cigar and burned the note. The two undersecretaries bowed and left the office, their real instructions safely in mind.

6

ON A cold morning at the edge of dark, Lord John and Sir Frederick met for the last time in St. Petersburg. Snow swirled about them, blurring their persons from anyone who cared to observe them. "Look for me at White's in St. James's Street, John," said Sir Frederick.

Lord John nodded. He reached inside the breast of his fur coat for a leather packet. "These are the letters and documents that you shall need, Freddy. They should be sufficient to open the way wherever you go. There is also a *podorojni*."

Sir Frederick looked at his friend with newfound respect. "I'd like to know how you managed that one, John. Never mind. I am glad to have it. The postmasters at the stations will be double quick about furnishing new horses when I wave *that* under their noses." He held out his gloved hand to Lord John, who took it in a tight grasp. "Good bye, John. I am glad the old man decided at the last moment that the sea trip was to be yours. I am always wretched on a ship. It is that awful rolling, I think."

Lord John grinned. "Good-bye, Freddy. And God-speed."

Sir Frederick stepped up into the covered sleigh. He waved briefly as the driver spoke to the horses and the sleigh glided away. Swirling snow obscured Lord John's sight and he turned to his own sleigh. Within seconds he was being carried swiftly toward a shuttered house on the Peterhof road.

Sophia stood looking through a crack in the wooden shutter that covered a front window. She was tense as she waited on the sleigh. When it finally arrived, she let out a

sigh of relief. It had been her constant fear that Josef
would detect something different in this visit to her
mother's house and would return early with company,
having raised the alarm. She had sent him back to her
aunt's house with instructions to return in two hours' time,
as she had made a practice of doing a few days before.
Princess Kirov had commented briefly on Sophtia's
absences at odd hours, but she had not questioned her
niece closely. Sophia knew that her aunt believed that she
was rendezvousing with Lord John, and that was exactly
the impression she had wanted to establish.

When Lord John had contacted her again through
Mistress Wheeler, Sophia had felt confident in suggesting
her mother's house as their meeting place. Now she was
not so certain. Josef surely must have suspected from her
nervousness, that this rendezvous was different. Always
before when Josef returned, Sophia had been waiting for
him. When he came this time, there would be no one.

Sophia flew out the door and then turned to securely
lock it. Standing in the snow, snowflakes swirling about
her head, she stared up at the house that held so many dear
memories of her mother and childhood.

Then she turned and walked swiftly away, the bundle
she carried bumping against her leg. She had smuggled
little by little her most precious mementos and a few
clothes from her aunt's house, not wanting to leave Russia
empty-handed.

She reached the sleigh as Lord John jumped down.
"Allow me, my lady," he said, taking the awkward
bundle. Its weight surprised him as he put it in the sleigh.
He handed Sophia up into the sleigh and climbed in beside
her, calling a command to the driver.

The driver called to the horses and the sleigh began
gliding once more down Peterhof road toward the docks.
Lord John glanced at his companion and was surprised by
the gleam of excitement in her eyes. Somehow he had
thought she would be frightened and tearful and in need of
reassurance.

"You are remarkably calm, my lady," he said, careful

not to address her by name in the driver's hearing.

Sophia laughed softly, her breath frosting on the frigid dawn air. "I was afraid you would not come before Josef returned, but now I know that we will soon be far beyond even my aunt's formidable anger. She will not realize what has happened for an hour or more."

"And what will your aunt realize?" asked Lord John curiously.

Sophia's cheeks flamed, but her gaze was merry. "My aunt will believe that I have eloped with my lover."

"What!" Lord John was aghast.

Sophia laughed again. "I do apologize, my lord. I have used you shamefully. Somehow my aunt discovered that I had met you at Mistress Wheeler's home. She concluded that we were lovers. I allowed her to think what she would because she gave me permission to continue to meet with you," said Sophia matter-of-factly. She smiled at his expression. "You are shocked, my lord? Pray attempt to understand my aunt's thinking. She believed a desperate affair of the heart would make me more amenable to an unwanted marriage. And she knew also that you were leaving Russia very soon. My aunt took pleasure in informing me of that, I assure you. From her point of view my eyes would be opened to reality and I would have no more dreams of love and permanence."

"Your aunt is a selfish monster," exclaimed Lord John. He caught back his anger with difficulty. "Forgive me, my lady. I should not have spoken so."

"Why not, when it is true?" asked Sophia, shrugging.

The sleigh had reached the docks and Lord John was spared the necessity of a reply in the bustle of getting himself and Sophia on the merchant ship. When at last everything was arranged and they stood at the railing to watch the city slip slowly past, he was free to think again of all that Sophia had said. He glanced down at his slight companion, wondering about the character of a young woman who thought so little of leaving the only family she knew and who could talk so calmly of love affairs.

The gilded towers and park of Peterhof slipped away

into the distance. The ship sailed past the town of Oranien-
baum. The banks became low and the land flat as the ship
proceeded up the Gulf of Finland. Sophia stared toward
the receding shore, unmoving. Crystal tears slid down her
cheeks, but she uttered no sound. The breeze ruffled the
dark fur of her cape. Lord John found her gloved hand on
the railing and gently folded her fingers in his. They stood
together, hands clasped, and watched great Russia disappear.

7

THE DAY was cold and gray, but a faint softening of the air hinted at an English spring. Without fanfare an unprepossessing carriage drove up the curb before a respectable London town house. The door opened and a gentleman stepped out. He turned to assist a young woman dressed in a travel pelisse and gray velvet bonnet out of the carriage to the pavement. The young lady's fur-trimmed bonnet tilted as she looked up at the town house. Shadows of uncertainty and apprehension darkened her blue-gray eyes.

"Courage, Miss Wyndham," said Lord John. Sophia smiled at him gratefully and nodded. He gently took the bundle that she clutched and escorted her up the steps to the door. Lord John banged the knocker sharply.

The porter who opened the door was astonished to learn their identities. He immediately ushered them to the drawing room and went to inform his employers of their visitors.

When Sophia met Lord John's glance, she smiled, but she did not address him. She seated herself on a silk-upholstered settee, only to get to her feet again. She looked about her at the drawing room's tasteful mahogany furniture and russet and green hangings with a cool pretense. Despite her previously expressed confidence in her relatives' certain welcome, she had had several weeks to develop doubts and she felt some apprehension over the coming meeting with her aunt and uncle. She had not seen them in over six years. Her sudden unannounced arrival now could come as an inconvenient surprise.

Lord John understood his companion's withdrawal and he did not press her for conversation. He stationed himself next to the fireplace, far enough away not to intrude and yet near enough to assist Miss Wyndham's case if he should be needed.

Sophia and Lord John had not long to wait before the drawing-room door was thrown open and a middle-aged couple entered. The woman was pleasantly plump, with soft brown hair and eyes, and wore a fashionable mauve morning dress rucked with lace. "Dearest Sophia! I am so glad you have come to us at last," she said warmly.

Sophia felt her nervousness vanish. Without hesitation she went to her aunt and the women exchanged a tight embrace. "Aunt Matilda, you have no notion how wonderful it is to see you again."

Her aunt released her and Sophia found heself face to face with her uncle. His fine blue eyes were kind in expression and his face achingly familiar. "Welcome, dear little Sophia," he said, taking her hand and lifting her fingers to his lips.

"Oh, Uncle Charles." Sophia's eyes filled and she threw herself into his arms.

He awkwardly patted her shoulder. "Shush, child. You are home now."

Sophia straightened, half-crying and half-laughing. "You gave me such a start, Uncle. You looked at me just as Father used to."

"I suppose it is to be expected. We were twins, after all," said Charles Wyndham humorously. He looked beyond his niece to the tall quiet gentleman who observed their reunion. "My fellow informs me that you are Lord John Stokes. I must thank you for escorting our niece to us, sir."

"Lord John did more than escort me across town, Uncle," Sophia said, turning a warm smile on Lord John. "He helped me escape from Russia. If it had not been for his lordship's kindness, I would not be here now. Instead, I would have been married against my will to a Russian prince of disgusting habits."

"What is this, Sophia?" Charles Wyndham's voice was sharp. He shot a hard questioning look at Lord John.

Lord John realized how like an elopement Sophia's artless words had made their adventure sound. "Pray allow me to explain, sir. Miss Wyndham found herself in a rather peculiar situation." He gave the elder Wyndhams a concise account of all that had transpired from the moment that he had overheard the fateful conversation between Sophia and her aunt in a Russian ballroom. Sophia listened to him with a half-smile curving her lips, enjoying the sound of his voice and the changing expressions in his eyes.

The Wyndhams uttered exclamations of astonishment at his account. When Lord John had concluded, Charles Wyndham said gravely, "Certainly we owe you more than we can ever repay, my lord."

"Indeed we do. I shudder to think what our Sophia's life would be like if you had not acted so gallantly, Lord John," said Matilda. She suddenly bethought herself of her duties as hostess. "Do forgive me, my lord. I don't know where my manners have gone. I have not even offered you refreshment. I shall ring at once for tea."

Lord John forestalled her. "Pray do not concern yourself over me, ma'am. I am expected at my sister's house directly and must take my leave."

"Oh, if you are certain. But pray visit us again, my lord," said Matilda.

"Indeed, my lord. You shall always be certain of a welcome with us," said Charles, shaking hands with Lord John.

Lord John turned at last to Sophia, who had been watching him quietly. He lifted her hand and she felt the warm brush of his lips. "Good-bye, Miss Wyndham. I am happy that it has all turned out so well for you."

"Thank you, my lord. I shall remember your kindness always," said Sophia.

He bowed and left. Sophia heard the front door open. She went to the window, parted the lace curtain, and watched Lord John emerge from the house and stride swiftly down the steps to enter his carriage.

Her aunt came to stand beside her. "Lord John is a true gentleman, being gallant, kind, and compassionate. You were very fortunate to meet him, Sophia," said Matilda as she also watched the carriage drive away.

"I know it well, Aunt," said Sophia quietly. She let the curtain drop and turned somber eyes on her aunt. "I fear I have fallen in love with him. And I hope to marry him."

"Oh, my dear." Matilda Wyndham could think of nothing more adequate to say and turned helplessly to her husband. But Charles' startled expression gave her no inspiration in how to deal with such an amazing declaration.

As Lord John rode away in his carriage, he reflected that he and Miss Wyndham had parted as the best of acquaintances. It seemed odd to him that they had not developed a warmer footing after being together on the same ship for so many weeks, and part of him regretted it. His admiration for her had been initially kindled by her beauty and courage in a formidable situation. He had been further intrigued by the glimpse of humor she had revealed in the outrageous conversation about the view Princess Kirov had taken of their relationship.

But from the moment that the merchant ship entered the Gulf of Finland, Sophia had experienced seasickness and she had subsequently spent most of the voyage in her tiny cabin. Lord John exchanged hardly more than polite inquiries with her before reaching England, and the opportunity to satisfy his initial curiosity about the young lady he had aided was lost. He knew little more now about Miss Sophia Wyndham than when he first observed her in a Russian ballroom. She would remain forever a glimmer of mystery and beauty in his thoughts. Lord John laughed at himself. That was probably best, for Miss Wyndham's real nature probably could not compare to the image of her that he held in his mind's eye.

The elder Wyndhams were obviously pleasant enough, but Lord John did not anticipate making more than the one morning call that his sense of honor dictated.

By the time the carriage pulled up to a certain address, Miss Sophia Wyndham no longer occupied Lord John's thoughts. His responsibility was at an end and he was free to make plans for himself. The first decision he had made was to call on his sister Caroline and her husband, Richard. With any luck at all the Richardsons would offer him a fine dinner and a soft bed for the night. There would time enough tomorrow to make a decision about where he was to reside.

Lord John found his sister at home and was ushered into the drawing room. The lady reclining on the settee was still in her twenties, dressed fashionably in a muslin and lace day dress. Her riot of tawny, red curls was threaded with a sky-blue riband and the face she turned to her visitor was at once sweet and pert. Her green eyes widened in recognition and she threw down the novel that she had been reading. "John!" She came toward him, her hands outstretched.

Lord John caught her up in a bear hug and she squealed, scolding him good-naturedly to put her down at once. He did so and glanced at her softly rounded figure. "What, Caroline, again?"

She blushed and laughed. "Yes, isn't it marvelous? Richard hopes for a girl."

"Is this number five or six?" asked Lord John teasingly.

"It is the third, and well you know it, John," said Caroline with dignity. She abandoned her solemnity a second later. "Oh John, it is good to have you home! Are you on leave? How long can you stay before you must go back to that horridly cold place?"

"Thank you, Caroline. I am not on leave, but instead have been reappointed to London," said Lord John, amused.

"But how marvelous, John. I am so happy for you." A thought struck her and she stared at him anxiously. "It is all right, isn't it? I mean, you haven't disgraced yourself in some fashion."

Lord John laughed. "Quite the contrary. I've performed beyond my assigned duties. I don't know yet what to expect, however. I may be in London indefinitely or I could be sent to Timbuktu week after next. I shall know more after I have reported in to the Home Office."

"Do you mean that you have just arrived in town?" asked Caroline, astounded. "But it is four o'clock!"

"Yes, dear Caroline, and I am famished," said Lord John with a soulful look.

Instantly his sister was all solicitude, and she summoned the butler with a vigorous pull of the hanging bell. Caroline rapidly ordered a cold collation—wine and side dishes to be set out for her brother—and a room to be made up for him, for she would not hear of him going to a hotel. Lord John sat back at his ease in a wingback chair as he listened and grinned. As he well knew, Caroline's maternal instincts were strong and often spilled over to include the mothering of various and sundry relatives, friends, and stray animals. At this moment he did not mind in the least that he was one of their number.

Lord John spent a pleasant hour or so alone with his sister. Afterward the children were allowed to come down from the nursery. His two young nephews were delighted to become acquainted an uncle who thought nothing of getting on his knees to play with their tin soldiers. When the boys' father came home that evening, he was greeted with delighted cries and offered the instant information that Uncle John had come to visit.

Richard Richardson held out his hand to his brother-in-law. "Well, John, it appears that you are a favorite."

"How are you, Richard?" said Lord John. The gentlemen chatted for several minutes, obviously taking pleasure in each other's company. Caroline was content to sit almost unnoticed on the settee and watch her family. She was delighted to have them all together.

When dinner was announced the children returned to the nursery, and the Richardsons and Lord John sat down to a leisurely meal. Richard conveyed his surprise that Lord John had been posted back to London so unexpectedly.

Lord John grinned. "I fear it is all my own fault. I chanced to be in a position to play knight-errant, and later, despite my best efforts, I found myself permanently cast in the role."

Caroline pricked up her ears. "But what happened, John? Was there truly a damsel in distress?"

"I doubt you would be satisfied with less, Caroline," said Lord John, grinning.

His brother-in-law laughed and glanced with fondness at Caroline. "John has you there, my love. You are a dyed-in-the-wool romantic."

Caroline shrugged. Her smile was bewitching and provocative. "And you are my true knight, Richard." Her husband reddened and coughed in embarrassment. Having completely unmanned her husband, she turned her eyes innocently on her brother. "Now give us the round tale, John."

Lord John was amused at their warm byplay. Fleetingly he wondered if he would ever find just such a warm relationship for himself. He obliged their curiosity and made his last experiences in St. Petersburg an amusing adventure that had them both in stitches.

When he was finished, Richard dried his watering eyes. "'Pon my soul, John. I wish that I had seen your face when Kirov threatened to split you on the spot. Only you could have stepped into such a pretty tangle. But at least it is well ended."

Caroline had a far-off look in her eyes. She focused suddenly on her brother. "This Sophia Wyndham—is she very pretty?"

"Miss Wyndham is a paragon beyond compare. The slightest glance from her magnificent eyes and my manly heart was mortally pierced," said Lord John, pressing a hand to his chest with a deep sigh.

Richard, who had taken a sip of wine, spluttered a laugh.

"John, do be serious," said Caroline. "What is Miss Wyndham's family like? I mean the English branch, of course."

"The Wyndhams are quite a respectable sort," said Lord John.

"Wonderful. And Miss Wyndham is pretty, I believe you said," said Caroline.

Lord John looked at her in surprise. She wore a speculative expression and he sat bolt-upright. "Now, none of that, Caroline. I shall not have my peace cut up by your matchmaking efforts yet again. Richard, pray speak to her. Last visit I was positively compelled to end my leave three days early to escape that clinging ninnyhammer friend of hers."

"Estelle does not cling. Nor is she a ninnyhammer," said Caroline with dignity.

"My dear, John does have a point," said Richard gently.

"Oh, very well. Estelle is a bit bird-witted, I'll grant you that. But she was a very good catch, nevertheless," said Caroline.

"Did you say 'was'?" asked Lord John quickly.

Caroline's tone was oppressive. "Estelle had the good fortune to accept an offer from a gentleman of impeccable lineage, credentials, and background only last Season. She is very happy."

"Praise God!" exclaimed Lord John fervently.

His brother-in-law subsided into unrepressed laughter.

Caroline sent an annoyed glance toward her spouse. "Really, Richard! One would think that you do not care for John's future welfare and happiness at all."

Richard valiantly choked back his amusement, but he could not prevent a last chuckle from escaping him even as he assured his wife that her brother's welfare was indeed dear to his heart. He sought his wife's slim fingers and enfolded them warmly. "But, dearest love, I believe John is best-suited to the task of finding himself a bride."

"Thank you, Richard. I shall owe you my sanity," murmured Lord John.

"I do not altogether agree with you, Richard. My brother is notorious for his heedless decisions," said Caroline, ignoring Lord John's frivolous statement.

"My what?" exclaimed Lord John, indignant. "I am the most logical creature alive, Caroline. I'll have you know that I weigh carefully every possible consequence of my actions before I make a move."

"Then, how ever did you come to leap to the rescue of Miss Wyndham?" Caroline asked sweetly.

Lord John was momentarily speechless. He turned to his brother-in-law. "Outrage overcomes me. I am forced to remonstrate with you, Richard. You should beat her more often. My sister has grown unusually pert."

"You have just not been about her often enough, John." Richard lowered his voice and rolled his eyes back at his wife. "I tell you, it is sometimes like bathing in vinegar."

Caroline tried to arrange her features into severe lines. She utterly failed and began laughing. "Indeed, Richard. Then you must provide the oil in our amiable marriage."

The dinner ended on this convivial note. Lord John was persuaded by Caroline to enlarge on his days in St. Petersburg and it was hours later when he finally said good night and allowed a footman to show him to the room that had been prepared for him.

The next morning when he sauntered downstairs to join his sister and brother-in-law for breakfast, Caroline informed him that she was already planning a social function to mark his return to London. She asked him very casually if he had any preference in which young lady he was to escort to dinner.

Lord John looked at her for a moment. He said gently, "I hope that I have a wide choice, Caroline."

"Of course you do, John. Whom do you wish it to be?" asked Caroline. She looked over her list and began to hum.

Lord John glanced at his brother-in-law. Richard grimaced and shook his head. Lord John meekly said that Caroline could choose his dinner partner for him, which greatly pleased her. He watched his sister with pensive eyes while she happily made notes on her guest list.

Lord John was beginning to realize that it would definitely be to his advantage to locate a town house for himself. Otherwise he foresaw that he would spend the entire Season fending off Caroline's unending supply of marriageable candidates, unable to retreat. With his own establishment open, he could gracefully decline any social engagement when he chose.

Since he had anticipated being away from England for some years, he had made the present lease on his own town house a lengthy one. His tenants could not very well be put out on the street without notice. Perhaps if he waited and gave the tenants a few weeks' time to find a new address, he would not have to go to the trouble of locating another residence. Lord John had half-persuaded himself that this was the best course to take. Then Caroline mentioned a particular debutante in exceedingly glowing terms and he decided on the instant to take care of his housing problem that very day.

Lord John left the Richardsons' town house soon after breakfast, and even though he knew it was still early, he requested his carriage driver to set him down at his solicitors' address. He was impatient to tell the fellow that it was of the utmost urgency that a suitable establishment be found and a decent household staff engaged.

8

DURING THE next several days Sophia became better acquainted with her aunt and uncle. They had always shown kindness to her as a child and she was glad to find that her memories had not misled her. Charles and Matilda quickly put her at ease with their sincere delight in her presence. They scrupulously included her in their activities and their conversations and expressed warm interest in her opinions.

As Sophia came to feel more at home, she told the Wyndhams little by little of her mother's death and her life under Princess Kirov's roof. Sophia spoke so matter-of-factly about being a pawn in Princess Kirov's schemes to further the Kirov family interests that Matilda was moved to protest.

"My dear, how distressed you must have been," said Matilda, her generous heart touched with pity.

Sophia shook her head. Her eyes gleamed with laughter. "Perhaps you should pity Princess Kirov more, Aunt. Her expectations for me were so high. I utterly deflated them."

Charles Wyndham laughed. "Quite so. But Tilda and I are happy that you did, Sophia. We enjoy your company immensely."

"Indeed, my dear. You have made us most happy by coming to us," said Matilda, smiling at her niece.

"And I am so grateful to you both for opening your home to me," said Sophia.

Later, when the elder Wyndhams had retired to the privacy of their bedroom for the night, Matilda was thinking over the earlier conversation with Sophia and what it had been like to have her living with them for the past week. She had been delighted to discover in Sophia a well-bred young woman. Sophia had proven herself considerate of those about her and participated readily in whatever plan was proposed to her. Matilda was particularly grateful for Sophia's even temper and lively interest. She knew of so many young ladies who were self-centered and spoiled. But she supposed Sophia's life had not allowed for much self-indulgence.

Matilda had dismissed her maid some moments before and now she sat down at her dressing table to perform for herself the last task in her nightly toilet. She drew a brush slowly and steadily through her heavy brown hair. Her thoughts were still on her young niece. "Charles, what do you think of our Sophia?"

Charles Wyndham was reading, seated in an overstuffed armchair. Without lowering his book, he said, "I have immensely enjoyed her presence this past week. Indeed, she is much like I imagined a daughter would be."

Matilda's hand froze in midstroke. Stricken, she stared in the mirror at her husband. "You have never before expressed regret, Charles."

Surprised, Charles lowered his book. What he saw in her face made him immediately go to her. He gently took the brush out of her hand and carried her fingers to his lips. "My dearest Tilda, I never express regret over a situation that cannot be changed."

"I am sorry, Charles. I have failed you so miserably." Matilda averted her face.

Charles gently raised her chin. There were tears in her eyes. He lovingly traced her trembling lips. "Sweet love, I have never regretted the wonderful times with you. Perhaps children would have made those times richer. I do not know. But I do know that I love you as passionately and irrevocably now as I did on our wedding day. Nothing could ever add or detract from that."

"Oh, Charles." Matilda rose and went into his embrace. He kissed away her tears. After a while Matilda leaned away from him and anxiously met his eyes. "You truly do not mind?"

"I am a selfish brute, Tilda. When I think of what it would have been like to share you with a brace of sturdy children, I shudder," said Charles with mock humor.

But Matilda recognized the underlying note of sober truth in his voice. With a sigh she settled her head against his shoulder. "We have a daughter now, Charles, and she is of marriageable age. Shall you be able to watch Sophia marry?" she asked teasingly.

"I should think so," said Charles with emphasis.

"What do you think of this infatuation of hers for Lord John?" asked Matilda, her thoughts carrying her logically to the point of concern.

"Sophia strikes me as an independent young woman. I suspect it is best that we do not tax her about it. She will eventually decide things for herself," said Charles.

"But, Charles . . ."

He gave her no further chance to speak but kissed her thoroughly, leaving her disheveled and breathless. He said softly, "Dearest Tilda, pray cease speculating about our niece's romantic fancies. I have a few of my own, you know."

Matilda blushed and laughed and went willingly to bed with him.

Even though Charles Wyndham's opinion carried considerable weight with his wife, Matilda Wyndham was nevertheless doubtful that something should not be said to Sophia. Therefore, a couple of days later, when Sophia chanced to mention Lord John Stokes, Matilda took advantage of the opening.

"Sophia, do forgive me if I speak out of turn. But are your emotions truly attached to Lord John? Quite naturally you feel gratitude to him, but . . ." She ended with a delicate shrug.

Sophia laughed. She swiftly hugged her aunt. "I appreciate your concern for me, Aunt Matilda. But what I feel for Lord John is much more than mere gratitude. Of course, I am grateful but there is so much more in my heart." There was a luminous glow in her eyes. She paused, then said softly, "I am happy when my thoughts dwell on him. I dream of him. And I want passionately for him to return my regard. Is that love, Aunt?"

"It is near enough, child," said Matilda with a smile.

She allowed the subject to drop, wise enough to recognize
that she should not press her niece too hard. She was not
thoroughly convinced that Sophia's emotions were irrevocably attached, however, and made a mental note to introduce her niece into English society as quickly as possible.
Once the Season began, Sophia would be caught up in a
whirl of activity and have the opportunity to meet scores of
young men. Matilda thought the exposure to society would
be a true test of Sophia's avowed affection for Lord John.
If Sophia remained steadfast in her preference during the
next few months, then Matilda felt that she would be
satisfied that her niece's regard for Lord John was more
than an impressionable young girl's admiration. Then her
responsibility to Sophia could very well include encour-
aging Lord John to make his addresses. The ghost of a
smile flitted over Matilda's face as she watched Sophia
skillfully knot silver strings into a reticule. Matilda decided
that Charles was very clever to give their niece time to
make her own decision. But Matilda meant to be quietly
waiting to help Sophia if she was needed.

Caroline Richardson's party was one of the first of the
Season. The Wyndhams received invitations to it with a
particularly warm note urging them to attend. The
Wyndham ladies were surprised. They did not know the
Richardsons.

"Is Caroline Richardson a friend of yours, Sophia?"
Matilda asked doubtfully.

"I have never met her," said Sophia, equally puzzled by
the personal note.

Matilda turned the invitation over in her hands. "The
address is quite a respectable one. Perhaps they are acquaintances of your uncle's. Being a physician, Charles
often forms new connections. I suppose we should
attend." Sophia agreed and they turned their attention to
other matters.

The personal invitation was not again wondered at until
the evening that the Wyndhams were in their carriage on
their way to the Richardson soiree. Charles Wyndham said
casually, "By the by, who are these people, Tilda?"

She looked at him, astonished. "Why, do you not know them, Charles?"

"No. Should I?" asked Charles curiously. He was amused by the bewildered look exchanged between his wife and niece. "I gather that none of us knows why we are attending this party. Well, well. It may prove to be quite an interesting evening."

The mystery became clearer when the Wyndhams met their hostess. Caroline Richardson welcomed them warmly. She glanced at Sophia with more than idle curiosity. "Miss Wyndham, how pleased I am to meet you at last. My brother, Lord John Stokes, speaks quite highly of you."

Sophia blushed at the implication of her hostess's greeting. "I am happy to make your acquaintance, Mrs. Richardson. Forgive me, but I am still somewhat bemused by your gracious invitation. Lord John had not told me about any of his family."

"John is so discreet that he is positively boring," said Caroline easily. She turned then to the elder Wyndhams and assured them of welcome. She drew the Wyndhams after her into the gathering and introduced them to several acquaintances. Presently she left them on their own while she attended a new arrival.

The musicians struck up a country dance and almost immediately Sophia was asked to stand up in a set. Matilda graciously gave her permission and the young gentleman swept Sophia onto the floor.

Matilda looked up at her husband. "Well, Charles, it seems that we have been invited this evening at Lord John's express wish."

"So it appears," said Charles. He studied the throng about them with interest. "I recognize only a few faces here and there. Unless I miss my guess, I suspect we are a bit out of water." He shrugged, and bowed elaborately to his wife. "At the very least I intend that we shall have an enjoyable evening. Pray give me the honor of this set, madam."

Matilda laughed, delighted by his extravagant gallantry,

and allowed herself to be swept onto the dance floor. Their
complete enjoyment in the entertainment provided was in
time noted. Later, when they were drawn into conversation
by various personages, their quiet manners endeared them
to those about them. Unknown to the Wyndhams, they
had successfully taken the first step toward acceptance by
the *haut ton*. The Wyndhams would thereafter be considered valued guests because they were genial and inclined
to enjoy life and those around them. The crowning cachet
was that they were discovered at a gathering hostessed by
Caroline Richardson, who was a popular hostess.

When Lord John made his appearance, Caroline immediately whisked him off to do his duty. On the face
Lord John accepted his fate with equanimity. He was uni-
formly gracious to the young ladies and the dowagers,
careful not to show any hint of partiality, and he found the
task not unlike his former diplomatic duties.

It was more than an hour before Lord John discovered
that the Wyndhams were in attendance. He immediately
approached Charles Wyndham, who stood leaning on the
back of his wife's chair. "Well met, sir! I am glad to see
you and Mrs. Wyndham here." He and the Wyndhams exchanged pleasantries. Charles and Matilda were curious
about him since he had apparently asked his sister to
extend a social invitation to them and swiftly established a
more familiar footing with him. After a few moments,
Lord John glanced about. "I have not seen Miss Wyndham. Did she not accompany you this evening?"

The Wyndhams exchanged an unfathomable glance.
Unknown to him, they wondered what his intentions were
toward their niece. "Oh, yes. Sophia is in this set. She
enjoys the dancing very much," said Matilda, nodding
toward her niece, who was at that moment being swept
through the country dance by an exuberant partner.

For a long moment Lord John watched Sophia, struck
by the difference in her from the last time he had seen her
dance. Sophia's eyes twinkled with lively fun and she
laughed merrily at her partner's utterances. Lord John unconsciously smiled, glad for her enjoyment. Charles

Wyndham's brows rose at the warmth of his lordship's expression.

"It is clear that Miss Wyndham is thoroughly enjoying herself," Lord John said, turning back to the Wyndhams. He raised Matilda's hand, preparing to take his leave. "Madam, I am your devoted servant." He was surprised when Matilda detained him.

"Pray do not leave us so quickly, my lord. We have enjoyed your conversation and I know Sophia will be happy to renew her acquaintance with you. Look, the set is just ending," said Matilda.

Charles Wyndham cleared his throat and became suddenly interested in the decorative plaster on the ceiling. Matilda ignored him.

"My lord! How wonderful to see you again." Lord John turned to find Sophia approaching with her recent partner in tow. She held out a gloved hand to him, and smiling, he took it. Sophia did not wait for him to speak but turned at once to her companion. "George, this is Lord John Stokes, whom I met in St. Petersburg. He was attached to the British embassy there."

"Oh, I say!" The young man enthusiastically shook hands with Lord John. "Your servant, sir. I am George Hetherby, Esquire. I was just confiding to Miss Wyndham that I was considering the diplomatic service as a career. I should think it frightfully exciting."

Lord John regarded Mr. Hetherby's eager young face with amusement. "Quite, Mr. Hetherby. You don't know from one moment to the next whom you might meet or what you will be required to do." His eyes briefly met Sophia's gaze and she colored faintly.

"Have you met many of the royalty, sir?" asked Mr. Hetherby.

"Oh, dozens," said Lord John easily. He regretted his own offhandedness when he saw the awe in the young gentleman's face. "Of course that is nothing in Russia. Every province of that huge country has its prince. I suppose they could be considered something like our own lesser nobility. However, life in St. Petersburg was in itself odd and wondrous.'' Lord John launched on a lively description of the duties and functions of an attaché in a foreign capital. Mr. Hetherby hung on his every word, occasionally asking a diffident question. Matilda and Charles were equally fascinated and gained further insight into their niece's background. When Lord John touched upon aspects of Russian life that seemed more than Mr. Hetherby or the others in his audience could readily accept, he appealed to Miss Wyndham for corroboration.

"Oh, yes, in the spring when the snow and ice have melted it is not at all unusual to discover an entire cart and its horse fallen into a hole in the road. A dozen men are needed sometimes to pull the cart and horse out,'' said Sophia.

"Well! I have never heard of such a thing,'' said Matilda. Her niece laughed at her wonderment.

"Russia is a giant in every sense of the word, Mrs. Wyndham. Her citizens' lives are proportionately dramatic,'' said Lord John.

"You speak as though you admire the country, my lord,'' said Charles, curious.

"Russia is a country worthy of respect, sir. However, I am also wary of her. She is a giant of unbridled power and passion, and that can be a dangerous combination,'' said Lord John.

"Extraordinary. My brother, Sophia's father, once said much the same thing. I confess that I am fascinated. I should like to discuss the political side of Russia in more depth with you, Lord John,'' said Charles.

"I would be happy to do so, sir, and I await your pleasure,'' said Lord John.

"Then you must come to dine with us next week. We are having a small dinner party on Thursday. I will send you an invitation,'' said Matilda, on the instant deciding that it was time to begin the Season's entertaining.

Lord John bowed and expressed his anticipation of a pleasant evening. A familiar figure caught his eye and he stared a moment, then turned to the Wyndhams. "Forgive me, but I have this instant seen someone that I must speak to straightaway. I look forward to our next meeting. Your

servant, sir, madam." Sophia gave her hand to his lordship in farewell. "My lord." Lord John bowed to the
ladies and, after a casual word to George Hetherby, left
them.

"Lord John is an extremely pleasant gentleman. I shall
be happy to entertain him," said Matilda, with a glance at
her niece. Sophia was smiling and her eyes followed Lord
John's tall figure. Satisfied, Matilda turned her attention
to young Hetherby. "I should like you to join us as well,
Mr. Hetherby."

"Oh, I say! I am much obliged, ma'am," said George,
reddening with pleasure. He turned to Sophia and with an
awkward bow, said, "The new set has struck up. Should
you care to dance again, Miss Sophia?"

"Thank you, George. I care to dance above all else,"
said Sophia with a merry laugh. The two went off.

Charles, who had stood by silent the last few seconds,
leaned close to his wife's ear. "This dinner party has come
up rather sudden, my dear. What are you up to, Tilda?"

"Trust me, my dear Charles. I simply think it time that
our niece enter society so that she can meet any number of
nice young people," said Matilda.

"I see. 'Pon my word, we have quite an interesting
Season ahead of us this year," said Charles.

On the other side of the crowd Lord John had found the
gentleman that he had glimpsed. "Freddy! I didn't know
you had gotten into town," said Lord John. He grasped
his friend's hand hard, genuinely glad to see him. "I had
almost given you up for lost."

"So did I, once or twice. The distressed damsel's cousin
came roaring after me, you know. It was that huge bearish
Kirov fellow who threatened to kill you that night in St.
Petersburg. Remind me to tell you about it," said Sir
Frederick. He had his glass in his eye and was in the
process of surveying the graceful women who passed by.

"I shall be all ears. But how do you come to be at the
party tonight, for I know that if Caroline had known you
were in London she would have mentioned it to me," said
Lord John.

"Nothing simpler, my dear fellow. I ran into your

brother-in-law at White's this afternoon. I had just taken rooms at a hotel and decided to step around to the club for some civilized conversation. He naturally invited me to come by this evening," said Freddy absently as he continued to ogle the ladies present. His eyes brightened. "Look there, John. Do you see her? What an absolutely stunning creature she is."

Lord John was amused to find that his friend had singled out a cool brunette of classic beauty, who had earned the sobriquet "Ice Maiden." He took Sir Frederick's arm. "Come, Freddy, that one makes a habit of breaking hearts. Let me introduce you instead to a sweet, fresh young lady of my acquaintance."

Sir Frederick hung back, giving him a suspicious look. "What is this, John? Are you taking a leaf from Caroline's matchmaking book?"

Lord John laughed. "On my honor, no! But you did say that you wished someday to meet our own fair damsel in distress. Miss Wyndham is here tonight."

"Is she, by Jove? Then do lead on, John," said Sir Frederick, his curiosity instantly aroused.

9

THE GENTLEMEN crossed the ballroom to where Sophia stood with her relatives. Lord John introduced Sir Frederick Hawkesworth to the Wyndhams. Charles and Matilda's attention was claimed almost immediately by another acquaintance and the gentlemen were able to speak to Miss Wyndham. Lord John made the introductions. He was astonished by Sir Frederick's reaction. Sir Federick stood as though stricken dumb. A moment passed and Sophia glanced at Lord John. Sir Frederick came to himself then and flushed, stammering a greeting.

Sophia was amused by Sir Frederick's openmouthed admiration, and touched by his subsequent embarrassment. She held out her hand to him and warmly grasped his fingers. "I am most happy to meet you, Sir Frederick. You are, after all, one of my shining knights. Lord John has told me of the role you played in aiding my escape from St. Petersburg. I am grateful for your gallant heart," she said, smiling in a friendly fashion.

Her almond-shaped blue-gray eyes rested on him warmly and Sir Frederick reddened at once. He made an effort to pull himself together. "I was happy to oblige, Miss Wyndham. But pray call me Freddy."

Sophia was instantly wary of his attempt to establish such quick familiarity, and laughed to ease her set-down. "Thank you, my lord, but I think it best if I do not."

"But everyone does. I rarely answer to anything else." Sir Frederick appealed with desperation to his companion. "John, bear me out."

"It is quite true, Miss Wyndham. His friends know from past experience that they cannot engage Freddy's full attention with any name more formal," Lord John said.

"Then I may count myself one of your friends, Sir
Frederick?" asked Sophia teasingly, still undecided.

"Oh, quite. Quite right. I am most honored," he
assured her fervently.

Sophia abandoned her playful air, deciding that Sir
Frederick Hawkesworth was harmless. She shook her
head. "I can see even on our short acquaintance that you
are too trusting, Freddy. I shall take great advantage of
you, I promise you."

"I shall try to bear it stoically, Miss Wyndham," said
Sir Frederick happily, with a bow.

"Have you been back in England long, my lord?" asked
Sophia.

"For a few days only. The overland trip from Russia
took longer than your sea voyage did. And I was delayed
somewhat, too," said Sir Frederick, with a sideways glance
at Lord John.

Sophia was quick to interpret his look. She lowered her
voice. "I sense that you were delayed on my account. Pray
tell me what happened." Sir Frederick hesitated. Sophia
smiled. "You need have no reservations in confiding the
truth to me, sir. Believe me, I would not be at all surprised
if the Kirovs made some attempt to retrieve me."

"I think you may tell us, Freddy," said Lord John,
slowly. He had not thought about it, but aiding Miss
Wyndham would naturally have repercussions.

Sir Frederick was dubious, but he shrugged. "I suppose
it is all right to do so. Very well, then. My driver drove like
lightning, all the while singing encouragement to his
horses. He was a splendid fellow who spoke French and
German besides his Russian. I was obligated to him ten
times over before we reached Poland, believe me. I would
have had a devil of a time making myself understood at
some of the places we stopped to change teams."

"You were about to tell us of the Kirovs, Freddy,"
prompted Lord John.

"Quite right. I am coming to it. We were several
hundred vests out of St. Petersburg when the Cossacks
appeared," said Sir Frederick.

"Cossacks?" gasped Sophia. Her eyes darkened.

Sir Frederick nodded. "There we were, my fellow and I, skimming over the eternal ice and snow. We flashed past a stand of birch trees, then suddenly Cossacks dashed by on horses. They came singly without order, these deadly lances in their hands. It quite gave me a start, I can tell you. They were rough, bearded fellows dressed in gray garments that opened out in huge hoods for their heads. The Cossacks headed off the sleigh's horses and these other horsemen appeared. One of them was this huge, blond fellow, all arrogance and fire."

"Misha!" exclaimed Sophia, easily recognizing her cousin in Sir Frederick's succinct description.

"He announced himself as Prince Mikhail Kirov," said Sir Frederick.

Sophia nodded. "Yes, that is my cousin. Aunt Elizaveta must have sent him personally to bring me back. Pray go on, sir. What did Misha say?"

"His highness was enraged that you were not in the sleigh. Naturally I claimed all ignorance, not liking the looks of those Cossack lances. My driver was trembling like a blancmange, poor fellow, and I was more than a little shaken myself," said Sir Frederick with a burst of candor.

"Did Misha . . . threaten you?" asked Sophia hesitantly. She did not like the thought of one of her relations behaving with such a lack of civility, but she knew of old her cousin's temper.

"I should say he did! He vowed all sorts of revenges upon my person and my descendants, if I lived to sire any. I had a very warm time of it. I have never been in a more uncomfortable position in my life," said Sir Frederick feelingly.

"I am sorry," said Sophia, dismayed that she had been the cause of such an unpleasant experience.

"Well, he cooled down a little after the Cossacks had torn apart the sleigh," said Sir Frederick. "Then he apologized as though all had become sunlight and roses, and galloped away."

"What did you say, Freddy?" asked Lord John sharply.

Sir Frederick looked at him in surprise. "Why, that the prince apologized and—"

"No, about the sleigh."

"Why, he had his men tear everything out of the sleigh. You know how the sleigh was packed, John, with the luggage in the bottom and over it that bed covered with black moroccan leather. Prince Kirov suspected that Miss Wyndham was secreted under the bed," said Sir Frederick. He shook his head with a glimmer of a smile. "How he could have thought a lady would be willing to ride across half of Russia under a bed, I don't know."

"But I might have thought to do it. Misha knows my determination as well as I know his. We are much alike in some ways," said Sophia quietly. It troubled her that even while in a blind rage Prince Kirov had been able to project her possible choices. He apparently knew her thinking better than she would have imagined possible.

Lord John was watching her expressive face. He said quietly, "You believe that the prince will come for you here, my lady?"

"Yes," said Sophia simply. It was a certainty in her heart.

Lord John took her hand in his and felt her fingers tremble. "Pray do not be anxious, Miss Wyndham. I suspect that Prince Kirov, if he comes, will discover that London is a far cry from St. Petersburg. He shall not touch you here."

"You may depend upon it, my lady. I myself shall guarantee your safety," said Sir Frederick, swift to reassure in his turn.

Sophia laughed and gently pulled her hand from Lord John's comforting grasp. "My thanks to you both, noble sirs. I apprehend that I still have two faithful knights for my protection." A shadow crossed her face. "Though I do wish that you had left Russia with pleasanter memories, Sir Frederick."

"Freddy," he corrected quickly. He grinned. "But I do have fond memories, Miss Wyndham. Did I not tell you of

the caravan of sleighs that I saw emerging from a dark
forest? There must have been upward of a hundred of
them in a string with a driver for every seventh horse.''

"You saw the traders," exclaimed Sophia with delight.
"I saw them often in the marketplace. They carried wares
from every corner of the world throughout Russia.''

"These fellows appeared more like apparitions of the
snow than mere traders," said Sir Frederick. "The sun was
just rising, throwing rays across the snow and trans-
forming it into a surface of diamonds. The cold of the
night had settled like a cloak upon the caravan, for every
man and horse was encrusted with frosty particles and the
long beards of the men and the manes of the horses
glittered in the new light. It was a wonderful sight.''

"Oh, how I would have loved to have seen it," exclaimed Sophia. Her aunt called to her. She made her
excuses to the gentlemen and gracefully moved away to
join Matilda Wyndham.

The gentlemen watched her go. "I am glad that you were
able to turn her mind to pleasanter memories," said Lord
John. He glanced at Sir Frederick, his grin suddenly
teasing. "I never knew you to be so poetic, Freddy.''

"I am inspired to more than poetry, John," said Sir
Frederick solemnly. His eyes rested still on Sophia
Wyndham's face and thick gold hair.

"What! Not again, Freddy. You tumble into love more
often than the seas break against Dover's white cliffs,"
said Lord John, laughing. "I'll wager that in a fortnight
you'll have forgotten Miss Wyndham and your heart's
desire shall be a statuesque brunette, or a vivacious red-
head.''

"On the contrary, John. This time is very different. An
aloof part of me that was never before affected has been
struck at last. From this moment forward I am Miss
Sophia Wyndham's devoted servant," said Sir Frederick
solemnly.

Lord John stared at him, speechless. He had never seen
his carefree, fanciful friend so serious of mien.

Sir Frederick clapped Lord John on the shoulder.

"Thank you, John. I might not have met my angel but for you. I must go strengthen my acquaintance with the Wyndhams, for I intend to call on them often in the future." He left Lord John to approach the Wyndhams and engaged them in conversation.

Lord John was bemused. Sir Frederick was an extremely engaging fellow, generally indolent in nature. This new purposefulness in him was astonishing at the very least. Lord John felt a plucking at his sleeve. He turned.

"John, I should like to present to you Lady Priscilla Eversly. Pris, this is my dear brother, Lord John. I know that you shan't mind if I leave you in John's capable hands," said Caroline, and with a sweet smile up into her brother's consternated eyes, she swept away.

"How very pleased I am to meet you, Lord John," said Lady Priscilla in a soft voice, and held out her hand. Her green eyes were very bright when she glanced up at him.

Lord John took her proffered fingers and bowed. "Likewise, my lady. I believe you are an old friend of Caroline's?"

Lady Priscilla inclined her head. "But it has been more than a year since we have visited. I was in mourning for my late husband, you see, and could not go about. However, I have now reentered society and I very much look forward to the Season."

Lord John gave a pleasant smile and turned the conversation to less personal matters. Inwardly he groaned. Already Caroline was beginning her matchmaking efforts. If he read aright the determination in Lady Priscilla's eyes, she meant to have the prize before Caroline could point anyone else in his direction. Lord John recognized that his situation could prove perilous since he could not very well exit the function until the guests began to leave. His sister's meddling was a damnable nuisance. As for Lady Priscilla herself, he rather thought it would be the better part of discretion to rid himself as quickly as possible of her possessive presence. In due course Lord John maneuvered another gentleman into place and gracefully extricated himself. The lady's green eyes flashed, but she could only watch as Lord John sauntered away to greet an old acquaintance.

Lord John spent the better part of the evening escaping the attentions of the various ladies to whom Caroline introduced him. His temper was somewhat frayed when he again met with Sir Frederick.

"Here, now, John, what is this frown? It has been a pleasant-enough evening, surely," said Sir Frederick.

The lines deepened between Lord John's heavy blond brows. "On the contrary. I do not enjoy playing the fox while Caroline is the master of the hunt," said Lord John.

Sir Frederick cast a more penetrating look at him. "Your sister is at it again, I gather."

"I am all out of patience with her, Freddy. I realized it was coming, of course, and so I asked my solicitor to find me another establishment and a decent staff. But I do not know for how long I shall be able to stand having my peace cut up," said Lord John explosively.

"You don't want another establishment, John. Trust me, as soon as the lease is signed, you'll receive another overseas position or your tenants will take wing before their term is expired, and then you will be saddled with the upkeep of both residences," said Sir Frederick earnestly.

"What do you propose, then? I tell you, Freddy, another forthnight at Caroline's mercy and I shall go mad," said Lord John feelingly.

"Join me at the hotel, John. There is a vacant apartment adjacent to mine which is for let," said Sir Frederick. "You will need a small staff, of course, besides your valet. But nothing could be simpler than to find a porter and a fairly decent cook, and in the meantime you are welcome to take your mutton with me."

Lord John grasped his hand. "I am in your debt, Freddy. I shall pack up and be over at first light. Now all that remains to be decided is how I am to break the news to Richard and Caroline."

"What's to fear, John? After all, you are a trained diplomat," said Sir Frederick cheerfully.

Lord John started to laugh. "Quite. I had forgotten. I

am obliged to you for reminding me, Freddy."

The gentlemen exchanged a few more words before Sir Frederick went in search of his hostess to take his leave. Lord John's good spirits were restored and he was able to look on the remainder of the evening with admirable calm.

10

THE NEXT morning Caroline took breakfast in her room and so was not immediately aware of the quiet exit her brother's valet and luggage made from the house. Richard, who was on hand to express regret and his understanding to Lord John, chose not to enlighten her. He rather thought that he preferred to leave that task to Lord John.

When Caroline joined the gentlemen for luncheon she wondered at Richard's evasive gaze. She touched her husband's hand. "Dearest love, what is it? You have hardly spoken one word to me since I entered the dining room."

Lord John sent a glance at his brother-in-law's guilty expression and sat back in his chair. "It is my doing, Caroline. I asked Richard to allow me to break the news to you myself."

"What news?" Caroline looked from Lord John to Richard and back again to Lord John.

"I have found a hotel and I moved in this morning," said Lord John quietly.

"Whatever do you mean? You cannot leave us. It is too utterly ridiculous. You are my only and dearest brother. I would be a beast to allow you to stay anywhere else but here," Caroline said.

"My decision is made, Caroline." Lord John saw that she meant to protest further and threw up his hand. "Pray do not, dear sister. I love you well, and Richard and the boys, but I cannot endure each day being put on the block like a bullock for stud."

"John! I never did—I do not!" said Caroline indignantly. Her brother's gaze remained steady on her and

in a moment she shrugged uncomfortably. "Oh, very well.
I do understand how you might perhaps think so, but it is
not at all what I intended."

"I am certain that it wasn't, Caroline," said Lord John
dryly. He rose from the table. "I shall be dining with an
acquaintance this evening and with the Wyndhams next
Thursday, but I hope I shall be welcome to visit with you
next week."

"Of course, John." Caroline put up her cheek for Lord
John's kiss. When he had left the room, she said,
"Bother!"

"I did warn you, my dear. John is not the sort to be
driven," said Richard.

Caroline tossed her head. "I am not confounded yet,
Richard."

Richard sighed. "You are incorrigible, Caroline. Well, I
shall leave you to it. But I feel devilish sorry for John. I
will be at Tattersall's this afternoon. Shall I ask for the
carriage to be brought around for you before I go?"

Caroline's smile was unexpectedly sunny. "Thank you,
Richard. I do indeed wish to make a call or two," she said.

Richard was glad to see that her frown was gone and left
her to call for the carriage. Caroline did not burden him
with the cause of her renewed good humor. He would not
understand the necessity for her to call on Mrs. Wyndham
and her delightful niece, Miss Sophia Wyndham, but of
course it was important to establish a friendly relationship
with them. After all, her brother John had mentioned that
he would be dining with the Wyndhams on Thursday next.
Miss Wyndham must hold quite an attraction for him.

At the Wyndham residence, breakfast was always a
cheerful time, and Sophia had grown fond of the hour.
The topic that morning was naturally the soiree that they
had attended the evening before.

"I was never more surprised than when Lady Jersey herself came over to say a kind word," said Matilda, pouring
Charles a cup of coffee.

"But why should that surprise you? Lady Jersey seemed to me very gracious," asked Sophia.

"Your aunt means that we do not as a rule associate with the *haut ton*. Caroline Richardson introduced us to several personages that we have not mixed with before," said Charles. He glanced at his wife and said teasingly, "Shall you be able to bear our own respectable circle any longer, Tilda?"

"How nonsensical you are, Charles. I know where our true friends are to be found," said Matilda comfortably. "But the experience has led me to reflect. Our niece should be enjoying more of society, Charles. Therefore I wish to bring her out this Season."

"What?" exclaimed Sophia, pausing with her own cup halfway to her mouth. She set down her tea. "Aunt Matilda, you cannot be serious."

"I quite agree, Tilda. This dinner party for Thursday that you concocted so suddenly yesterday evening may be just the thing. I suggest that you have in the dressmakers and whomever else you shall need," said Charles.

"Thank you, my dear," said Matilda. Charles rose from the table and she put up her face so that he could kiss her. "You shall be off, then?"

"Yes. Pray don't look for me before luncheon. I shall be making several calls this morning," said Charles. He waved to Sophia and left the room.

"Aunt, what can you and my uncle be thinking?" asked Sophia, disturbed.

"Why, my dear, we are thinking of you. You are young and deserve the opportunity to establish your own friendships and life," said Matilda. She saw the footman push open the door a crack and she put her napkin on the table. "Come, Sophia. It is past time that we allow Henry to clear away breakfast. If you would, pray join me later in the sitting room. I would like to talk more about your coming-out."

"Yes, and so do I," said Sophia.

The ladies left the breakfast room and separated to attend their toilets. While washing in the waterbasin in her

bedroom Sophia could only wonder at her aunt's intention
to introduce her to society. Sophia considered the idea
absurd. She was not a fresh young debutante. She had
been out in St. Petersburg for some time and certainly
social functions no longer held the same mysterious allure
for her. Sophia admitted to herself that she sometimes
missed social activities. Yet she really did not see any
reason why her Uncle Charles and Aunt Matilda should go
the bother and expense of a London Season for her.

As Sophia finished with her toilet and smoothed her
hair, she decided that she must make her aunt understand
that she had no particular interest in embarking on a
Season. She had never actually expected to have one and
she was astonished that her aunt should wish to sponsor
her.

Sophia returned downstairs and joined her aunt in the
sitting room. When the ladies had taken up their embroidery, Sophia immediately addressed the subject of her
Season. "Aunt Matilda, pray do not think me ungracious,
but I do not wish for a Season. I do not miss society all that
very much. Indeed, I am quite content as I am."

"Nonsense, child. You need the company of other
young people. We are too dull for you," said Matilda.

"You aren't anything of the sort. I have enjoyed every
moment with you and Uncle Charles," said Sophia with
spirit.

"Perhaps. But being with us will not bring you to the
notice of Lord John Stokes," said Matilda.

Sophia was silenced, recognizing the truth in her aunt's
words. Matilda watched her thoughtful expression and
smiled, aware that she had scored a telling point. For
several minutes the ladies enjoyed a comfortable silence,
each applying needle to her hoop.

The butler came in to announce a caller and Matilda
asked him to show in the visitor. She and Sophia were
equally astonished when Caroline Richardson entered the
sitting room. Matilda quickly recovered. "Mrs. Richardson! This is an unlooked-for pleasure. Pray be seated."

Caroline laughed. "Thank you for that kind welcome,

Mrs. Wyndham. Quite frankly I feel that I am very very bold to call on you and Miss Wyndham upon such short acquaintance." She sat down on the striped-silk settee and began to pull of her soft kid gloves.

Matilda and Sophia exchanged glances at this open indication that Caroline Richardson intended to make a lengthy visit. "Shall I call for tea for our visitor, Aunt Matilda?" asked Sophia.

"That would be nice, Sophia," said Matilda. Her niece rose and Matilda stopped her with a gesture and a smiling shake of the head. "The bell, Sophia."

Sophia blushed. She sheepishly reached out for the bell-pull. "I fear that I may never become accustomed to the bellpulls here in England."

Caroline Richardson was astonished. Hesitantly she said, "Forgive me, but I cannot help but ask. Do you not have bellpulls in Russia?"

Sophia shook her head. "Oh, no. I cannot tell you how many times since I returned to England that I have startled the servants by appearing in person with a request. They believe me quite mad."

The butler entered and Sophia turned with a gracious word to request the tea board. He bowed and left.

"I am informed by Sophia that the Russian ladies normally shout for whatever it is they need," said Matilda.

"How extraordinary. I should not like the exertion and and I know my dear Richard would detest it. Our boys are quite noise enough," said Caroline, her eyes dancing.

The Wyndham ladies joined in her laughter.

The tea board and urn were brought. Sophia offered to pour the tea, and without appearing to do so, Caroline watched her closely. She had found that how someone poured tea for visitors was almost always a good indication of the quality of their upbringing. Caroline was pleased by Sophia's gracious manner and thought that even if Russia was too backward to have bellpulls, the ladies were at least taught proper serving skills. On the thought, Caroline said, "I had never before appreciated the small differences between England and Russia, Miss Wyndham. Do you know, I rather envy you the unique experience of living in both countries.''

Sophia looked at Mrs. Richardson for any sign of condescension, but there was none in Caroline's open expression and wide green eyes. "Indeed, I am quite fortunate.''

"I was saying to my niece just moments before your arrival, Mrs. Richardson, that I am particularly looking forward to this Season because she is staying with us. I shall be able to introduce her to our English society. Sophia was presented ages ago in St. Petersburg, of course, but I wish her to feel that London is her true home,'' said Matilda.

"But I already feel at home," said Sophia quietly.

Caroline looked at them, her brows raised. "I believe that I sense a disagreement of philosophy here.''

"Indeed, Mrs. Richardson. Sophia insists that she is perfectly comfortable with the company of her dull aunt and uncle, but I have told her that is not the way to meet an eligible young gentleman," said Matilda with a sly glance at her niece.

Sophia blushed deep rose, well understanding the allusion to Lord John. "Aunt Matilda!''

Caroline laughed, delighted by Sophia's confusion. It spoke well for the young woman's modesty. "Oh, I quite agree, Mrs. Wyndham. Your niece must certainly enter society and enjoy a few flirtations. If you would not take it amiss, I shall myself recommend Miss Wyndham for sponsorship by one of the hostesses of Almack's.''

Matilda's jaw dropped for an instant. She quickly recovered. "Why, that is most kind of you, Mrs. Richardson.''

Sophia recognized by her aunt's reaction that Mrs. Richardson had paid her a fine compliment. "Thank you indeed, Mrs. Richardson," she said.

"It is settled, then," said Caroline. She introduced a more general topic, and after a few more moments of pleasant conversation, Caroline decided it was time to take her leave. Well-satisfied with her visit, Caroline began to draw on her gloves. "I have kept you ladies for too long, I know, so I shall be on my way."

"We have certainly enjoyed your company, Mrs. Richardson. Pray do call again," said Matilda. She and Sophia rose with their visitor to walk with her to the door.

"And I, too, have enjoyed myself. I shall be driving in the park later this week. May I call on you to join me?" Caroline asked, holding out her hand to each lady in turn.

"Of course. I know that Sophia in particular would enjoy a drive. She has seen little enough of London since her arrival," said Matilda.

"We shall between us correct that, Mrs. Wyndham," said Caroline with a smile. She turned away and the door was closed behind her by the porter.

When Matilda and Sophia returned to the living room, they looked at each other in shared amazement. "How extraordinary, Aunt. I have never met anyone quite so friendly," said Sophia.

"Nor have I, Sophia. I would almost suspect that Mrs. Richardson is determined to establish a friendship with us for one reason or another except that the lady is so open and kind. I certainly never expected that she would take such an interest in your welfare," said Matilda.

"I gather that Almack's is rather exclusive," said Sophia dryly.

"Quite. The hostesses grant entry only to those sponsored by such well-known persons as Caroline Richardson. Almack's is the epitome of good *ton*, my dear, and all debutantes are hopeful to enter its doors," said Matilda.

"It sounds rather pretentious, actually," said Sophia, wrinkling her nose.

"Almack's is also called the Marriage Mart," said Matilda. She chuckled at her niece's expression and again took up her embroidery. "When your uncle returns for luncheon I shall ask him to take us about this afternoon. It is high time that you become familiar with some of the sights of London."

"Thank you, Aunt. I think that shall be a good deal

more comfortable than discussing Almack's," said Sophia with a smile.

Her aunt laughed, happy that she had been able to tease Sophia. Matilda thought it a good sign when Sophia could take it in stride.

Two other ladies called that morning, both of whom were old friends of the Wyndhams. Matilda introduced Sophia and they were gracious in welcoming her to London. One remembered Sophia's parents and even recalled Sophia herself as a child. Sophia discovered a certain poignant pleasure in listening to stories about her parents, and the morning flew for her.

When luncheon was announced, the visitors rose to take their leave, declining Matilda's invitation to stay. So it was only Charles, Matilda, and Sophia who sat down to the laden table. The conversation was desultory, Charles telling a story about one of his patients. Matilda recalled her promise to Sophia. "My dear, I have told Sophia that we might go about London this afternoon, if you do not have a great many more calls to make."

Charles thought a moment. "I am free for most of the afternoon. There is only old Peters for this evening and I doubt if he wishes anything more than to play a hand or two at cards and grumble about his gout," he said.

"Poor old gentleman. Is his gout worse, then?" asked Matilda.

"When he sticks to the diet I have prescribed for him, he is much better. But old Peters is a stubborn old fool. He won't give up his port wine for long," said Charles, shaking his head.

"I have often wondered, Charles, if Mr. Peters does not go back to his port so that he will have the excuse to send for you. You are the only person who will sit with him long enough to give him a good card game," said Matilda, her eyes twinkling.

Charles stared at her, astounded. "Do you know, I believe that you may have something there, Tilda. I shall try a change of tactics with him this very evening."

"Your Mr. Peters sounds to be an eccentric, Uncle," said Sophia, amused.

"Aye, but he has a good heart. It is a pity that he has no family or friends left to care about him. He has outlived them all. His is a very sad, lonely existence," said Charles.

"Then you must find him some companions of his own age, Uncle," said Sophia.

Charles' jaw dropped. "I never thought—but of course you are right, Sophia." He smiled at his wife and niece. "I am fortunate to have the company of two such insightful ladies. Pray tell me what you wish to do this afternoon. I will endeavor to make it a memorable outing."

"Sophia, what do you choose?" asked Matilda, turning to her.

"If you should not mind, I would like to see the museum. I enjoyed very much the displays in St. Petersburg and I know that the English collections must be as beautiful," said Sophia.

"An excellent choice, Sophia. Tilda and I have not been to the museum in quite some time and it will be a novelty for us as well," said Charles.

Matilda rose from the table. "Sophia and I shall leave you now to your wine, Charles, and make ourselves ready. We will meet you in the sitting room in just a few moments." Her husband agreed, and Sophia followed her aunt from the dining room. The ladies went upstairs to change out of their morning dresses.

When Sophia returned downstairs, she had put on a dark-blue merino walking dress, frogged across the breast and trimmed with sable at the collar and cuffs. She carried a muff of the same dark fur. She had swept her gleaming blond hair under a shako, the soft fur framing her slanted eyes and slender face. As Sophia entered the sitting room, she said, "Aunt Matilda, do you think this dress too Russian? I—" She suddenly saw that her aunt was not alone. "Oh!"

Sir Frederick rose from his seat in deference to Sophia's entrance. He stared at her openmouthed, lost in admiration.

Matilda glanced at him and then addressed her niece. "Sophia, Sir Frederick has but this moment come to call upon us."

Sir Frederick quickly stepped forward to make his bow
to Sophia. "I am happy to find you still at home, Miss
Wyndham."

Sophia gave her gloved hand to him. "It is a pleasure to
see you again, Sir Frederick." She realized that Sir
Frederick was holding her hand longer than necessary. He
smiled at her. Sophia threw a helpless glance toward her
aunt, who was an interested spectator.

Matilda recalled her duties. "Pray be seated, Sir
Frederick. Sophia, if you would so good as to hand me the
embroidery, I shall do a few stitches while we wait on your
uncle."

Sophia did as she was asked and then seated herself on
the settee beside her aunt.

Sir Frederick sat down across from the ladies. "I realize
that you and Miss Wyndham are preparing to go out, Mrs.
Wyndham. I hope that my visit is not detaining you," said
Sir Frederick.

"Not at all, Sir Frederick," said Matilda, and would
have said more except that her husband came quickly into
the sitting room. She set aside her embroidery and rose to
meet him.

Charles Wyndham nodded to the visitor. "Sir
Frederick." He took Matilda's hands and kissed her on the
cheek. He said quietly, "I am sorry, my dear, our visit to
the museum must be postponed. I have but this moment
received word that Mrs. Haversham is entering her con-
finement."

"You must go, of course," said Matilda, patting his
arm.

Sir Frederick cleared his throat. "If the ladies are
agreeable, I shall be more than happy to escort them
wherever they wish."

Charles looked inquiringly at his wife and niece.

Matilda said graciously, "We accept your timely
invitation, Sir Frederick."

Charles Wyndham left to make his call on Mrs. Haversham and Sir Frederick joined the Wyndham ladies in their
carriage. Sir Frederick was momentarily surprised that

they wished to go the museum, but he was of an agreeable nature and was determined to enjoy himself.

The outing turned out better than either Sophia or Sir Frederick could have imagined. Sir Frederick was delighted when Matilda eventually decided to rest on a bench and waved on her niece to enjoy the pieces of sculpture and paintings around the room. The privacy thus afforded Sir Frederick the opportunity to establish a firmer footing with Miss Wyndham, but mindful now of her cooling toward him when he had insisted on her use of his first name at their last meeting, Sir Frederick was careful to be only a pleasant companion. As a consequence, Sophia felt more at ease with him. She enjoyed his wit and the mild flirtation that he indulged in, knowing that his words were meant to be taken in a light manner. When they rejoined Matilda and Sir Frederick escorted them home, Sophia was almost sorry that he had not again insisted that she address him as Freddy. It pleased her when Matilda announced that she intended to make up an invitation to Sir Frederick for the dinner party.

As for Matilda, she could not help but wonder if Lord John Stokes was already in danger of being supplanted in Sophia's heart.

11

THE FOLLOWING two days it rained heavily and the Wyndham ladies did not receive any visitors or call on anyone themselves. Instead, Matilda had requested Sophia's help with planning the dinner party. Matilda also decided that it was time for Sophia's wardrobe to be expanded and she showed Sophia the different various fashion plates in the ladies' magazines. Once Matilda had gotten past her niece's initial reluctance to put her to any expense, she and Sophia spent several agreeable hours deciding which styles Sophia should have made up for the Season. When the clouded skies began to show signs of clearing, Matilda promised that she and Sophia would visit a modiste that Friday.

On Thursday, Caroline Richardson called to take the Wyndham ladies for a drive. Matilda had already made arrangements to sit with an old friend who was recovering from a serious bout of influenza. She expressed her disappointment in missing the treat, but urged Sophia to go ahead without her, and Sophia soon found herself settled in Caroline Richardson's landau. The day was bright and warm, a break from the last of winter, and Caroline had requested that the top of the landau be put down. Sophia was enthralled with the signs of spring that she saw, especially when they reached the park. "How wonderful that here spring begins so early," exclaimed Sophia, her slanted blue-gray eyes alight.

"But surely the trees would be budding in St. Petersburg as well," Caroline said, amused by her guest's enthusiasm.

"Oh, no, the Russian spring comes late and it is then so very fleeting. St. Petersburg would still be a city of ice today," said Sophia.

"I shudder to think about it. I much prefer the warmer months," said Caroline.

"I do not mind the cold. I suppose that I am conditioned to it. But spring is my favorite time of the year. There is something glorious about it. I do thank you for inviting me to drive with you today, Mrs. Richardson," Sophia said.

"Pray call me Caroline. I intend to be a friend to you, you know, and the sooner we are on familiar terms, the better I shall like it," said Caroline. She laughed at Sophia's startled expression. "I am quite sincere, I assure you. My interest springs from the role my brother played in your arrival in England. John made light of it, but it must have been such an adventure for you! My heart pounded to hear how John whisked you out of the capital and spirited you away on the ship. It was the stuff of a romantic novel."

Sophia colored faintly. "I am in debt to Lord John and he has my everlasting gratitude. However, it was not such an adventure as you believe. I was seasick almost from the instant we boarded the ship. If it had not been for Lord John's unwavering solicitude, I believe I would have leapt overboard rather than endure the passage to England."

"Oh." Caroline was taken aback. Sophia's open confession destroyed whatever suspicions she had harbored that Miss Wyndham and Lord John had enjoyed a light flirtation while sailing to England. But Caroline was a hardy romantic. She decided not to give up so soon on Miss Wyndham. After all, Lord John had gone to a great deal of trouble on the young lady's behalf. "I have always been fascinated by John's adventures in foreign countries. He is forever teasing me with half-glimpses of the people he has met and the places he has seen. I hope that you will not also laugh off my eager questions," said Caroline.

Sophia liked the ready smile in Caroline Richardson's green eyes. "I shall be happy to tell you what I know of St. Petersburg, but I have actually seen very little of Russia."

"But St. Petersburg is the capital," said Caroline.

Sophia laughed. "Quite true."

Lord John, who was astride a large gray gelding, espied

his sister's landau and directed his mount to it. "Good afternoon, ladies. I see that you, too, are taking advantage of this sunny day."

"John! How fortuitous, for we were just discussing you," said Caroline ingeniously.

Sophia felt her face flame. Bravely she held out her gloved hand to Lord John. "Your sister was asking me about St. Petersburg, my lord."

"Indeed." Lord John directed a quizzical look at his sister, whose expression was all innocence. "Caroline is as inquisitive as a child. Be careful or ere long she will worm out your deepest secrets along with your memories."

"You are despicable, John," said Caroline cheerfully, immured to his gentle insults. "Sophia shall tell me all the things that you will not about St. Petersburg and Russian society. I have not asked a single personal question, I will have you know."

"But you will. You are incorrigible," said Lord John, and grinned at his sister's ferocious scowl. He turned to Sophia. "If you have a dire deed on your conscience or a favored young gentleman's name locked in your heart, Miss Wyndham, I strongly advise you to decline future invitations with my sister."

"Pray do not be anxious on my account, Lord John. I am as close as a clam when I wish," said Sophia, smiling.

"Really, John, this is too bad of you," complained Caroline. She instructed her driver to go on. "And I shall thank you to come to dinner next week, John, so that I may give you a proper scold."

He laughed and turned his mount to accompany the carriage. "Actually I am rather glad to have your invitation, Caroline. The cook my solicitor found for me leaves much to be desired. Truth to tell, I am compelled to beg a dinner invitation from whomever I chance to meet."

Sophia laughed up at him. Her eyes were shining. "It is only that you have become too accustomed to rich living, my lord."

Lord John bowed to her. "Alas, I fear you may be correct, Miss Wyndham."

Caroline was astonished by the easy camaraderie that existed between her brother and Miss Wyndham. It pleased her, however, to discover that Miss Wyndham was not as nonchalant about Lord John Stokes as she had pretended. "John, you know that you are always welcome at Richardson House. And if you like, I shall inquire around to find you another cook."

"Thank you, dear Caroline. I cannot describe to you the heartfelt gratitude in my breast and my stomach," said Lord John solemnly.

Sophia had difficulty keeping a straight face. "You are a fool, John," said Caroline, laughing. He bowed.

The occupant of a passing carriage waved and Caroline asked her driver to stop. "How are you, Madame Aralov," she said, addressing the older woman who had hailed her. She nodded to the mounted gentleman who accompanied Madame Aralov's carriage.

Madame Aralov inclined her head. Her dark gaze slid over Sophia to come to rest on Lord John. She openly admired his broad shoulders and blond head. "I am well, Mrs. Richardson. I see that you take the air also this afternoon. I do not know your escort."

Caroline was less vivacious than Sophia had ever seen her. "This gentleman is my brother, Lord John Stokes. And this is a friend, Miss Sophia Wyndham."

Madame Aralov's gaze swung to Sophia. "Wyndham? Ah, yes. You are the niece of Princess Elizaveta Kirov. My friends in St. Petersburg have written to me about you."

"Indeed." Sophia did not allow her own eyes to waver under the older woman's avid gaze.

Madame Aralov showed her teeth in a small smile. She turned her head. "Comte, do you know Mrs. Richardson?"

"We have met," said the gentleman, his haughty expression unchanging. Sophia received a fleeting impression of dark good looks and a cold manner. Caroline inclined her head in a cool nod.

Madame Aralov laughed shrilly. She again turned to Sophia. "Miss Wyndham, you are a naughty child to create such a scandal. I am told that even the czar has heard of you. Now I meet you in London, and in such company." Her dark slanted eyes slid suggestively to Lord John. Her smile was deliberate. "I shall have much to relay to my friends in St. Petersburg." Without notice, Madame Aralov gave a sharp order to her driver and her carriage rolled away.

"Who was that detestable woman, Caroline, and the gentleman with her?" asked Lord John.

"Madame Aralov is a member of the Russian circle here. She is a horrid vulgar gossip, but yet she is received everywhere. As for the Comte de Chaleur, I understand that he is a displaced nobleman. He spends his days as a hanger-on with whoever is willing to pay for his company. I, for one, cannot see why anyone would, but the count is known as fortunate at cards and perhaps that makes him acceptable to some," said Caroline with a certain distaste.

"I did not care for Madame Aralov," said Sophia quietly. She looked up at Lord John. "My lord, do you believe what she said is true about there being a scandal in St. Petersburg?"

Lord John met her gaze. "Undoubtably there was a scandal, Miss Wyndham. But whether your disappearance caused such wide consternation as Madame Aralov suggested I find rather difficult to believe. Forgive me when I say this, Miss Wyndham, but you were not a particularly important personage." He ended with a smile.

Sophia could not help laughing. She shook her head. "You have wonderfully deflated my sense of importance, my lord."

"Pray do not give that horrid woman another thought, dear Sophia. I'll wager there is not more than a handful of people who care what happened in St. Petersburg, and three of them are now present," said Caroline, giving Sophia's fingers a quick reassuring squeeze.

"I am well and truly among friends," said Sophia, returning her companion's smile.

"On that note I shall take my leave of you ladies. This mount of mine needs a good run before I return him to the stables," said Lord John. He bowed from the saddle and then spurred his horse.

The ladies watched him go, each with feelings of reluctance. "I suppose it is time that I return you home, Sophia. My boys will be wondering where I am. I always spend time with them in the afternoons before supper," said Caroline.

"Then certainly we must make haste," said Sophia.

The carriage did not take long to pull up before the Wyndham town house. The driver helped Sophia down to the pavement.

Caroline leaned out and said, "We must go driving again, and soon. Or you may choose from Richard's stable if you wished instead to ride alongside the carriage."

"Oh, no. I do not ride if I can possibly help it. I am half-ashamed to admit it, but horses awe me," said Sophia.

"Good. We can talk better if we are both inside the carriage," said Caroline with satisfaction.

Sophia laughed and waved as the carriage rolled away from the curb. Then she ran up the stairs to the door and the porter let her in.

The Wyndham dinner party was a relatively small, quiet affair of about thirty people. Sophia knew several of the guests present from previous meetings. The two ladies who had called on Matilda, and who had spoken graciously of Sophia's mother, had brought their husbands. Lord John Stokes and Sir Frederick Hawkesworth made themselves companionable at the table to those on either side of them. George Hetherby was there, appearing a bit shy but pleased about the company with which he found himself placed. There were a few others, acquaintances of Charles' and Matilda's that Sophia had met. On the whole there were not many younger people of Sophia's own age, but she did not mind. Many of those present had known her parents and they made her feel quite at ease. After dinner the ladies moved to the sitting room so that the gentlemen could enjoy their wine. When the gentlemen rejoined them, it became a convivial evening of conversation over

the loo table while soft music was played on the pianoforte
by one of the ladies.

Before the evening was done, Sophia received gracious
invitations from several of the ladies. Matilda was well
pleased. "Sophia can now begin to enjoy herself more out
in society, and as she makes an ever-widening circle of new
acquaintances, I hope she will be able to make a certain
judgment on her feelings for a particular gentleman," she
said quietly to her spouse.

"I did not know that you had a devious streak, Tilda,"
said Charles teasingly. She shook her head at him, smiling,
and moved away to speak to one of their guests.

Sophia and Lord John were seated on a settee, momentarily left undisturbed by the company. "You have at last
debuted into English society, Miss Wyndham," said Lord
John, nodding at their dinner companions.

"Indeed, my lord. My aunt and uncle have been very
gracious to me in that direction. I had not given much
thought to it before, but England is now my home and I
must learn her ways," said Sophia, glancing about at the
others.

Lord John looked at her in surprise. "You sound almost
timid, Miss Wyndham. Your poise has always been such
that I did not suspect that you felt any sort of
trepidation."

Sophia laughed and her warm blue-gray eyes twinkled.
"I am well taught in the universal social graces, Lord
John. But even so, I have been in Russia for many years.
At times I feel oddly out of place here."

"You are not alone in that, Miss Wyndham. It is just the
same for me whenever I first enter a foreign capital. I may
know the language but still there is something different
and a bit exciting about the people and their city," said
Lord John. He took her hand and reassuringly pressed her
fingers. "You will come to feel perfectly at home, I assure
you."

Sophia was very conscious of his touch. She raised her
head and her pulse quickened at the warmth of his gaze.
She colored faintly. "Thank you, my lord. You have a
wonderful knack for soothing one's anxieties."

Lord John laughed and released her hand. "It is my diplomatic training. It is so ingrained in me that I sometimes error by overly emphasizing the pleasant side of things."

"Your sister, Caroline, once said much the same thing, except that she used the phrase 'discretion bordering on boredom,' " said Sophia mischievously.

Lord John looked startled, then amused. "I shall have to speak to Caroline. I am not at all boring, even in my sleep."

Sophia laughed, as he had meant for her to, and he smiled.

"So, John, I should have known that you would attempt to monopolize Miss Wyndham," said Sir Frederick.

He smiled down at them pleasantly. But there was a half-speculative look in his glance that Lord John could easily read. His friend's flirtations commonly did not last over two weeks and he was actually impressed by the strength of Sir Frederick's devotion to Miss Wyndham. Lord John decided on the spot to relegate his own mild interest in Miss Wyndham to the background so that Sir Frederick would have a better opportunity to give full rein to his ardor. After all, Miss Wyndham could possibly be the lady to win Sir Frederick's flighty heart. Lord John felt a twinge of regret for his decision, which surprised him. Lord John rose from the settee, remarking, "You are a suspicious dog, Freddy. I am merely an imperfect substitute for your suavity and charm."

Sir Frederick grinned and Sophia laughed. Lord John left them alone on this bantering note.

Sophia regreted Lord John's departure but she reminded herself that she was sophisticated enough not to wear her heart on her sleeve. Therefore she turned to Sir Frederick with a welcoming smile. "I am delighted that you were able to come this evening, Sir Frederick. It is awfully comforting to have a familiar face among a room full of near strangers."

Sir Frederick bowed, acknowledging her gracious words. He seated himself beside her on the settee. "I wish that you could learn to call me Freddy," he complained.

Sophia laughed at his comic expression. "I apologize, Freddy. I don't know how I could have forgotten. We are old friends, after all."

Sir Frederick's eyes were unsually warm as his gaze rested on her animated face. He took her hand and raised her fingers to his lips. "Indeed we are, Miss Wyndham. And I trust that our friendship shall grow ever deeper and more valued."

Sophia stared at him, startled. The open admiration and intensity in his warm brown eyes struck her. Oh, Lord, she thought, dismayed. He is half in love with me. She gently disengaged her hand from his and remarked in a disjointed fashion on the warmth of the weather. "It is so unusual for March. At least, it would be in St. Petersburg. But I suppose here the coming of spring this early is common-place."

Sir Frederick agreed to it with a faint grin, thinking that his chosen lady was flustered into shyness by his near declaration. For her part, Sophia wondered how she was ever to discourage Sir Frederick without unnecessarily wounding him. She had never before faced such a dilemma. The situation would have been easier if she could have withdrawn to a more formal footing with Sir Frederick, but she thought that would be difficult now, since she had agreed to call him by his given name.

Sophia was relieved when a few moments later her uncle requested that she join him and two of his old friends, who, he said, had been close to her father. Sophia assented and, as she rose, said a few gracious words of farewell to Sir Frederick.

Much later, after the guests had left, Sophia confided in her aunt. "And I very much fear that Sir Frederick is becoming besotted with me, Aunt," she ended, troubled.

"What is wrong with that?" asked Matilda calmly.

"Why, I do not wish him to be. I don't want anyone to think of me in such a fashion, for it is futile. Do you not remember, Aunt? My heart is not my own," said Sophia.

"Well, perhaps Sir Frederick's infatuation with you will engender a little jealousy in Lord John," said Matilda, mischief in her eyes.

"Aunt Matilda," gasped Sophia.

Matilda laughed at her, then sobered. "I do understand, Sophia, truly I do. But you must be prepared. There will be other gentlemen besides Sir Frederick who will admire you and become smitten with you."

"But Sir Frederick!" exclaimed Sophia.

"Pray put it out of your head, Sophia. If you have not yet discovered it, young gentlemen often tumble into love and just as quickly tumble out of it. You have only to be patient with Sir Frederick, and perhaps in a few weeks time he will transfer his allegiance to some other charming young lady," said Matilda.

"You make him sound very fickle, Aunt Matilda," Sophia said. She was not certain if she liked the thought that a gentleman could be so faithless.

"I do, don't I?" agreed Matilda comfortably. Sophia laughed and hugged her gratefully. She went up to bed with her spirits much improved.

12

SOPHIA'S ENJOYMENT of the Season was complete. She had always reveled in society and even as a debutante had never experienced the extreme shyness that beset some young ladies. After Sophia had gotten over her initial trepidation at the Wyndham's dinner party, she had readily taken to English society. Lord John had been correct in his assurances that she would quickly feel at ease. It puzzled Sophia that in Russia the English were reputed to be cold and arrogant. Sophia thought she could never have expected greater kindness nor warmth than she had received since her arrival in London. It did not occur to her that her situation was unique. Her relatives were respectable and had entry in a small way into the better circles. In addition, since her arrival Sophia had also gained the friendship of a few notable hostesses, prominent among them being Caroline Richardson, who had gone to lengths to establish Miss Sophia Wyndham as a desirable addition to any hostess's guest list. Sophia herself cemented her social acceptance with her warm charm and exquisite ability to appear entertained by whomever she was with.

As Sophia's most recent admirer led her onto the dance floor, she looked around the crowded ballroom, gladness bubbling within her. She enjoyed so much mixing with people and talking with them. She had early on discovered in herself a knack for finding something of interest in each individual she spoke to, and as a consequence, she was very rarely bored. Sophia was blithely unaware as she laughed with her partner that her enjoyment of the company in which she moved was to be disturbed.

When the set was finished, Sophia was escorted by her

partner back to the empty chair beside Matilda. He
lingered a moment before he bowed and took his leave.
"You have made another conquest, Sophia," said
Matilda, laughing.

Sophia smiled and shook her head. "You have said so
about each and every gentleman who has claimed my hand
for a dance this evening, Aunt Matilda. You cannot expect
me to take you seriously." She glanced down at her dance
card for the name of her next partner.

"But of course I can. You are a lovely young woman of
wit and charm. What gentleman could be so addled that he
does not take notice?" said Matilda teasingly.

Sophia was staring at her dance card. "I believe I am
able to name at least one, Aunt Matilda," she said in a
strangled tone.

"My dear! Why, you are as white as a sheet. Whatever is
the matter?" asked Matilda, alarmed.

"When did this man sign my card?" asked Sophia,
pointing at a flourishing signature.

Matilda peered at the name. "Why, it must have been
during one of the sets. I recall that you laid down your card
very briefly, but I am afraid that I did not notice who
could have picked it up."

A deep voice spoke behind Sophia. "I have come to
claim the dance saved for me, mademoiselle."

"Misha," said Sophia faintly. Matilda's mouth
dropped open in recognition. With an effort, Sophia
gathered her composure and turned, only the slightest
lifting of her brows to indicate her surprise. "I am
astonished, Misha. I did not know you were even in
England," she said.

Prince Kirov laughed. "And why should I not be?
London has its attractions, cousin. Little Sophia, let us
join the set. I have a desire to dance with you again. It has
been so long." He held out his hand commandingly for
hers. Sophia hesitated, wondering if she could trust him.
Prince Kirov seemed to read her mind. He grinned. "Dear
Sophia, I swear to you that I have planned nothing more
than a pleasant turn about the ballroom."

Sophia stared up into his blue eyes, searching for any hint of guile. "Misha, I warn you—"

Prince Kirov waved aside whatever she meant to say. "Come, Sophia, have I not sworn it? May I become my mother's worst enemy if I speak a lie." He pressed his hand fervently against his breast in exaggerated melodrama.

Sophia burst into laughter. "That is indeed a mighty oath! Very well, Misha. I shall believe you."

"Sophia, do you not think . . ." began Matilda. But Prince Kirov swept Sophia away before she had finished.

"That is your English aunt?" asked Prince Kirov, nodding in Matilda Wyndham's direction. At Sophia's nod, he said disaparagingly, "She is like a timid sparrow. She flutters with her agitation, but futilely. She is a weak woman."

"That is most unkind and unfair, cousin. I shall thank you not to insult my aunt again," said Sophia quietly.

Prince Kirov laughed at the challenge in her blue-gray eyes. "I am relieved, little Sophia. I feared that England would soften your spirit."

"Quite the contrary. I am resolved to remain here, Misha. There is nothing you can say that will change my mind," said Sophia, tilting up her chin.

Prince Kirov held her closer and spun her a little faster. His voice was teasing, caressing. "Dearest Sophia, let us not spoil our waltz. I do not wish to speak of unpleasant things when at this moment I am so glad to find you."

"But that is why you have come to England, is it not?" asked Sophia persistently.

"We shall not speak of it now," said Prince Kirov. He saw that she was about to retort and whirled her faster until they were flying around the ballroom floor.

Prince Kirov and Sophia made a striking couple as they flashed past the others on the floor, he tall and extraordinarily handsome and she blond and graceful. The other couples parted before them like the seas and soon the ballroom floor had become theirs alone.

"Good Lord!" exclaimed Richard Richardson as he watched Prince Kirov's and Sophia's whirling progress.

Humble envy invaded his soul for their sheer poetry of motion.

Caroline had a fair idea of the turn of his thoughts. She pressed his arm reassuringly. "Dearest love, there are areas in which you have no equal," she said softly.

Richard turned a startled expression on her. He grinned at the coquettish light in her wicked green eyes and glanced again at Prince Kirov and Sophia, still whirling in solitary splendor. "That fellow was pointed out to me as Prince Mikhail Kirov, newly arrived in London, but two days ago."

"Do you mean that gorgeous man is Sophia's cousin? The one who threatened John?" exclaimed Caroline, her gaze sharpening on the couple.

"The very one. I wonder if John knows that Prince Kirov is in London. Prince Kirov is on unexpectedly easy terms with Miss Wyndham, don't you think? I would have thought there would be an estrangement between the two after what took place in St. Petersburg," said Richard.

Caroline did not answer. She was appalled by the several implications of Richard's observation. First and uppermost in her mind was concern for Lord John's safety. But the question about Prince Kirov and Sophia also bothered her. Richard was right. Surely Sophia would not dance with Prince Kirov with such obvious enjoyment if there were a strain between them. Caroline's active imagination supplied a possibility that she did not particularly care for. But what did she know of Russians and their ways, after all. Perhaps theirs was more than a cousinly relationship. If that were the case, Prince Kirov would secretly be rather pleased that Sophia had run off to England rather than be forced into marriage. It gave him the opportunity to pursue his own liaison with her without the complication of a jealous husband.

Caroline thought she had never enjoyed a party less. She plucked at Richard's sleeve. "Richard, let us go pay our respects to Mrs. Wyndham," she said urgently. With a glance at her face, Richard agreed and they started across the ballroom.

When the set ended, there was a smattering of applause

and Prince Kirov led Sophia in a regal manner back to her chair. Sophia was breathless and half-laughing with the exertion. She had felt as though she were flying, and it buoyed her mood. Her eyes were sparkling and her face becomingly pink when she walked up to Matilda. She was surprised to see Sir Frederick Hawkesworth and the Richardsons standing with her aunt.

Sir Frederick came forward to take her hand in greeting. To Sophia's surprise he did not release her fingers, but instead looked challengingly at Prince Kirov. "We meet again, your highness," he said.

"Indeed, and under much more friendly circumstances," said Prince Kirov, smiling. He nodded at their clasped hands. "I see that you are known to my cousin."

"I am Miss Wyndham's devoted admirer," said Sir Frederick emphatically.

Sophia gasped. She suddenly understood what Sir Frederick was doing. She tried to pull her hand free, but Sir Frederick held on to her firmly.

Prince Kirov's brows rose. "The word was 'devoted,' was it not?" he asked softly.

"It was," said Sir Frederick calmly.

The two men stared at each other. Prince Kirov appeared thoughtful, but there was the beginning of a hot glitter in his eyes.

Sophia felt her heart constrict at that look in her cousin's eyes. "Freddy, you mustn't. You do not know him. Oh, Misha, pray do not," she said in great agitation.

Prince Kirov looked at her then and smiled. "He means so much to you, little cousin?" His voice was deceptively smooth.

Sophia gazed unflinchingly at him. She was honest with him and hoped it was enough. "Sir Frederick is a dear friend, Misha, who has taken my concerns to heart. He, too, knows why you have come to London." Sophia turned on Sir Frederick. "Freddy, will you please let go my hand," she hissed. He was taken aback by her vehemence and unconsciously loosened his grip. She snatched her hand away. Prince Kirov threw back his head and laughed.

"I see nothing amusing in this," said Sir Frederick with dignity.

Prince Kirov was still smiling. "You are fortunate, milord, that I am amused." A dark-featured handsome gentleman sauntered up and Prince Kirov greeted him with pleasure. "My excellent count! I had wondered where you had gotten to."

"I was nearby, your highness. But I did not wish to interrupt when you were so obviously involved," said Comte de Chaleur. His hard dark eyes rested momentarily on Sophia, then traveled to Sir Frederick.

"Ah. You will be amused to hear that my little cousin fears evil intentions from me, Comte." Prince Kirov threw up his hand when he saw that Sophia was about to retort. "No, cousin. As I told you, we shall discuss our differences at another time. Comte de Chaleur, allow me to present you to my cousin, Mademoiselle Sophia Wyndham, and her devoted gallant. It was 'devoted,' was it not, sir?" Prince Kirov grinned at Sir Frederick's stiff bow, then swept a hand around to include the others who had stood by in silent fascination. He said chidingly, "You forget your manners, Sophia. Present me to your friends."

"Of course, Misha," said Sophia quietly. She briefly introduced the Richardsons and Matilda Wyndham. The count came in for his own introductions and received only a vague nod from Caroline Richardson. Prince Kirov bowed and said all that was polite. Then he sauntered off in the Comte de Chaleur's company.

"How I detest that man," said Caroline, staring after them.

Richard was startled. "Prince Kirov? I admit that he is a bit overwhelming, but he does have a certain foreign charm."

"Not Prince Kirov but the Comte de Chaleur," said Caroline impatiently.

"The count is a known leech, my love. I would be very surprised to find that anyone is much enamored of him. He is a friend only as long as one's pocketbook is full and

generous, as Prince Kirov will undoubtedly discover," said
Richard disparagingly.

Matilda found the Richardsons' observations fascinating and she turned to ask Sophia if she knew anything
about the Comte de Chaleur. Matilda was startled when
she realized that Sir Frederick and Sophia, whose quiet
conversation she had not paid particular attention to, were
in violent disagreement.

"I was attempting to help you, Sophia," said Sir
Frederick in a low exasperated tone.

"And how many times must I repeat that antagonizing
Misha is not the way to do so!" Sophia grasped his arm
urgently. "Listen to me, Freddy. Prince Mikhail Kirov is a
dangerous man. He is not to be taken lightly. In Russia—"

"This is England, Sophia. Prince Kirov isn't likely to lay
a knout across my shoulders here or have me incarcerated," said Sir Frederick.

"But he can kill you," said Sophia bluntly. He looked at
her with an expression of disbelief. "Freddy, Misha has
fought nine duels. He killed all but one of his adversaries,
and for much less reason than you gave him tonight when
you pretended there was an understanding between us."

"Dueling is illegal," said Sir Frederick.

Sophia looked pityingly at him. "Really, Freddy."

Sir Frederick grinned a little sheepishly. "I take your
point, my lady. Very well, I shall not go out of my way to
ruffle any feathers. I trust that satisfies you?"

"Thank you, Freddy," said Sophia, smiling at him
again.

"Sophia, did your cousin say anything to you about why
he is in London?" asked Matilda with concern.

Sophia shook her head. "It was the oddest thing, Aunt.
He refused to broach the subject, saying only that he
would discuss it at a later time."

"I am certain that he will," said Sir Frederick. "I must
let John know that Prince Kirov is here. Caroline, have
you seen him?"

"Not for the past hour when I noticed him in Lady
Priscilla Eversly's company," said Caroline.

"Lord John may have already left, then," said Matilda. "I thought I saw him speaking with our hostess only a few minutes ago."

"John has been seeing quite a bit of Lady Priscilla, hasn't he?" asked Richard, looking at Caroline. She would not meet his eyes, well aware that he disapproved of her matchmaking efforts. "I expect I shall catch him later at the hotel, then," said Sir Frederick.

It struck Caroline as significant that Sir Frederick would want to apprise Lord John so promptly of Prince Kirov's arrival. If John were in danger from Prince Kirov, she hoped that she would be told. But Caroline knew of old that Sir Frederick wasn't likely to be very informative. He, like John, was too much in the practice of holding his own counsel. "Botheration," she said under her breath.

Sir Frederick soon took his leave of the ladies and departed to search for Lord John.

Sophia was less absorbed by the implications of Prince Kirov's appearance than was Caroline. Her mind was taken up with the information that Lord John had been in the company of Lady Priscilla, who was known to be on the lookout for a new husband. Her aunt had not said so, but perhaps Lord John had left with Lady Priscilla. Sophia did not dare ask Matilda. But jealousy threatened to choke her, especially when Lord John had not even taken time to wish her good night. For Sophia the ball had definitely palled. She turned to her aunt. "Aunt Matilda, would you mind it terribly if we made our excuses? I am suddenly not in a dancing mood."

Matilda rose promptly, believing her upset over Prince Kirov's untimely appearance. "Of course not, my dear. I am a trifle tired myself."

Sophia and Matilda Wyndham said their good-byes to the Richardsons and to their hostess. They left the ballroom and soon were settled into their carriage. Sophia stared silently out of the window as the streetlamps passed. Her spirits were at a low ebb. It had seemed to her in the last week that Lord John was more attentive. She had dared to hope that he was beginning to feel something for her. But he had left that evening without even the courtesy of wishing her good night and she had convinced herself that Lady Priscilla had been on his arm. Those were hardly the actions of a gentleman who was interested in her. And now her cousin, Prince Mikhail Kirov, was in London. Sophia had no doubt as to why he had come, and the knowledge further damped her naturally exuberant outlook. Altogether the evening had ended for her in a dismal fashion.

13

SOPHIA DID not sleep well that night and the following morning she wakened hollow-eyed. She was unusually bad-tempered and snapped at her maid twice before she was dressed. She went downstairs to breakfast without feeling her usual anticipation of the pleasant hour to be spent with her aunt and uncle.

Charles and Matilda both noticed their niece's subdued air. Charles raised his brows questioningly at Matilda, who only shook her head. They did not tax Sophia about her unusual quiet and she was grateful to them. She felt their concern, but she could not bear just then to open up to them.

After breakfast Sophia excused herself, saying that she meant to spend a quiet morning in the library.

Matilda took her announcement as a hint that she wished to be alone. "Quite all right, my dear. I was telling Charles earlier this morning that I wished to visit with a couple of our old friends, and I knew that you would probably prefer not to accompany me after such a late evening," she said.

"Oh!" Sophia was disconcerted that Matilda so readily took her at her word. "It is only that I am feeling a bit under the weather this morning. Pray do not give me another thought, Aunt Matilda, but enjoy your outing."

"Thank you, my dear," said Matilda. She set aside her napkin and rose. "I shall return in time for luncheon."

Charles took out his watch and then stood up also. "I must be going as well. I promised Mrs. Haversham that I would call on her and her new little boy early this morning." He bent to kiss Sophia's cheek and smiled warmly at her, thinking that he understood the reason for her mood. "Tilda told me of Prince Kirov's appearance at the ball. You must not fret over him, Sophia."

"I shan't, Uncle Charles," said Sophia, returning his smile. He was gone then. Minutes later, when she left the breakfast room, Sophia found that Matilda had already left in her carriage. Except for the servants, she found herself alone in the town house.

Contrary to what Sophia had thought, she did not feel relief at being left alone with her thoughts. Restlessly she paced, unable to settle for long with a novel or her embroidery. She simply could not forget what Richard Richardson had said about Lord John spending his time with Lady Priscilla Eversly. Sophia had met Lady Priscilla only once, but she had been immediately struck by the lady's magnetic beauty. Her magnificent emerald-green eyes and slim figure most certainly appealed to the gentlemen despite her reputation for husband-hunting. Sophia thought it would be strange indeed if Lord John did not also share the general admiration for Lady Priscilla, but the reflection did not make her feel any happier.

When the butler entered the sitting room to ask if she wished to receive Sir Frederick Hawkesworth, Sophia's first impulse was to refuse. But almost instantly she changed her mind. Sir Frederick was an amusing companion and she wanted very much to be amused. And Sophia knew that Sir Frederick was attracted to her. At least he did not seek out Lady Priscilla Eversly's company over hers. "Wait. I shall see Sir Frederick, after all. Pray show him in," said Sophia. She seated herself on the settee and took up her once-abandoned embroidery.

The butler hesitated a fraction of a second, then bowed. Sophia smiled to herself, almost reading his scandalized thoughts. A respectable young lady rarely received a gentleman caller without a chaperone present. But Sophia was beyond caring. She felt a burgeoning recklessness.

When Sir Frederick was shown into the sitting room, he was surprised to find Sophia alone. He was even more surprised when she rose and met him in the middle of the room, her hand extended. He took her hand and bowed.

"I know I find you well, Miss Wyndham. Have I chosen an inconvenient time to call? I see that Mrs. Wyndham is not with you."

"My aunt shall not be joining us this morning," said Sophia. She glanced toward the butler, who still lingered at the doorway, and said, "That will be all, Andrews."

The butler bowed stiffly and there was no doubt at all of his disapproval.

"Perhaps I should not stay," said Sir Frederick.

"Nonsense, when we are such good friends. Pray sit beside me here on the settee, Freddy," Sophia said, smiling.

Sir Frederick could not believe his good fortune. His chosen lady was smiling at him with invitation plain in her fascinating blue-gray eyes. His confidence was suddenly shaken with doubt. His instincts urged him to action, but he did not know if he dared to trust them.

Unaware of the spectacular effect she was having on Sir Frederick's whirling thoughts, Sophia set herself to be at her most charming. She flirted outrageously with Sir Frederick, who so patently admired her. He was not Lord John, of course, but he was Lord John's best friend and in some perverse way Sophia took comfort in that.

She was astonished when Sir Frederick suddenly groaned and dropped his head into his hands. "Freddy, what is it? Are you ill?" she asked, alarmed.

Sir Frederick laughed. He straightened. "Indeed, I could truthfully say so."

Sophia's concern deepened. She laid her hand on his forearm, all coquettishness forgotten. She hardly noticed when his free hand came up to press her fingers close against his sleeve. "Pray tell me, Freddy. I shall help you if you will allow me."

Sir Frederick met her gaze and she was shocked by the intensity of longing in his eyes. "I am in love with you, Sophia. You must know by now that I am."

"Oh, Freddy," said Sophia softly. She gently tried to withdraw her hand. She felt awful. She had played to his admiration to boost her own faltering self-esteem and never gave a thought to how he might interpret it.

But Sir Frederick was not willing to let her go so easily. He turned on the settee and took both her hands. "I know that I am speaking too early to you, that I should allow you more time to come to know me," he said. "But my excuse must be that I love you quite passionately."

Sophia pulled at her hands and this time he allowed her to go. She rose from the settee and walked quickly to the window. "I am so ashamed of myself. I did not realize . . . But it is impossible. I cannot love you as you wish. Oh, how I wish that you had never said anything to me."

A swift step fell behind her. Strong hands fell on her shoulders and turned her so that she faced him. Sir Frederick stared down at her. "But I have told you. And love between us is not impossible, Sophia. You may come to care for me as much as I care for you," he said earnestly.

Sophia shook her head. Her palms pressed against his broad chest. "No, no. You do not understand, Freddy." He kissed her then. It was a long, tender expression of his devotion. Sophia felt a mild stirring of her senses, and also compassion. When Sir Frederick raised his head, Sophia hid her face against his shoulder. "Oh, Freddy. You have made it so difficult for me," she whispered.

"I am happy to hear it. At least you have not refused me outright," said Sir Frederick, soft amusement in his voice.

Sophia firmly took herself out of his embrace. "Freddy, I must make you understand. I am in love with another gentleman."

Sir Frederick was momentarily startled. Then he said diffidently, "Has the other fellow declared himself?" Sophia shook her head. He brightened and said, "Then he has at least expressed an interest?"

"No," said Sophia honestly, although it cost her pride and pain to admit it.

"There we are, then. I have a chance," said Sir Frederick cheerfully.

"You are really quite incorrigible. Has anyone ever told you?" said Sophia, somewhat irritated.

Sir Frederick grinned at her. "On several occasions. However, I have never let it cast me down, and I shan't now. Guard your heart as best you may, Miss Wyndham, for I intend to lay siege." He then took his leave, and though Sophia protested again that he had spoken in vain, Sir Frederick only laughed.

Sophia discovered that Sir Frederick was as good as his word. He sent her flowers every other day. Those days that she did not find flowers waiting for her in the downstairs hall, she could depend upon a visit from him. Her uncle began to tease her about her persistent beau. Sophia soon learned that her explanation that Sir Frederick was only a friend fell on indulgent but somewhat deaf ears.

Sir Frederick made a point of being seen with Sophia at every function she chose to attend. It was not long before others took notice and began to comment.

"It seems to me that you should concentrate your talents on a match between Lady Priscilla and John, Caroline, and abandon any thoughts of Sophia as a sister-in-law. Miss Wyndham seems inordinately fond of Freddy these days," said Richard with wicked amusement.

Caroline turned her shoulder on him, but privately she was forced to agree with him. It was a pity for she truly liked Sophia Wyndham, whereas she found it more and more difficult to tolerate Lady Priscilla's posturing. Caroline instantly regretted the uncharitable thought. Lady Priscilla was a beautiful woman and was naturally aware of it. Caroline only hoped that her feelings of growing dislike would disappear once the baby was born. Then perhaps she could smile at her future sister-in-law. That is, if John was such a fool as to offer for the shallow creature, thought Caroline. Caroline laid her palm against her enlarged belly and again scolded herself.

Prince Kirov had also taken note of Sophia's constant escort. He did not like Sir Frederick Hawkesworth's attentions and mentioned it to the Comte de Chaleur. "My cousin is a little fool. Sir Frederick Hawkesworth is a man of tissue paper. I tell you, I would gladly see him dead rather than allow Sophia to marry such a one," he said contemptuously. The count gave a calculating glance at Prince Kirov, but he said nothing.

Despite her misgivings, Sophia found it difficult to resist Sir Frederick's company. He was always an agreeable companion and he served to take her mind from other things. Lord John was frequently with them, but he never seemed inclined to seek her out himself. Sophia covered her bruised feelings with laughter and quick wit. She lived as fast as she dared and even ignored Prince Kirov's hovering presence. Her cousin had never referred to the reason he had come to England, and Sopia knew that he was attempting to play on her nerves, so she did not allow his presence to bother her. When she thought of Prince Kirov at all it was as only a small gray cloud on her horizon.

Lord John and Sir Frederick left White's later than usual in the small hours of the morning. The nearly deserted street was an indefinite gray and wisped with fog. The gentlemen paused on the walk in the light of a lamppost, allowing the chill predawn air to cool their heated brows. Lord John leaned tiredly on the straight walking stick he affected. A hackney cab stood at the curb and the driver called a soft inquiry.

Sir Frederick yawned hugely. His eyes were bleary as he blinked at his friend. "I will be off now, John. I n-need a few hours of sleep to clear this thick head of mine."

Lord John waved away the hackney cab. "I'll walk with you, Freddy. I want to stretch my legs a bit," he said.

Sir Frederick was already moving in a careful manner up the walk. "Happy to have you, of course." He attempted a short bow and stumbled.

Lord John steadied him with a hand on his elbow. "You're badly dipped tonight, Freddy."

"Devil a bit," said Sir Frederick cheerfully. He hiccuped. Immediately he proferred an apology, which Lord John graciously accepted. They walked companionably to the corner.

Lord John heard the unhurried clop of hooves and

glanced over his shoulder. The hackney cab was following them at a short distance, perhaps in hopes of yet making a fare. "There's a cab, Freddy. Shall I flag it down?"

"Non-nonsense. It's only a step away," said Sir Frederick. He waved negligently and stepped off the curb out of the lamplight. Lord John shrugged and followed him.

One of the lamplights had gone out and the side street was darker. Lord John sensed the swift scurry of feet on the cobbles. His instincts clamored. He grasped his walking stick and twisted the head to free the blade hidden inside. He swept up the short sword as hulking shapes rushed out of the gray-dark. "Freddy!" he shouted in warning.

Lord John heard his friend's startled exclamation. Then the footpads were on him. He ducked the club aimed at his head and thrust deep into the man's unguarded chest. The footpad grunted, then began to crumple. Lord John yanked free his sword and spun on his heel. A second footpad was leaping toward him. The sword darted forward. The footpad roared in pain and stumbled back.

"John! To me! To me!"

Lord John whirled. Sir Frederick had been forced across the sidewalk as he grappled with an assailant and was backed against an iron railing. Another attacker maneuvered for an opening, an ugly club raised high. Lord John leaped toward the trio, but he was not quick enough. He watched horrified as the club descended. The blow caught Sir Frederick above the ear and he fell heavily to the pavement. Lord John roared and descended on the footpads like a madman. His attack was so savage that the two footpads quickly fled.

The hackney cab pulled up. The driver jumped down. His voice was squeaky with nervous excitement. " 'Ere, guvnor! Oi came as quick as Oi saw wot was 'appening."

Lord John knelt beside the Sir Frederick. He found an erratic pulse in the unconscious man's neck and let out a soft sigh. He looked up at the cabdriver and said shortly, "Help me to get him up into your cab." Lord John took

Sir Frederick's shoulders and the cabdriver his legs. Together they maneuvered Sir Frederick into the carriage,
where he sprawled on the duty floor. The cabdriver
climbed up on his box and unsnubbed the reins. "One
moment!" Lord John cast about in a shallow circle. When
he found the hollow walking stick, he wiped his sword and
slid it into hiding. Then he gave the cabdriver short, terse
directions and stepped up into the cab, closing the door.

The hotel was only a short distance away. When it was
reached Lord John leapt out of the cab and went inside.
Within seconds he returned with Sir Frederick's valet and
porter, both exclaiming over the attack. Lord John dis-
patched his own porter for a doctor. Sir Frederick was
tenderly carried upstairs by his own servants while Lord
John remained behind to settle with the hackney driver.
The watch had been an interested observer of the pro-
ceedings and now came up to inquire into the matter. Lord
John explained briefly about the attack. He saw when his
porter returned with Charles Wyndham, who carried a
black bag. They disappeared upstairs. Lord John satisfied
the questions of the watch and was finally free to go
upstairs to Sir Frederick's apartment.

When he entered Sir Frederick's bedroom, he found that
the unconscious man had been stripped of his coat and
boots and was laid down in the bed. Sir Frederick's valet
was removing a basin of reddened water from the bedside
while Charles Wyndham gently probed an ugly swelling on
the side of Sir Frederick's head.

"How bad is it, sir?" asked Lord John. There was a
grim set to his mouth.

"On the whole, much better than it first appeared. The
wound bled profusely, but it seems to have ebbed now. I'll
put a bandage on it tonight and return in the morning,"
said Charles Wyndham. He worked with quick compe-
tence even as he glanced across at Lord John. "And you,
my lord? Did you sustain any wounds?"

Lord John was taken aback. He had to think a moment
before shaking his head. "I was fortunate enough to be
armed. Poor Freddy was not."

"Quite." His work completed, Charles Wyndham straightened up and began to repack his bag. "I shall look in on Sir Frederick tomorrow morning and again in the evening. My main concern is that he could suffer concussion."

"Freddy has one of the hardest heads I know," said Lord John, smiling faintly. "Perhaps that will work to his advantage."

Charles laughed. "I hope that it does, my lord. I shall wish you what is left of a good night."

Lord John grasped his hand. "Thank you, Charles, for coming." He walked to the door with the older man and showed him from the apartment. After a few quiet words with Sir Frederick's porter, Lord John reluctantly left his friend's apartment.

Lord John slept for only a few hours. After breakfast he went to check on Sir Frederick's progress.

At the door the porter told him that Sir Frederick had wakened early when the doctor had been to see him. Lord John bounded upstairs to his friend's bedroom. He found Sir Frederick lying in bed, a new bandage decorating his pallid brow. "Good Lord, Freddy! You look as pale as a mawkworm," he said. Lord John straddled a chair, beside the bed and keenly studied his friend's face. He was glad to see that Sir Frederick's eyes appeared clear and lucid, free from confusion.

Sir Frederick smiled crookedly. He touched the bandage. "The least you could say is that I present a sympathetic picture, John. I've my reputation as a romantic figure to think of, you know."

Lord John laughed. His eyes gleamed. "I shall send Caroline to you. She would find your present circumstances highly appealing."

"Thank you, but there's no need to bother," said Sir Frederick hastily. He was silent a moment, then began to move restlessly. "When I think how the blackguards laid me low practically at my own door!"

"I'd say you were dashed fortunate to come away with only a cracked head, Freddy," said Lord John.

Sir Frederick agreed. "I was never so glad for anything in my life, John, when you pulled out that sword. The villians pelted off fast enough when faced with cold steel. I don't like to think how I might have fared if you had not been with me. Thank you, John."

"You would do the same for me," said Lord John with a grin, and shrugged.

"Has it been since Prince Kirov's arrival in London that you began to carry the sword stick?" asked Sir Frederick. He smiled when Lord John inclined his head. "You have always been the cautious one, John."

"I endeavor to be, Freddy. But have you seen Lady Priscilla Eversly? I may have met my match with her. She means to have me, you know," said Lord John jokingly.

Sir Frederick smiled but there was the gathering of a frown in his eyes. "Do you know, John, that attack was the oddest thing."

"Quite. The rascals have become uncommonly bold," said Lord John.

"I wasn't thinking of their boldness, John. I could have sworn those footpads cursed me in Russian," said Sir Frederick.

"What!"

At Lord John's stare, Sir Frederick gave a half-embarrassed laugh. "Yes, I know. I was bosky as a coach wheel. They couldn't have, of course. Queer what a blow to the head will make a man think."

"Could you make out what was said?" asked Lord John. His brows had drawn together.

"You aren't serious, John!" Sir Frederick saw that he was, and shrugged. "That is what convinces me that I was hallucinating. The one with the club ordered the other to be quick. I gathered the impression it wasn't a few pounds that interested them, not when I saw the gleam of a knife. Then you started toward me. And that is all that I remember, except an exploding pain."

The frown had deepened in Lord John's eyes. "Then you felt that you were their specific target?"

"That is it exactly," said Sir Frederick. "But I've no

enemies to speak of. At least, none who bear me such potent ill will.''

Lord John did not immediately reply. A suspicion had gathered in his mind while Sir Frederick related his startling observations. Sir Frederick was spending a great deal of his time dangling after Miss Wyndham. Of late his intentions to her had become so marked that Lord John had heard speculation in social circles that an engagement between Sir Frederick Hawkesworth and Miss Sophia Wyndham was imminent.

Lord John wondered if Prince Kirov had also heard the rumors and had become alarmed by the possibility that his cousin might accept the suit of an Englishman. Lord John knew that Prince Kirov had publicly expressed hopes of persuading Miss Wyndham to return to Russia with him. That certainly would not come about if Miss Wyndham chose to marry instead.

Lord John did not take the attack on Sir Frederick lightly. He thought it entirely possible that Sir Frederick's devotion to Miss Wyndham had made him a target. Lord John sitll vividly recalled his own first meeting in St. Petersburg with Prince Kirov, the man's hot rage and promise of revenge for an imagined slight on the Kirov family honor. It was the reason that Lord John, when he learned of Prince Kirov's arrival in London, had taken to carrying a sword stick.

Lord John did not like the direction that his speculations led him. However, he did believe that Sir Frederick would continue to be in danger so long as he paid court to Miss Wyndham. But Sir Frederick could not be expected to end his attentions to the young woman that he so obviously adored simply for fear of another attempt on his life. Lord John would never ask it of him. Instead, he would simply have to think of a way to protect Sir Frederick.

''John? Is there something wrong?''

Lord John was startled out of his reverie. ''What? I am sorry, Freddy. I was only woolgathering.'' He did not think it time to air his speculations to Sir Frederick.

''That's all right, then. John, I shan't be going to

Tattersall's with you, after all. My head feels a bit wobbly just now. Do you know, I have the worst luck when I drink wine," said Sir Frederick with an attempt at his old humor.

Lord John obliged him with a laugh. Sir Frederick had grown pale with the effort of entertaining his visitor. Lord John could see that he was fast tiring and thought it was past time to take his leave. "I shall be off now, Freddy. I will keep an eye out for a regular jumper for you."

Sir Frederick raised a hand in acknowledgement as Lord John left him.

Outside the hotel, Lord John did not immediately turn his steps toward Tattersall's. He stood on the pavement a few moments, lost in thought. Coming to a sudden decision, he hailed a hackney cab, and as he climbed inside, he directed the cabdriver to take him to the debtor's prison.

14

On A Thursday two weeks later Caroline Richardson and Sophia had been waiting at Almack's an hour before Lord John finally made a promised appearance. Sophia had repeatedly scanned the ballroom for Lord John's tall figure. She felt her heart leap when she saw him at last. But she left it to Caroline to make the initial greeting.

"John! We were beginning to wonder if you were coming at all," said Caroline, extending her hand to him.

"I would never disappoint two such lovely ladies." Lord John clasped his sister's fingers warmly and bent to kiss her cheek. He admired Caroline's blue satin gown and lace overdress. "You look incredibly lovely, Caroline."

"I look like a whale, but thank you all the same, John," said Caroline.

Lord John laughed and turned to greet Sophia, who stood smiling close by. He raised her fingers to his lips. "And you, Miss Wyndham, are ravishing tonight."

"Thank you, my lord," said Sophia, coloring faintly. She had chosen her midnight-blue satin gown with its low-cut bodice rucked in delicate silver lace specifically to attract his admiration.

"I hope that you have saved a set for me, Miss Wyndham," said Lord John with an utterly charming smile.

A warm melting feeling suffused through Sophia's limbs. She spoke a little breathlessly. "Of course, my lord. We did not know how late you meant to be, however, and it is still two away on my dance card."

"I timed it neatly, then. I was never more glad of anything than to be able to say that I had committed myself to Almack's tonight," said Lord John.

"Was the dinner party truly that tedious, John? I would have thought that having all those diplomats together would make for utterly fascinating conversation," Caroline said.

"You have forgotten how many such dinner parties I have attended these several weeks, Caroline. But at least tonight I was thrown a crumb of hope," said Lord John.

"Oh, my Lord! Have you at last been given a post?" asked Sophia.

Caroline had told her in confidence some time before that Lord John was restless and wished to return to active duty abroad. "Yes, do tell us, John. I am all on edge," said Caroline.

Lord John grinned at them. "Nothing is at all official, so not a word to anyone yet. But there is talk of Paris."

"Paris, John! Why, that is wonderful," said Caroline.

"Indeed, my lord. It is a great honor," said Sophia, smiling at him. She did not want to think about what an appointment for him could mean to her, but wanted only to feel happy for him. There would be time enough later to think about his going away from London. Her next partner came up to claim his dance with her and Sophia made Lord John promise to tell her all that he knew as soon as she returned. He laughingly agreed and watched as she and the young gentleman entered the set for a country dance.

"John, that is truly wonderful news. I am so happy for you. Richard, too, will be glad for you. He knows how much you detest idleness. You may now look forward to putting dull old London behind you," said Caroline.

Lord John turned his gaze away from the dancers on the floor to glance down at her. There was a faint smile on his lips. "It has not been altogether dull, Caroline. You have devoted your best efforts to saddling me with a bride and I have just as energetically resisted. And of course there has been the business with Freddy. I have not had more than a handful of truly boring hours, other than perhaps those dinner parties peppered with prosy diplomats."

Caroline laughed. Her eyes were filled with mischief. "I

shall not open myself to comment on my matchmaking tendencies. However, I have not heard anything more since it became general knowledge that he was in bed with a concussion."

"Charles Wyndham has been looking after him, as you know, and seems to think Freddy will soon be back on his feet. I am astonished that Miss Wyndham has not mentioned it already," said Lord John, his gaze on Sophia as she spun by.

Caroline followed his glance. "You assume a great deal, John." She frowned. "John, I should like to talk seriously to you for a moment."

Lord John transferred his gaze to his sister's face, his brows raised in surprise at her tone. "What is it, love?"

Caroline decided to be blunt. "I wish to know what game you are playing with Sophia Wyndham, John. Since Freddy was set upon, you have practically lived in her pocket."

"Have I?" Lord John's tone was cool, a warning to her.

Caroline was not to be put off. "You know very well that you have, John. And I like Sophia too much to want to see her hurt or made the butt of gossip. Your sudden attentiveness these past two weeks is beginning to cause comment, believe me. Indeed, some unfriendly souls have even put forward the notion that you are taking advantage of Freddy's enforced bed rest and are trying to cut him out with Sophia."

Lord John was astonished. It had never occurred to him that his recent activities could be so misconstrued. He had deliberately set out to make himself a more prominent presence in Miss Wyndham's circle of admirers because he hoped by doing so it would deflect the unhealthy interest in Sir Frederick's devotion to the lady. Lord John had reasoned that the more he was thought to be a favored suitor of Miss Wyndham's, the less likelihood there would be of a second attempt on Sir Frederick's life later. Lord John had brushed aside any consideration for his own safety. Prince Kirov already regarded him with enmity and nothing would be changed in that regard. But he had never meant, nor expected to be, seen as standing in competition with Sir Frederick, and it came as an unpleasant revelation to him.

"You must know that is not true, Caroline," he said, frowning at her. "I would never attempt to do such a thing. Quite the contrary. All along I have been careful to maintain a friendly, yet formal standing with Miss Wyndham because I knew how Freddy felt about her."

Caroline looked at him in silence while she digested what he had said, as well as what he had not voiced. Finally she said, "You are a fool, John. You are in love with Sophia and have been from the start. But you won't admit it even to yourself because of some sense of obligation to Freddy."

"That is ludicrous, Caroline," said Lord John, greatly irritated.

"Is it? I think not. Has it never occurred to you that Freddy may not be Sophia's choice? After all, she does have some say in the matter, John. Sophia could very well prefer you or any one of her other admirers over Freddy," Caroline said. She nodded toward Sophia and the young gentleman who had started in their direction with the end of the set. "What if Sophia prefers young Endicott instead of Freddy? Would you feel the same obligation to stand aside, John?"

Lord John was spared the necessity of a reply as Sophia and her young admirer reached them.

"Thank you so much, Oswald," said Sophia. She smiled up at her escort and the gentleman flushed brick red.

"N-not at all, Miss Wyndham. It was m-my pleasure," he said. He bowed to Lord John and Caroline as he took his leave.

Sophia wondered at Lord John's deep frown but she did not have time to think long about it. The music struck up a waltz and Lord John bowed to her.

"I believe this is the dance promised to me, Miss Wyndham," he said.

"Indeed, my lord," said Sophia. She laid her fingers in his and felt his arm encircle her waist. Then he guided her onto the floor and Sophia gave herself up to pure pleasure. It was moments like this that she knew she would treasure all of her life. She was acutely aware of Lord John's arm firm about her waist, the nearness of their bodies as they turned in perfect unison on the lilting melody. She had been so happy for the past couple of weeks. Lord John had made the last fortnight one of magic for her. He had called on Sophia nearly each day and had been quick to appear at her side at social functions. And not once had he forsaken her for Lady Priscilla Eversly's company. Sophia thought she could hardly be any happier, unless Lord John should choose to request an interview with her uncle to ask for her hand. She really felt that, unlike Priscilla Eversly, she would make an ideal diplomat's wife. She was gracious and attractive and intelligent. Her education had been a good one. She was fluent in English, Russian, French, and German. She would get along very well in Paris or anywhere else and . . . Sophia cut off the direction of her thoughts, smiling at herself.

"A penny for your thoughts," said Lord John. He had been watching her expression and the happy light in her eyes made him curious.

Sophia blushed. "I was thinking of your appointment to Paris, my lord. I know that you must look forward to it."

Lord John wondered what there could be about his appointment to cause her to blush. "Indeed. The most difficult part will be waiting for word that it is official. But I hope to hear within a few weeks."

"A few weeks? I did not know it would be so soon," said Sophia, dismayed. She had thought—stupidly, she saw now—that it would be months before Lord John heard anything.

"You do not sound so glad for me now, Miss Wyndham," said Lord John teasingly.

Sophia blushed hotly. "I was only thinking, my lord, how much I shall miss you. We have been friends these many weeks."

"I am flattered, Miss Wyndham," said Lord John. He was strangely stirred by the vulnerability in her eyes. Not for the first time, he thought Sophia Wyndham was a very beautiful woman. Through the Season he had felt more and more frequently the allure of her attractiveness and for Sir Frederick's sake had to fight against it. He knew instinctively that she would fit perfectly under his chin if he were to take her in his arms and . . . Lord John realized with shock what he was thinking.

Sophia was made nervous by his intense gaze and silence. "Do you go to the masque at Vauxhall Garden, my lord?" she asked in an effort to rekindle their conversation.

"What? Forgive me, Miss Wyndham, but did you say something about a masque?" asked Lord John, hastily regathering his troubled thoughts.

Sophia laughed at him. "Yes. On Tuesday next at Vauxhall Garden."

Lord John frowned. "You do not mean to attend that function, surely."

"But why ever not? I have heard any number of people talking about it," said Sophia in genuine surprise. Then testing him, she said, "I have heard, too, that Lady Priscilla Eversly means to attend."

"Perhaps Lady Priscilla is sophisticated enough to be able to find amusement in the dissolute company one finds at such functions. But a masque at Vauxhall Garden is not at all the sort of thing your aunt and uncle would find acceptable for you," said Lord John.

"My aunt and uncle found no fault with the invitation, my lord. It will be quite a respectable party, I assure you," said Sophia, annoyed both by his criticism and by his obvious view that Lady Priscilla was more worldly than she. Sophia had the feeling that he looked on her as a naïve debutante. It did not occur to her that he might consider her and her relatives too little versed in some facets of society to be able to make the most prudent judgments.

There was a moment of silence. "Then naturally I can have no further objections," said Lord John in a neutral tone.

"Oh!" exclaimed Sophia. She did not know what to

think about this apparent loss of interest. They finished the waltz with very little else to say to each other. Sophia was upset doubly by the irritation she felt toward him and the sense of guilt it caused her. Surely she should not harbor such antagonistic feelings about the gentleman she loved.

Sophia remained remarkedly subdued as Lord John accompanied her back to her seat. Caroline was talking animatedly with a friend, but broke off a moment to acknowledge their appearance. "Lord Dunnsel, I believe you know my brother, Lord John. And this lady is a good friend, Miss Sophia Wyndham."

"It is my pleasure," said Lord Dunnsel. He was a portly gentleman who sported loudly colored waistcoats and a ridiculous little mustache. Sophia found him charming on first sight. She was talking to him with much more animation before many minutes had passed and barely acknowledged Lord John's leavetaking.

Caroline quickly noticed Sophia's unusual coolness toward Lord John. She said in a low voice, "John, what have you done to upset Sophia?"

"Miss Wyndham is merely piqued that I do not share her enthusiasm for a certain function, Caroline," said Lord John. He did not mean to say more and Caroline realized it. She sighed, aware that was all the answer she would get, and waved to him as he left.

Lord John left Almack's for White's to play a few hands of whist. He reached home much later that night and was met by his porter at the door. Mims conveyed the intelligence with a decidedly superior sniff that a very low and vulgar person was waiting for his lordship in the parlor. The porter confided that he thought it would be the safest place for the visitor, as there were no small valuables lying about in the room. In the disparaging description, Lord John swiftly recognized the man he had wanted to speak with for several days. Throwing his hat and gloves to Mims, he crossed the hall and entered the parlor. He shut the door firmly against his porter's curiosity.

An unprepossessing burly individual in a leather waistcoat turned quickly at his entrance. The man's long face

was scarred and his broad nose flattened and misshapen
from being broken too many times, the sure sign of a bare-
knuckle pugilist. There was a guarded expression in his
brown eyes. He held a worn cap between his hands.

After a moment's appraisal that was returned, Lord
John came forward with his hand outstretched. "How do
you do?" he said in his soft drawling voice.

The man searched his features for any sign of mockery
before he hesitantly took the proffered hand in his own
large hard-calloused palm. "Seeing as 'ow ye got me out of
the Roundhouse, werry well. I don't ken yer lay, though,"
he said gruffly.

Lord John smiled. He noticed that the man's speech was
better than that of most cockney Londoners. "It's very
simple, my friend. I wish to have a certain task done
without a lot of fuss."

The wariness in the man's countenance deepened. "And
the task ye be set on?" His eyes had become very hard. He
considered himself an honest man. He would have no part
in dirty work like murder, even if he were to be sent back
to jail for it.

Lord John studied the stubborn set of the fellow's
square jaw and wondered if he had chosen the wrong man.
His reply was almost casual but he watched alertly for the
man's reaction. "A friend of mine was set upon by
footpads two weeks ago. I do not believe it was a random
attack. I wish you to follow my friend and observe who
might have too much of an interest in him."

The man's surprise was plain. "Ye 'ave got windmills in
yer 'ead, guvnor!"

Lord John said gently, "Far from it, fellow. And I shall
thank you to remember it. Let us say only that I have an
overriding interest in my friend's continued welfare."

The man glanced speculatively at Lord John. He had
sensed the underlying steel in his lordship's soft speech.
There was more to this richly dressed flash sprig than met
the eye, he thought. He grinned suddenly. "If ye're trying
to cut a wheedle, Oi lay odds it won't work. By-the- by, me
name's Will."

Lord John stared, momentarily startled by the man's unexpected affability. Then he flashed a grin. "You're right, Will. Ye'll 'ave ten bob when yer finished," he said. He had always had an ear for languages and mimicked perfectly the man's accent. Lord John laughed at the man's expression. "I want you to know from the first that I have paid your debt. Therefore, you are free to go whenever you wish it." He waited, knowing that the execution of his plans now hung on the man's own code of honor.

There was a moment's silence. "Ye're queer as Dick's hatband, guvnor. Where did ye learn to speak loike a cockney?" asked Will. His voice was gruff, and was the only indication of his inner feelings. Quiet, fierce joy ran through his veins. He had dreaded this meeting. He had heard it whispered that certain members of the quality "bought" a man from prison and, under the threat of return, forced him to do whatever filthy deed was required. Then, once the dirty task was done, the "bought" man was once more cast into prison, a tool used and forgotten. He could hardly believe his good fortune in escaping a similar fate.

"My porter taught me a bit of the slang. He was a bowman prig in his misbegotten youth," said Lord John, half-smiling. He knew that the man had made his choice. "Have you any other questions?"

"Why did ye not call in a redbreast, then?" asked Will, testing him.

Lord John did not intend to admit that he had indeed considered an appeal to the Bow Street Runners, but discretion had won out in favor of the man before him. "Don't be daft, man! They are as easy to pick out as a mail coach. Freddy and whoever is after him would be certain to know something was in the wind," said Lord John.

Will nodded, satisfied. "Ye have a good 'ead on yer shoulders, even considering ye're daft."

Lord John laughed. He was not at all offended at the slur cast on his mental powers now that they had come to an understanding. "I believe we shall deal well in this,

Will. Your man is Sir Frederick Hawkesworth. I shall tell you his habits. You are to follow him on the streets and report to me, preferably at night. My porter, Henry Mims, will let you in through the kitchen. I'll have him show you to a room of your own in a moment. I wish you to begin tomorrow. I will give you a description of Sir Frederick's friends, and one or two others that I want you to watch for as well.''

Will frowned, shaking his head. ''Guvnor, it's 'elp that Oi will be needing. Oi can't be expected to run after them all. But Oi ken some bright lads that would be glad of a few extra megs,'' he said.

''Then get them. I will pay their way,'' said Lord John. He proceeded to give Will a few quick descriptions.

An hour later the disapproving porter was called to the parlor and told to take Will to the extra room at the back of the apartment. As Lord John wished the big man good night, he said, ''There might be a good mill in this if my instincts are right.''

Will's eyes gleamed with relish; his large hands unconsciously flexed. He had been out of the ring for several years, but a worthwhile bout of fisticuffs now and then was just the thing to keep a man alert and young.

Lord John noted his reaction with amusement. ''Perhaps I shall give you a few rounds myself.''

Will nodded, dubious but happy. He turned to the porter and said, ''Lead on, cully.''

The porter's expression bordered on apoplexy. Lord John controlled his quivering lips only until the door closed, then laughed outright. He would wager that no one had dared to address Mims in such terms for decades. Lord John decided that he very much liked the big man, Will. Perhaps he could persuade Will to stay on after the danger to Sir Frederick was over. But Lord John somehow doubted it. Will's suggestion to use urchins, who were everywhere in the London streets and never really noticed, was proof that he was a man of foresight and individual thought. Lord John thought such a man would have a definite notion about his own future and it was unlikely to include employment with one of the gentry.

emerged from beneath the trees onto a graveled
arriage stood motionless directly before them.
did not guide their steps around it as Sophia
e would.

he stopped beside the carriage door and opened
gers slipped up above her elbow and there was
no mistaking the pressure in his grasp. Sophia's
n to pound. She moistened her lips. "Release me
ir," she said coldly.

unt laughed softly. "What? Are you not still
o me, mademoiselle? It is no matter. I am certain
cousin will more than make up for your change
Prince Kirov is very, very rich."

tried to pull herself free and at the same time
t at him. But de Chaleur was too strong. He only
er nearer to the open carriage door. Sophia
then and the count laughed at her. "No one pays
a woman's screams at Vauxhall Gardens,
selle Wyndham!"

tail of his words a gentleman suddenly burst out
rubbery. He launched himself at the count and
nia from his grasp. A second gentleman followed
aught Sophia as she stumbled free.

ia! Are you all right?"

cognized the gentleman's voice and she clutched
orting arm. "Freddy! But how did you—"

came and told me that you meant to attend the
It was his idea that we come to keep an eye on
deuced glad that we did," said Sir Frederick in a
one.

was the sound of a crushing blow and Sophia
uickly. The Comte de Chaleur crashed back
e side of the carriage. He hung there a moment,
e horses snorted nervously, and even though the
oke soothingly, the carriage rocked. Lord John
a fighter's crouch, his feet well-planted and his
d. Somehow in the struggle his mask had been
ay and his hard features were plainly recogniz-
e moonlight.

Lord John threw himself into an easy chair in front of
the hearth and idly watched the flames dancing behind the
grate. He thought that Sir Frederick's reaction would
probably border on the profane if he ever discovered that
he had a bodyguard. Lord John laughed to himself. "I
wish I could tell you about it, Freddy, if only to see your
face," he said aloud. He contemplated the toe of his boot
and laughed again.

15

SOPHIA WAS not enjoying the masque. Her party consisted almost entirely of strangers. She had come with George Hetherby, a young gentleman she had liked for some time as a casual friend, and his elder sister, Mrs. Helen Dorsey. It had been Mrs. Dorsey who had sent Sophia an invitation to join the party for dinner at the masque, and now Sophia very much regretted her acceptance. Her first suspicion that she would not particularly enjoy the evening came when she discovered that Lady Priscilla Eversly and the Comte de Chaleur were also attending. Sophia had never really liked either of them and she doubted that she would have included herself if she had known that these two were also of the party.

Dinner itself was delicious and featured lobster for the entree, but for Sophia it was somewhat marred by the overly raucous laughter and talk around her. But it was not only her own party who seemed so unusually boisterous. Sophia looked out from her box at the other boxes and the masqued company that milled on the dance floor to lively music. She had never witnessed such free manners and uninhibited conversation between the gentlemen and ladies. She happened to glance at a masqued couple who were sharing a passionate kiss. The gentleman's hand roved to his lady's breast. She squealed at his sly pinch and addressed him in a way that made Sophia's face flame. Sophia turned her head away from them only to meet the gaze of a masked gentleman in the adjoining box. The gentleman's stare was unnerving and Sophia hastily glanced at his companion, who appeared profoundly bored as he leaned on folded arms on the box edge.

Sophia wished suddenly that she were gone from the op-

pressive scene. She glanced over ⁣ she could persuade George to ⁣ keenly disappointed. George Het⁣ his chair, snoring loudly. There ⁣ her in that direction. She doubted ⁣ George after the excessive amoun⁣ imbibed. Sophia still brooded whe⁣ her elbow and nearly leapt out of

"I did not mean to startle you, ⁣ Comte de Chaleur.

"No. I am quite all right, I assur⁣ breathlessly. Her heart was still po⁣

"I cannot help but notice that y⁣ self, mademoiselle. Perhaps you w⁣ gardens for a moment. It was coo⁣ earlier," said the count.

His dark eyes were clear and ⁣ Sophia had never cared for the Fren⁣ at that moment she regarded him wi⁣ Comte." She rose with his finger⁣ Together they left the box, their exit ⁣ the two gentlemen sitting in the adj⁣

At first all Sophia was aware of ⁣ caressing her heated brow, then she⁣ ways were slightly overgrown by sh⁣ in places ill-lighted. More than on⁣ and sensuous laughter from couples⁣ She was glad when the count steere⁣ trysting places, and she began to re⁣ all evening. She glanced at her silen⁣ to you for your suggestion, mons⁣ found the atmosphere of this place⁣ expected. Our walk has at least ma⁣ able."

She glimpsed the flash of his whi⁣ "I hope that you may continue ⁣ selle," he said. There was a curiou⁣ voice.

Sophia was still wondering ab⁣

when they⁣ lane. A c⁣ The coun⁣ assumed ⁣

Instead⁣ it. His fir⁣ suddenly ⁣ heart beg⁣ at once, s⁣

The co⁣ grateful t⁣ that your⁣ of heart. ⁣

Sophia⁣ lashed ou⁣ pulled h⁣ screamed⁣ heed to ⁣ Mademo⁣

On the⁣ of the sh⁣ tore Sop⁣ and he c⁣

"Soph⁣ She re⁣ his suppo⁣

"John⁣ masque. ⁣ you. I am⁣ hurried t⁣

There ⁣ turned q⁣ against th⁣ dazed. Th⁣ driver spo⁣ waited in ⁣ fists pois⁣ ripped aw⁣ able in th⁣

The count stared at him. "You!" he hissed. There was full-blown hatred in his tone. Suddenly he moved, almost swifter than the eye could follow. He leapt to the box of the carriage, knocking aside the driver, and grabbed the reins to whip the team into a frenzied run. The open carriage door slammed madly as the carriage raced swiftly away.

Sophia tore herself out of the protective curve of Sir Frederick's arms. "John!" She flew toward him.

Lord John turned. He caught her up close and she burst into tears as she clung to him. He stroked her soft hair. "It's over now, sweetheart," he said.

"He—he said Misha would pay him," hiccuped Sophia.

"He won't try again, sweetheart. We're on to him now," said Lord John. She raised her face, wet by tears and shimmering in the moonlight, and he caught his breath at her beauty. Without thinking he lowered his head and took rough possession of her lips. He tasted the salt of her tears. Then her lips parted sweetly beneath his and he crushed her to him. His arms held her so close to him that she could feel the pounding of his heart. His lips demanded total surrender from her. Sophia felt her senses swim. Unconsciously her arms wound around his neck to draw him close.

A few paces away Sir Frederick stood frozen. His expression was still, shocked. Without a word he turned and strode away into the dark.

It was several moments before Lord John began to think rationally again. He realized what he had done. "Freddy!" He abruptly released Sophia and looked toward the spot where his friend had stood. But he already knew that Sir Frederick would be gone.

"What is it, my lord?" asked Sophia softly, almost dazed. She felt as though there were a blazing light within her and it bathed her in warmth.

Lord John turned to her. His thoughts were in turmoil. He had betrayed his closest friend, and the knowledge was a massive weight against his heart. And yet, when he looked into Sophia's luminous eyes, he knew that he could not deny his love for her any longer. "Sophia, I think it best if I take you back to your uncle's town house now."

His sudden decision dissipated some of the chaotic emotion that buffeted her, and she, too, thought of Sir Frederick. Sophia agreed, only remarking that she was glad that he and Sir Frederick had watched over her so well. "I humbly admit that you were right about the masque, my lord," she said. "I shall not doubt your wisdom again."

Twenty minutes later Lord John had turned Sophia over into the care of her aunt and uncle, who were much distressed to learn what sort of entertainment the masque had been. By mutual agreement Sophia and Lord John did not mention the Comte de Chaleur's role in the disastrous evening. Sophia hoped that Charles and Matilda would never learn of it. They would only be upset and anxious on her account. But Sophia admitted to herself that her reluctance to burden her aunt and uncle stemmed as much out of concern for them as it did from shame. She did not find it a happy thought that her own cousin would be willing to pay for her abduction. Sophia somehow did not think that Prince Kirov had initiated the plan. She knew his open nature too well. But she could well believe that he would accept a *fait accompli*.

Sophia was reluctant to say good night to Lord John, and it showed in her eyes.

He smiled at her and kissed her fingers. "I will call on you in the morning, but now I think I need to find Freddy," he said quietly.

Sophia nodded. She had before been too wrapped up in her own concerns to immediately realize what Sir Frederick must be feeling. She too wanted to talk with Sir Frederick. She knew that he must have been gravely wounded by what he had witnessed between her and Lord John that evening. He would never have suspected that she was in love with his closest friend.

When Lord John left the Wyndham town house he went to White's, hoping to find Sir Frederick. But he did not find him and no one had seen him that night. An acquaintance stopped him with an appeal for his opinion on urgent matters. It was a half-hour before Lord John was at last able to engineer a graceful exit from the club.

Lord John returned to the hotel and went directly up to Sir Frederick's apartments. The porter let him in immediately and pointed in the direction of Sir Frederick's bedroom.

Lord John paused at the open door and looked across at his friend, who was sprawled in a wingback chair with a wine bottle at his elbow. "Freddy."

Sir Frederick glanced owlishly up at him. "I am getting thoroughly, disgustingly drunk, John. Do not attempt to stop me," he said.

"I do not intend to," said Lord John, his heart bleeding for his friend's inner pain. He advanced inside the room and sat down on the clothes chest at the foot of the bed. "Freddy, I am more sorry than I can say."

"I do not want you here, you know. But I suppose it is inevi—inevitable," said Sir Frederick in a conversational tone. "But I love Sophia, John."

Lord John groaned. He ran his fingers agitatedly through his thick blond hair. "I know, Freddy! I have always known it. And tonight I betrayed you. I had no right—"

"But why not? She told me ages ago that she was in love with someone else. The irony is that it was you all along," said Sir Frederick with a terrible calm. He lifted the wine bottle to his lips and tilted back his head for a long drink.

"What are you talking about?" said Lord John sharply. "She couldn't have. She didn't know me. I stayed my distance because I respected your prior claims."

Sir Frederick wiped his hand across his mouth. "I didn't want to believe her. I tried to change her mind. But Sophia has always been your lady, John. I know that now." He stared into the fire. The silence stretched several seconds before he sighed and looked up to meet Lord John's helpless gaze. He laughed bitterly. "We are a pair of royal fools."

Lord John leaned forward. "Freddy, pray listen to me. I—"

"Leave me, John. I wish to wallow awhile in my self-

pity." At Lord John's expression, Sir Frederick smiled
faintly. But there was dark pain in his eyes. "Never fear,
John. I shall come around eventually. I know now what it
is like to love and to lose one's heart. I shall be more
careful of my future ladies' hearts."

Lord John hesitated a moment, then left the room. Sir
Frederick remained as he was, alone and in the half-light
of the dying fire.

Sophia did not see Sir Frederick for several days. She
sent a couple of notes around to him, but there was no
reply. When Sir Frederick did call on her, therefore, she
was surprised because she had begun to wonder if she
would ever see him again. Matilda gently suggested that it
might be better if Sophia saw him alone, and she agreed.

When Matilda had quietly left the sitting room, Sophia
asked that Sir Frederick be shown in. When he entered she
was shocked by his hollow-eyed appearance. "Freddy!"
she exclaimed in concern. She flew toward him, then
abruptly stopped with her hand still extended.

Sir Frederick laughed quietly. "I look the devil, don't I?
Whoever would have thought my reputedly impervious
heart could have been struck such a blow?"

"Oh, Freddy." Tears sprang to Sophia's eyes. "I am so
very sorry."

He gently took her hands. "Pray do not pity me,
Sophia. I am the better for it, you know, as though I were
precious metal tempered by fire."

Sophia smiled tentatively at him. "I hope we may
remain friends."

A shadow crossed Sir Frederick's face, but he nodded.
"It is my wish that we might always be friends, Sophia."

Sophia pressed his fingers briefly and stepped back.
"Shall I see you at Lady Woodstone's ball?" she asked,
her voice a little choked.

"Of course I shall be there. Have you ever known me to
miss a crush?" asked Sir Frederick with a smile.

Sophia made an attempt to laugh and shook her head.
"No, that is true." Thereafter their visit was a little easier

as they spoke of the mundane. When Sir Frederick at last took his leave, she felt hopeful that they might actually remain friends.

Matilda returned to the sitting room and Sophia told her of the outcome. "I am very sorry for Sir Frederick, but it is for the best that he found out," said Matilda, busy with her embroidery.

"Yes. I only wish it could have happened differently," said Sophia, taking up the yarns that she was sorting by color for Matilda.

The butler came in to announce another visitor to the two ladies. Sophia's face paled slightly when she heard the gentleman's name. The yarns she held dropped unheeded to her lap.

Matilda anxiously regarded her. "My dear? Do you wish me to deny him?"

Sophia stared at her aunt. She quickly shook her head. "No, I shall see him. Misha is very obstinate. He has finally chosen to discuss his mission with me. If I do not see him now, he will but approach me elsewhere. I think it would be best to see him now, in private."

Matilda nodded and quickly gave instructions to the butler. When he withdrew, she said, "I shall remain if you wish it, Sophia."

Sophia smiled at her gratefully but she had no chance to reply before Prince Kirov strode into the sitting room. Sophia stared up at her cousin, disconcerted. She had forgotten how large he was in a small room. She heard her aunt's gasp of astonishment and sympathized with her. Prince Kirov was somewhat overwhelming. He positively dwarfed the sitting room, physically and in aura, and the impression was not lessened by his grave greeting and the bow he made to them. He was accompanied by his dwarf, Fedor. Matilda found the contrast between the little man and his master startling, but she was also struck by the dwarf's innate dignity.

"Pray be seated, Misha. And you also, Fedor. I do not believe you know my aunt, Mrs. Matilda Wyndham," said Sophia.

Fedor bowed, understanding enough English to know that his presence had been noted. Prince Kirov acknowledged the introduction and exchanged pleasantries with Matilda Wyndham, who answered him with murmurs as she continued to eye him with fascination. Soon done with the civilities, Prince Kirov turned to Sophia. He said in Russian, "My cousin, I desire to speak with you on an urgent matter."

Matilda recognized Prince Kirov's obvious desire for privacy. She sent her niece a questioning glance.

Sophia reassured her with a slight gesture. "We will speak English, Misha. I have asked my dear aunt to remain during your call on me," said Sophia quietly.

Prince Kirov frowned, but a moment later his expression cleared. "Of course, Sophia. I can have no objection. I know how dearly you count family, just as I do. In truth, it is my concern for you as a loving cousin that has brought me here this afternoon."

Sophia smiled, quick and spontaneously. "Oh, Misha, you have always been the most charming of my relations. And I have always been fond of you."

Prince Kirov relaxed into a grin. He leaned back in his chair. "We have always been of one heart, little Sophia."

"Yes. But no longer, Misha," said Sophia gently. She would not allow him to establish a basis for argument with such an appeal. She watched his eyes and sighed. "I am sorry, Misha. But you should not have wasted this long journey for my sake. Nothing you say will persuade me to return to St. Petersburg."

"Sophia! But you must return." Prince Kirov had forgotten Mrs. Wyndham's presence. He had left off his position of ease and now sat upright. "The marriage contract with Tarkovich must be fulfilled. It is an insult to the prince that you have fled. All St. Petersburg talks of nothing else. Even the czar has been overheard to express interest. Sophia, our family honor is in your hands! Do not crush it so heedlessly." He spoke passionately and tears filled his eyes. But Sophia remained unmoved.

"If a marriage must take place with Prince Tarkovich, then choose one of my many silly cousins to take my place," she said unfeelingly. "I left Russia because the question of my happiness was not weighed. I will never return, Misha."

"My mother was perhaps hasty in her judgment. You have always been stronger-willed than the other young women in our family," said Prince Kirov with a calming smile. "I shall speak to Princess Elizaveta for you, little Sophia."

"You are too late, Misha. I have found a new home where my happiness matters to those about me. My aunt and uncle look upon me as their daughter, and I have made friends in society." Sophia shook her head. She held out her hand in an appeal for understanding. Unknowingly she slipped into Russian. "Misha, my best of cousins, you must know that I hold you in deepest affection. But you can never offer me better than what I have already found here in England."

Prince Kirov rejected her with a swift chop of his hand. He leapt up and strode swiftly to the window, only to turn about again. Anger flared bright in his blue eyes. "It is this English lord, this Stokes, who has poisoned you against us. He seduced you with his blandishments and his promises and spirited you away from all that you have known and loved. But you are a Russian, Sophia. Your blood sings to the same rhythm as my own. Russia is your mother!"

"And England is my father," said Sophia, once more speaking in English. She was pale but composed, and her eyes were steady. She saw by Prince Kirov's expression that she had startled him with her bald statement. She felt Matilda's fingers grasp her arm briefly, reassuringly. "With my birth God granted me the blood of two strong peoples. I was therefore given a choice, Misha. And I have made that choice. My future lies here in England. I think now that it always has. My mother insisted so strongly that I learn English ways and I never fully understood why. But she must have sensed that one day I would leave Russia and she wanted me to be prepared. As for Lord John Stokes, he merely offered me the opportunity that I waited for."

Prince Kirov's eyes were hard. "We seem to always to

return to Lord John, do we not, Sophia? You are a little fool. What are you to him? What could you ever be to him?" His voice reflected contempt and derision.

Bright color flooded Sophia's face as her own temper cracked to life. "His lordship is my friend, Misha," she said.

"So! It is as I suspected. You see him still," exclaimed Prince Kirov. He saw the warning flash of her eyes. Deliberately he softened his voice. "My Sophia, this man has blinded you. I want only to gather you close, to protect you from such wolves."

"There are many wolves in Russia and some of them are called prince," said Sophia bitterly.

Prince Kirov completely lost his head. He shouted, "Sophia, I no longer ask. You are not in your right mind. You will do as I say. I demand that you return to Russia with me. Now, at once. I demand that you sever your degrading liaison with Lord John. I demand—"

"That is quite enough, young man!" Matilda Wyndham's voice cut across Prince Kirov's tirade like a knife. He stared at her in openmouthed surprise. Matilda stood stretched to her full height, outrage evident in the stiff lines of her carriage and in her expression. "You will take your leave at once, Prince Kirov."

He drew himself up in haughty affront. "You dare to speak to me thus, madame? I am a prince of the greatest empire in the world."

"I shall speak however I wish, sir, for I am queen in my own house," said Matilda crushingly. "And you shall show the deference due to me and my niece by acceding to my wishes. Good day, Prince Kirov."

Prince Kirov stared at her for a long moment, then abruptly bowed and strode to the door. He wrenched it open and stomped out.

The dwarf followed after him hurriedly, but he paused at a soft call from Sophia, who addressed him in Russian.

"Good-bye, good Fedor. Pray look after Misha. He is very angry and you know how heedless he is when in a rage," she said.

"I shall watch for him well, my lady," said Fedor, bowing. He quickly left.

"Well!" Matilda sat down abruptly. "My knees are actually trembling. Your cousin is a very formidable man, Sophia," she confessed.

Sophia threw her arms about her aunt and kissed her on both plump cheeks. "You were magnificent, Aunt Matilda. Truly I do not know of anyone who ever had the courage to order Misha out like that."

"I could not allow him to browbeat you, my dear. And as for his scandalous accusation about you and Lord John . . . well!" she said, shaking her head in absolute disapproval.

"Misha is not always overbearing and vulgar," said Sophia. she felt her eyes fill. The ferocity of her cousin's hostility was devastating to her. Sophia had believed that somehow Prince Kirov would understand. But he had not.

Matilda put her arms about her niece's bowed shoulders. "It is all right, my dear. Pain often comes hand in hand with love simply because we care so deeply. I am sure that underneath your cousin is a perfectly nice gentleman. At least he must be when he is not acting like a spoiled infant deprived of a sticky treat."

"Oh, Aunt!" Sophia burst into tears and yet she was laughing at the same time. "You are so good for me."

"Yes, dear," said Matilda, somewhat bewildered at her niece's meaning but perfectly willing to agree when Sophia appeared to be regaining her sense of humor.

16

WHEN FEDOR caught up with his master, he was concerned that Prince Kirov's rage had not begun to abate. His master's eyes flashed, his voice was fierce when he ordered his driver to follow while he walked. Worst of all, he snapped at Fedor to jump up beside the driver because he did not want company. Morosely Fedor rode on the box beside the driver, who navigated skillfully through the afternoon traffic to keep Prince Kirov's striding figure in sight.

Fedor was not pleased when the Comte de Chaleur chanced to meet the master and engaged him in conversation. The dwarf fingered the hilt of his dagger as he watched the count's head courteously incline to catch Prince Kirov's words. There was something about the Frenchman that Fedor did not like. The dwarf sensed that de Chaleur was not to be trusted.

The two gentlemen eventually resumed their walk, now heading in the same direction and at a purposeful pace. Fedor frowned, worried. His master's temper was well-known to him. While in a rage Prince Kirov was ripe for any reckless act that occurred to him or that was suggested to him. Fedor's cold eyes narrowed on the count's lithe figure. What had the Frenchman said to the master? His short fingers closed gently about the hilt of his dagger. He sat back to await events.

At White's in St. James's Street, Lord John and Sir Frederick were enjoying a game of whist with two gentlemen of their acquaintance. Lord John was dealing. He turned over the last card to establish trump, and the bidding proceeded.

"I heard an interesting rumor surrounding your recent return from duty in St. Petersburg, John," said Sir Peregrine Ashford as he tossed out his chips. He was a dark-featured man with piercing blue eyes, and his glance at Lord John was not an idle one.

"I am all ears, Peregrine. I would not have thought my dull career could stir much interest," Lord John said, studying his hand.

Sir Peregrine grinned. "It is quite a romantic tale, actually, about an elopement and a cuckolded lover."

Lord John looked up and his gaze was even. "How extraordinary, Peregrine."

Sir Frederick choked on his wine. He reared upright in his chair, spluttering and gasped, "My pardon. This damnable wine. It isn't fit to be drunk."

His companion on his left did not bother to look up from his cards. "You know you should never drink wine, Freddy. It brings you bad luck. That instance at Eton—"

Sir Frederick groaned and clapped a hand to his brow. "Pray say no more, Henry. I recall Eton all too vividly, and especially my dear mother's memorable reaction when I was expelled for the remainder of the term. I was caned within an inch of my life. I have never since ridden a donkey."

The gentlemen at the table all laughed. They well remembered the famous drunken race that had ended in disaster for their friend. Yet even as Sir Peregrine laughed with the others, his eyes rested thoughtfully on Lord John. His query had been effectively tabled by Sir Frederick's lively performance and he wondered now if that was entirely coincidental. He knew that Lord John and Sir Frederick were close friends and had both been posted to Russia about the same time.

"Gentlemen, I have a decent hand this once and I am anxious to pit it against all bids," said Mr. Henry Duckwood, Esquire, plaintively.

"Forgive us for wandering from the point, Henry," said Sir Frederick cheerfully. He pushed his chips across the green baize to add to the pile. The game quietly continued, the majority of the winnings eventually falling to Lord John.

Finally Henry Duckwood scribbled a last chit and tossed it across the table to Lord John. "My luck is out this afternoon and it is time to recognize the fact. But I shall retrieve my honor tomorrow evening if you are willing to meet my challenge, Lord John."

"You will be disappointed, sir. Lord John Stokes is not the man to take up an honorable challenge," said an arrogant voice in ringing tones. There was sudden silence in the room as every gentleman present turned to stare.

A stout gentleman prodded his neighbor with a sharp elbow and whispered sotto voce, "What is the Comte de Chaleur doing back here? He just left and here I was thinking it a good thing. Englewood should never have sponsored him, you know." His companion shrugged.

Lord John had looked up and now coolly surveyed the tall, burly gentleman who had spoken. Prince Kirov stared down at him with hard blue eyes. Lord John saw de Chaleur standing near the prince's shoulder and he wondered fleetingly what the gentleman's interest could be. In the appalled silence Lord John turned to his frozen tablemates. "Gentlemen, if everyone agrees we shall meet again tomorrow evening."

"Aye, and for deep play," said Henry Duckwood, casting a nervous glance up at the huge gentleman standing so near his chair.

"Henry, any deeper and you shall drown," said Sir Frederick, deliberately trying for a light note.

"I deeply resent that, Freddy," said Duckwood, his attention diverted. "I'm a shrewd-enough player. Anyone will tell you so."

"I bet a monkey that you shan't be able to win back but half your notes before the evening is done," said Sir Frederick.

"Done," said Henry Duckwood promptly, his gaming instincts aroused. He called for the club's betting book and a waiter brought it to him.

"I, too, wish to record a wager," said Prince Kirov

loudly. He showed his teeth as he glanced about the crowd. "I shall match whatever wager is offered that Lord John Stokes is a coward and will refuse to meet me on a field of honor." He picked up Sir Frederick's wineglass and contemptuously tossed the contents into Lord John's face.

Consternation and astonishment appeared on the faces of the gentlemen who had loosely crowded around, and there were several exclamations. "Who is that fellow? Who let him in? My word! We can't have this sort of thing at White's!"

"My lord!" Henry Duckwood pulled a lace-edged linen square from his pocket, but his offering was not noticed.

Lord John dashed the rivulets of wine from his eyes. He rose slowly. His eyes, normally pleasant in expression, were hard as gray steel. He walked around the table, the gentlemen parting a way before him.

"John!" Abruptly free from his paralysis, Sir Frederick leapt up. Behind him his chair crashed to the floor. He grabbed Lord John's arm, but he was shaken off.

"Leave it alone, Freddy," Lord John said in a low, deadly voice. He stared at Prince Kirov. He felt Sir Frederick's hand press heavily on his shoulder.

"John, think about what you are doing. Don't allow the damned fellow to manipulate you," said Sir Frederick urgently.

Lord John smiled. "Come, Freddy. When have you known me to be manipulated?" His fist shot out. The blow was solid. Prince Kirov stumbled back and threw up his hand to cover his nose. Blood seeped from between his fingers as he whistled in pain.

"I shall meet you when and where you choose, Prince Kirov," said Lord John with remarkable calm.

Prince Kirov stared at him with hatred. "The Comte de Chaleur will act as my second. I shall shoot you for the cur that you are, milord!" He turned on his heel and strode out of the club. The gentlemen in the club silently watched him go.

"Freddy?" said Lord John, flexing his bruised knuckles.

"You are all kinds of fool, John—but, yes, I shall be your second," said Sir Frederick roughly.

"Thank you, Freddy."

Sir Peregrine Ashford, who had also gotten to his feet, came to stand beside Lord John. "I shall also be happy to act as your second if I am needed."

"Thank you, Peregrine. I shall let you know," said Lord John. He glanced thoughtfully at the Comte de Chaleur, whose eyes held a curious expression of malicious satisfaction.

The count caught his glance and smiled coldly. "Sir Frederick has said the truth, milord. You are a fool. Pistols are said to be Prince Kirov's preferred weapon. When the time and place of your demise are known, I shall contact Sir Frederick. There will be no need for engaging another second for this minor affair." He bowed and then walked away, ignoring the club members who whispered and exclaimed.

"What utter cheek!" exclaimed Sir Frederick indignantly. "Your demise indeed. He speaks as though you shan't put up a showing at all."

Lord John laughed and slapped him on the shoulder. "I shall attempt to justify your faith in me, Freddy."

"I wager that you broke the fellow's nose, Lord John," said Henry Duckwood. He held a pen poised above the open betting book and cast a glance around at the several gentlemen present. "Have I any takers?"

"Aye. I say the fellow's nose was only bloodied," said a stout gentleman. Protests were raised. A heated discussion broke out and Mr. Duckwood busily recorded the wagers given him.

Under cover of the loud discussion Sir Peregrine cocked his brow at Lord John. "I believe that I have the answer to my earlier query. I hope the lady is worth the trouble, John," he said softly. He was unsurprised when Lord John merely shrugged and sauntered away without comment. A true gentleman would always protect a lady's good name, and Lord John was known to be discretion itself.

In the next few days, as the details of the duel were set,

the count was well-pleased. Ever the opportunist, de Chaleur had already conceived of a plan to use the information about the duel for his profit. He thought of himself as an observant man and he had seen the soft expression in Miss Wyndham's eyes whenever she gazed on Lord John. He but needed a moment alone with Miss Wyndham and she would fall neatly into his hands.

The count's opportunity came at Lady Griffith's ball two days later. Miss Wyndham had gone to pin a bit of torn lace on her gown. When she returned to the ballroom, she was displeased to find the count waiting for her. He actually stepped into her path to force her to pause.

"I will be honored to escort the so-charming Mademoiselle Wyndham," said the count with a bow.

"I have an escort this evening, monsieur," said Sophia with finality. She had no desire to be anywhere near the count after his attempt to abduct her, and her distaste was reflected in her curt tone.

De Chaleur shrugged, not at all put off. "Ah, it is Lord Stokes again, is it not? Milord is dear to your heart, I think. Perhaps too dear."

Sophia looked at him angrily. "You are forward, monsieur!"

The count bowed. "Pardon. However, you should perhaps know that Lord John is endangered."

Sophia, who had been about to brush by him, stopped to look at him in astonished suspicion. "Whatever are you talking about?"

"Did you not know, then? Two days ago Lord John challenged your cousin, Prince Kirov, to a duel," said the count.

"Pray do not be absurd! Lord John would never do such a thing," said Sophia with scorn.

The count smiled faintly. "I wish that I could bow to your judgment of the matter, mademoiselle. But unfortunately, I heard the challenge with my own ears."

"I do not believe you," said Sophia.

"As you will, mademoiselle." Comte de Chaleur turned away.

"Wait!" Sophia caught his sleeve. He turned back inquiringly and she dropped her hand. "If you indeed heard such a challenge, monsieur, you must also have heard when this supposed duel is to be fought." Her voice was still scornful, but there was a shadow of fear in her eyes.

The count had been fishing for such an opening. "*Naturellement*. The duel is to be at Whiting Greene half-hour after dawn this very Saturday," said the count suavely. He watched the consternation appear on her face and he smiled. "You believe me now, mademoiselle, *n'est-ce-pas*?"

"And the chosen weapon, monsieur?" asked Sophia faintly, feeling herself caught in a nightmare.

"Prince Kirov chose the pistol."

The color drained from Sophia's face, leaving her waxen pale. "But I do not understand. Why should they duel?"

"Mademoiselle, you would know the answer better than I," said the count meaningfully. He watched her expression of dread deepen a second longer, then he bowed and sauntered away.

Sophia was torn by agonizing emotions. Uppermost in her mind was fear for her beloved Lord John. She knew Prince Kirov to be a crack shot who had won nine previous duels, killing his man in all but one.

Sophia's first impulse was to immediately confront Lord John and beg him to withdraw. But she knew she couldn't do such a thing at a ball where there were many curious ears. It would create a scandal, and not only her name, but also that of Lord John, would be talked abroad. they would both be in disgrace. Lord John could additionally face legal punishment for dueling. Sophia did not know if Lord John would listen to her, but somehow she had to stop him from meeting her cousin on a field of honor. Saturday was but two days away. Sophia decided that her best option was to seek out Lord John at his hotel very early in the morning, before anyone was about.

When she rejoined Lord John and the rest of her party, she was unnaturally pale but resolved. Her aunt asked with some concern if she was feeling unwell. Sophia murmured that she had a touch of the headache. Matilda insisted that

they go home and Sophia did not object. It was unbearable
to her to be near Lord John and yet be unable to speak to
him as she so desperately wanted. The ladies made their
excuses and departed.

The following morning Sophia rose early and dressed
without the help of her amiable maid. Not wishing to be
recognized, she left the town house wearing a heavily
veiled bonnet. Common sense dictated that a common cab
would protect her identity from idle passersby better than
her uncle's carriage with a private driver would, so she
took a hackney cab to Lord John's hotel.

Inquiring directions inside the hotel, Sophia knocked at
Lord John's apartment. The porter who opened the door
regarded her with some surprise and allowed her to step
inside. Sophia asked to see Lord John and pretended not
to see the servant's increasing astonishment at her boldness. "I have some pressing business with his lordship,"
she said calmly, her fingers tight inside her muff.

The porter looked regretful. "I am that sorry, my lady,
but his lordship left directly after he breakfasted."

Sophia's mouth tightened. She had no intention of being
fobbed off. "Then I shall wait. Is there a fire in the sitting
room?" She began to pull off her gloves.

"But, my lady, his lordship is gone out of the city and
does not mean to return until tomorrow," blurted the
porter.

"He is out of the city?" repeated Sophia, stunned.

"Aye. His lordship said he wished to put some business
in order," said the porter. All she could think was that
Lord John must be setting his estate in order. Sophia
swayed, suddenly dizzy.

"My lady!" The servant leapt to support, but with a
massive effort Sophia straightened. Her fingers were
trembling as she took a calling card out of her reticule. She
folded it into a corkscrew to cover her name. "Would you
be so kind as to ask Lord John to send a message to this
address when he returns? It is imperative that I speak with
him before Saturday," she said.

The porter assured her that he would do so, and escorted

her downstairs. He hailed a hackney cab for her. As he returned upstairs he wondered who the lady had been. He had never known a woman to come so brazenly to Lord John's apartment.

Sophia directed the driver to set her down at home. She wondered what she could do. She suddenly thought it would be a good idea to confide in Sir Frederick. He was such a particular friend of Lord John's and could surely be counted on to help her. She almost tapped on the window to ask the cabby to turn around and return to the hotel, but her courage failed her. It had taken most of her nerve to call at Lord John's private apartments. She could not have stood another such visit and faced such astonished disapproval from the servant. When she returned home, she sent a message around to Sir Frederick's lodgings and settled down to wait for him to call on her.

Sir Frederick had not called before Matilda and Sophia were due to attend a morning tea. Sophia wanted badly to remain at home, but she was committed to accompanying Matilda and she did not know how to gracefully decline without drawing wholly unwelcome interest to her agitated inner state. Sophia could think of no way she could allay her aunt's certain concern, and so she went. It was an interminable tea, and when at last they returned home, it was one o'clock. Immediately Sophia asked the butler if Sir Frederick had called and was told that he had not. She assured herself that Sir Frederick was merely busy with his own social rounds and had not yet had an opportunity to swing by the Wyndham town house. Nevertheless she sent another message, this one worded with a bit more urgency. Matilda went out again and Sophia begged off, determined to be at home when at last Sir Frederick should come.

As the hours passed she slowly realized that Sir Frederick must have received her messages but had chosen not to humor her. Her assumption was confirmed when a hastily scrawled note was delivered from Sir Frederick, saying that he had an unavoidable engagement but would be happy to call on her Sunday. That left her with the inescapable conclusion that Sir Frederick was deliberately

avoiding her and there was only one reason why he would
do so: he must be involved in the duel and was afraid if he
called that she would sense he was hiding something from
her. "Of course, how could I have been so stupid!" exclaimed Sophia. Lord John's logical choice for second was
Sir Frederick.

Sophia was about to throw discretion to the winds and
call for a carriage so that she could confront Sir Frederick
at his lodgings when her uncle returned to the house. She
could not leave then because he would ask unanswerable
questions. He knew that she had no engagements that
evening and it was too late to use shopping as an excuse.

Sophia fidgeted throughout the evening, watching the
clock half in dread and half in anticipation. She knew her
only chance now to stop the duel and save Lord John's life
was to reach his hotel in the morning before he left for the
field of honor. She dreaded the inexorable passing of the
hours, yet at the same time she did not know if she could
endure the tension for an entire night.

At last Matilda urged her to go up to bed, remarking
that she looked pulled to death. Sophia again blamed a
headache for her unusual pallor and restlessness. When she
reached her room she allowed the maid to undress her and
got into bed. She did not go to sleep straightaway but lay
tense and staring into the dark. But at last she slept.

When Sophia woke it was to the breaking of dawn.
Horrified at the advanced hour, she threw on her clothes.
She knew she would be too late to catch Lord John at his
hotel. She only hoped that she would be in time at Whiting
Green. She hailed a cab and set out, urging the driver to
top speed with the promise of an exorbitant tip.

17

IT WAS cold and misting at dawn. A curricle followed by a gig rolled unnoticed over the gravel road that bounded a small green and wood. The small green was deserted when Sir Frederick and Lord John stopped the curricle. Sir Frederick turned on the leather seat, the reins still between his fingers. "John, are you certain you do not wish me to attempt a reconciliation through Kirov's second?"

"Quite certain, Freddy. He means to kill me. It is only sporting to give him the chance," said Lord John cheerfully. He climbed down from the curricle and walked toward the deserted green, his boots disturbing the tendrils of mist that trailed across the damp ground. Behind the curricle the doctor engaged for the meeting climbed down from his carriage. With black bag in hand he trudged down the slight rise to the middle of the green.

"Damn your eyes, John!" Sir Frederick snubbed the reins and leapt down after his friend. He caught up with Lord John and grabbed his arm, forcing him to a standstill. "Listen to me, man. I've nosed around a bit. This is not Kirov's first duel and this fellow is a deadly first-rate shot. You cannot simply delope and then stand there for him to—"

Lord John interrupted him. His eyes were hard. "I have no intention of deloping, Freddy. I am aware of Prince Kirov's reputation. I had heard about his duels while in St. Petersburg. It does nothing to alter my decision to fight. Prince Kirov forced this meeting on me for his own reasons. I have accepted the necessity for the contest and its risks, but I do not contemplate suicide." He grinned faintly at Sir Frederick's uneasy expression. "Would you rather that I had refused to defend my honor, Freddy?''

"Of course not," said Sir Frederick quickly, but his eyes remained troubled.

"Freddy, if I had not accepted Kirov's challenge, he would have found another way to accomplish his end and exact his revenge for my imagined slight. Some night I would assuredly be set upon by footpads, or perhaps discover an assassin in my own bedchamber. You know yourself of the Russian's ferocious tenacity. Therefore, I much prefer this duel of honor, Freddy. At least it is a known quantity," said Lord John quietly.

Sir Frederick sighed. "All right, John. I've taken your point. But pray hit him first. I don't fancy having breakfast over your cold body."

Lord John was laughing as he and Sir Frederick joined the physician.

The physician shot an alert look from under beetled brows at Lord John. "Solid nerves of steel, heh, my lord? You'll do, then." He took out his pocket watch and flipped open the face. "Five minutes past the hour. Perhaps we shall be able to go to breakfast earlier than we hoped, gentlemen."

Before the echo of his observation had died, a barouche swept around the bend into sight, followed by another smaller carriage. The physician snapped shut his watch and replaced it in his pocket. He shook his head and sighed. "A pity, that." He moved away to take up his position at a distance from the combatant's area and knelt on the wet grass to open his bag. As Sir Frederick watched with increasing unease, the physician laid out surgical tools of menacing appearance.

Sir Frederick averted his gaze and thought it best not to bring Lord John's attention to the physician's matter-of-fact preparations.

Lord John had his eyes on the tall, bearlike figure that descended from the barouche. Prince Kirov strode toward them, his golden hair glinting in the early-morning light and his cape billowing about him. He was pulling on dark gloves. Lord John took note that the prince's dress was sober and did not boast the usual bright gold buttons or gold epaulettes.

Beside the prince walked the Comte de Chaleur. In his hands he carried the long narrow box that contained a brace of dueling pistols. Lord John felt himself tense at sight of the box and unreasonably he was irritated at the count. "Damn fellow turns up everywhere," he exclaimed softly under his breath. He felt Sir Frederick's hand fall briefly on his shoulder, then his friend went to meet the Comte de Chaleur. The seconds met in the middle of the field of honor. The box was opened and the weapons were duly inspected by each. Sir Frederick chose the pistol for his principal and the count took up the remaining weapon.

The principles met with the weapons in hand. Lord John's gaze was steady when he met the hot stare of the Russian. Prince Kirov smiled, suddenly giving the impression not of humor but of ferocious anticipation. The principals turned, back to back with weapons held up at the ready beside their heads. On command, Lord John and Prince Kirov each stepped forward to count off their paces, then turned to face each other. They stood with their bodies positioned sideways so that they presented the narrowest target possible. Their weapons slowly lowered. The gentlemen took aim.

A woman's scream split the deadly quiet. "No! Do not!"

Lord John turned his head, startled, as he recognized Sophia's voice. In that instant his body turned, presenting a full target. A shot exploded. Fiery pain ripped into his side and threw him to one knee. Gasping, Lord John righted his aim. He squeezed the trigger. The explosion deafened him and the gun bucked in his hand. Through a darkening haze he saw Prince Kirov drop his smoking pistol from a suddenly limp grasp. Swearing, the Russian clapped a hand to his useless shoulder. Dark swirled around Lord John and he slumped to the ground.

"John!" Sir Frederick reached him first. He knelt and raised the unconscious man in his arms. Blood welled with frightening rapidity from a high chest wound. Sir Frederick felt an overwhelming, sickening sense of loss.

The physician and Sophia joined him at the same moment. Tears already streaked Sophia's white face. Her eyes were large with horror. She reached out a trembling hand to touch the still, white face of the man she loved. "Oh, my beloved," she whispered brokenly.

The physician spared her a brief irritated glance as he ripped open Lord John's coat and bloodstained shirt. "Pray do not dare to faint, miss. I have no time to attend vaporish females. This man's life is at stake."

"He is alive?" Sophia's eyes suddenly blazed with hope.

"For the moment. But I must stop this damnable bleeding or we shall lose him," said the doctor briefly, busy at his trade. He tersely ordered Sir Frederick to place Lord John back on the ground with something to pillow his head. Sir Frederick swiftly peeled off his own coat and rolled it to place under the wounded man's head. Thereafter he acted as a second pair of hands to aid the physician in fixing a compress tightly over the chest wound in an effort to staunch the ominous well of blood. Sophia crouched beside Lord John, holding his lifeless, limp hand against her cheek. Her eyes never wavered from his face as she watched for any possible sign of returning consciousness.

Footfalls approached, muffled by the grass. Sir Frederick looked up to find Prince Kirov standing over them. A silk handkerchief had been tied around his shoulder in a makeshift bandage. Two of his attendants flanked him. The Comte de Chaleur stood a few paces apart.

"You are somewhat *de trop*, Prince Kirov. What do you want here?" asked Sir Frederick coldly.

Prince Kirov regarded him dispassionately before his gaze dropped to the still form of his adversary. "Milord was a brave man."

Sir Frederick leapt to his feet, his fists clenched. His eyes blazed with pain and anger. "Damn your worthless hide, Kirov! I should beat you to a bloody pulp."

Prince Kirov stiffened. His attendants did not understand English, but they recognized the Englishman's stance as threatening and heard the rage in his voice. They moved to protect their master.

"*Nyet*!" Sophia was on her feet in an instant, a slim barrier between Sir Frederick and the Russians. She addressed her cousin in Russian. "Call down your dogs, Misha! You have done all that you meant to. There will be no more." There was contempt and bitterness in her voice.

When Prince Kirov met Sophia's eyes, he felt as though the breath was knocked out of him. His little cousin had never before looked at him with such loathing. "Little cousin—"

Sophia's brilliant eyes flashed. "You are no longer family to me, Prince Mikhail Kirov. I renounce you and all of Russia. I am English from this moment."

Prince Kirov stared at her, stunned.

The count broke the silence, saying silkily, "Miss Wyndham's sensibilities are naturally overset by the violence she has witnessed, Prince Mikhail. Mademoiselle will be more calm away from the field of honor."

Prince Kirov glanced at him. Purpose gathered again in his eyes. "True, I had forgotten that my cousin has been protected from the world." He gestured sharply at his attendants, giving rapid orders in Russian.

Disbelief gave way rapidly to fear in Sophia's expression. "No! I shall not go!" One of the servants reached her and she whirled to cuff him roundly.

Sir Frederick reacted swiftly. He leapt over Lord John's prostrate body to flatten one of the Russian servants with a powerful roundhouse. The man sagged, gasping, and he spun to deal with the other servant who struggled with Sophia. He stopped short at the sight of the small pistol that appeared in the count's hand.

"Be a wise man, monsieur, and you shall live," said the count softly. His eyes were very bright and hard.

Prince Kirov motioned his servants to take Sophia away. Sophia still resisted, striking out, but to no avail. Prince Kirov smiled at Sir Frederick. "You are a loyal man, Sir Frederick, but misguided. My cousin will come with me, whether you live or die. You would do better to look after your friend, for he is surely bleeding to death." He strode off toward the carriage. Despite Sophia's struggles, she was forced into one of the vehicles and the Russian servants climbed in with her. The count left the green more slowly, pistol trained on Sir Frederick, who raged at his helplessness. When the count had put sufficient distance between himself and Sir Frederick, he rapidly climbed into the barouche with Prince Kirov. The carriages drove away.

His fists clenched, Sir Frederick stared after the vehicles.

As the carriages were disappearing, a horse bolted from the shelter of the wood. Sir Frederick had a fleeting glimpse of a roughly coated individual. Then the horseman was gone.

"My lord, we must move his lordship, and quickly. I cannot do more for him here," said the physician, breaking into Sir Frederick's abstraction.

Sir Frederick turned at once to assist the physician in carrying Lord John to their curricle. They wedged him upright. "You must be careful or his lordship may fall over and the bleeding start again. I wouldn't give you odds on his survival if the wound does come fresh," said the physician.

"Never fear. I shall get him home in one piece. Follow us soon after," said Sir Frederick grimly.

Then began a nightmarish journey back to town that he shuddered over ever afterward. Each jolt that the carriage took made him clench his teeth and shoot a sharp look at the white bandaging over Lord John's chest. At last he reached Lord John's apartment at the hotel and was able to rouse the household for aid. Within minutes Lord John was lying in his own bed with the physician in attendance. Sir Frederick and the servants looked on anxiously, their tones hushed when they spoke.

The physician inspected Lord John again and nodded in satisfaction. "It looks well enough. Now we need only to extract the lead and our friend may begin to mend."

"Do you mean that his lordship will live?" asked Sir Frederick sharply.

"Oh, yes. He is a strong man, in healthy condition," said the physician cheerfully.

"Thank God for that," said Sir Frederick, closing his eyes briefly in relief.

"Yes, well, make yourself useful, my lord, and find me

someone to assist with the cutting," said the physician.

"I'll do it," said Sir Frederick. He swallowed a sudden lump in his throat.

"That you won't. You're as green as a pea now. I want you to get a stiff brandy to steady your nerves and something to eat. You'll need your wits about you to rescue that unfortunate young woman," said the physician sharply.

"Sophia!" Sir Frederick passed a tired hand over his face. "I had forgotten. I shall have to break the news to her family, I suppose."

The physician shot him a look of pity. "It is a shocking business, to be sure, my lord," he said.

Sir Frederick went downstairs to follow the good doctor's directive. The thought of food revolted him, but he managed to choke down some bread and cold ham. His mind was busy, casting about for options. He thought Prince Kirov would initially take Sophia back to the town house he had rented for the Season. Then later Sophia would probably be carried out of England on the first leg of the journey back to Russia. Sir Frederick had no doubt that was what was planned, and he was equally as certain that alone he could not accomplish Sophia's release. Prince Kirov was well-protected by his extensive entourage.

Sir Frederick decided to visit the Home Office to see if he could generate official pressure on Prince Kirov. Then afterward he would call on the Wyndhams, a task that he dreaded. He collected his hat and cane and went home to change into fresh clothes. It would not do to appear at either interview dressed as he presently was in bloodstained shirt and breeches.

Some time later Sir Frederick had accomplished his errands. The Home Office had at first been disbelieving, but once he had gained access to a former superior who knew him well, things went a bit more smoothly. He urged strongly that Prince Kirov be barred from leaving England to effect Sophia's release, but that was not granted to him. He had to have proof that Prince Kirov had Miss Wyndham. He was told a diplomatic protest on Sophia's behalf

would be lodged with the czar himself and would go out in
the next packet. The protest would probably arrive in St.
Petersburg before Prince Kirov. Sir Frederick was advised
to be satisfied with that. Not content, Sir Frederick then
traveled to Bow Street to request the services of some of
the famous runners, expert detectives of their time. He
hoped the runners could discover some way into Prince
Kirov's town house that he could use to rescue Sophia.

Then the interview with the Wyndhams took place. It
was all that Sir Frederick dreaded and more. He told
Charles and Matilda what he had set in motion on the
diplomatic end. It sounded pitifully little even to his own
ears, and he hurried on to tell them of his more satisfactory
interview in Bow Street.

Charles Wyndham furiously announced his immediate
intention of storming Prince Kirov's residence to demand
the release of his niece. Sir Frederick had visions of a
bloodbath. He spent the better part of an hour dissuading
the older man from his reckless course of action. Sir
Frederick listened to himself with disbelief and resignation, disliking his own seeming cowardice. In the end
Charles Wyndham gave way. Sir Frederick left only when
he had given him solemn oath to alert the Wyndhams the
instant he knew anything.

Exhausted and starved, Sir Frederick made his way back
to Lord John's establishment. He was relieved to find that
Lord John was showing signs of awakening and that the
physician was still with him. He asked to be called at once
when Lord John was fully awake. The porter Mims and
the cook hovered in the hall. Sir Frederick requested that a
cold collation be brought to him in the drawing room and
went back downstairs. He went immediately to pour himself wine from the decanter and then threw himself tiredly
into a wingback chair. It was there that a certain rough-
coated individual was shown in to his presence.

The man took off his cap and held it before him.
"Begging yer pardon, yer lordship. Yer lordship don't ken
me from Adam. But it's in me mind that we should meet
seeing as 'ow the guvnor is down in 'is bed," said the man.

Sir Frederick stared up at the big man from the depths of
his chair. He deduced instantly that "guvnor" must be
Lord John and he wondered why his friend would know
such a rough-looking customer. He noted with fascination
the man's flattened, crooked nose and the scarred knuckles
on the hands that twisted his cap. "Who the devil are
you?" he asked.

The man took his abrupt question in a friendly manner
and grinned. A couple of gaps showed where he had had
teeth broken or knocked out. "Oi am called Will, milord,
and Oi be the one who 'as shadowed yer lordship these
many weeks at the guvnor's request."

Sir Frederick choked on his wine. "What?" He had
never heard anything so outrageous.

Will's grin broadened. "Ah, ye never twigged me, then.
And as well ye didn't. But that is nah 'ere nor there." He
waved a broad calloused hand. "Wot Oi come to tell ye is
the whereabouts of the lass that was took. I followed the
blokes, belike, on me 'orse."

Sir Frederick, who was feeling varying degrees of
surprise and disbelief, suddenly remembered the lone
horseman that he had seen leave the scene of the duel. He
stared at Will with sharp interest. "That was you who
came out of the trees at the end? You say that you know
Miss Wyndham's whereabouts?"

"Aye. Oi've the address, all right." Will laboriously
repeated aloud an obviously memorized number. It was an
address that Sir Frederick was familiar with, and excitement coursed through him. "The lass is a rare 'un, spitting
and clawing even as the blackguards carried 'er inside. Oi
put friends on watch about the viper's nest whilst Oi
'urried back 'ere," said Will. "And seeing as 'ow the
guvnor is laid up, Oi kenned that yer lordship should be
told."

"Thank you. I cannot tell you how much this means,"
said Sir Frederick, jumping to his feet. He clapped Will on
the shoulder. "I've got solid news for Bow Street now,
thanks to your alertness."

"Runners, heh?" Will nodded judiciously and examined

Sir Frederick with a degree of respect. "That was very fast footwork, milord."

Sir Frederick grinned. "I'll send off a note directly to Sir Robert Peele." He scrawled the missive and called for a footman to immediately deliver a message. He poured a glass of wine and offered it to the big man. Will accepted it carefully, not wanting to break the crystal glass. "Now, Will, what was that nonsense about Lord John setting you on my tracks?" asked Sir Frederick.

Will chuckled, but he was hardly launched on his explanation before the door was thrown open. Mims eyed Will with distant disapproval and addressed Sir Frederick. "My lord, his lordship is awake, and very distraught."

Sir Frederick set aside his wine. Watching him, Will followed suit. "Thank you, Mims." He went out the door and Will followed. The porter made an attempt to detain Will. Noticing, Sir Frederick said, "It is all right, Mims. His lordship will want to see this man."

Will grinned impudently at the outraged porter before he followed Sir Frederick upstairs.

Upon entering Lord John's bedchamber they saw that the physician and the staunch valet, minus his coat and with his shirt sleeves rolled above the elbow, were having difficulty persuading Lord John to remain in bed.

Lord John sighted his friend. His eyes blazed feverishly. "Freddy! Thank God. Tell these morons to let me go!"

Sir Frederick advanced, shaking his head. "I am afraid not, John. You must do as the kindly doctor says, for you—"

"I'll be damned if I will. I've gotten it out of the doctor, Freddy. Kirov took Sophia, and I must go after her," snapped Lord John and with renewed determination attempted to throw his valet's weight off his shoulders.

Sir Frederick caught the valet's glance and signaled him. The valet obediently stepped back. All at once free Lord John fell back and stared at them all bemusedly.

"My lord!" The physician protested, his glance concerned for Lord John.

"No, Doctor. Allow his lordship to rise if he wishes," said Sir Frederick quietly.

Lord John grinned fleetingly at him. "Much obliged to you, Freddy." He raised himself with painful awareness of the wound in his chest, then swung his feet to the floor. He stood up shakily. "There, now. You see, Doctor? I'm right as a trivet." He swayed suddenly and abruptly his face whitened. Even as the valet reached him, Lord John caught himself on the bed hangings. He allowed the valet to help him back onto the bed. He looked up at Sir Frederick with a grim expression. "Damn your eyes, Freddy. You knew that I was too weak to stand."

"Yes, and now so do you," said Sir Frederick cheerfully. He dragged a chair near the bed and straddled the seat. "How is my stubborn friend, Doctor?"

The physician was chuckling to himself as he snapped shut his bag. "You've a rare understanding for patients, my lord. As for his lordship's condition, he is better than I first expected. After entering, the bullet lodged against his breastbone. The wound is not life-threatening, but his lordship lost too much blood. I am going now to instruct the cook in what is to be prepared for his lordship to build him up again."

"I take it that his lordship shall be dining on thin gruel and broth?" asked Sir Frederick blandly.

There was a twinkle in the doctor's eye. "As you say, my lord, and perhaps a little barley water as well." The physician bowed, preparing to take his leave.

"Good God," said Lord John blankly, revolted.

Sir Frederick and the doctor laughed. Then the valet offered to show the doctor to the kitchen and they left. Will leaned against a heavy wardrobe to watch the gentry, and waited until he was needed.

Sir Frederick was still grinning, his chin bedded on his folded arms on the back of the chair. "I am deuced glad that you are alive and kicking, John."

"You can't be any happier than I am," retorted Lord John. He sobered swiftly. "Freddy, we must rescue Sophia at once. I know that I am useless, but you—"

Sir Frederick interrupted him in a firm tone. "Not to

worry, my friend. I've already lodged a formal complaint
to be forwarded to the czar and have engaged the services
of Bow Street. Your man there, Will, was on hand to trail
Sophia's captors back to Kirov's town house. He informs
me that friendly allies even now encircle the establishment
so that Kirov and that scaly henchman of his, the count,
cannot spirit her away without our knowing.''

"Will?" Lord John was startled. He half-rose to peer
intently at the big, quiet figure that now advanced toward
the bed.

"Aye, guvnor. Me and 'is lordship 'ave 'ad time to meet
each other, and a rare pleasure it was," said Will
humorously.

Lord John threw a quick glance at Sir Frederick.
"Indeed? You did not have a go at him, I hope, Will?"

Will was affronted. "Not belikes. Wot would Oi be
doing taking a poke at 'im meself? The footpads is who
would do that, if Oi would let them." His reply seemed to
reassure Lord John.

Sir Frederick was bemused. "John, do not tell me that
you had Will follow me as a protector."

Lord John's expression was somewhat guilty. "Forgive
me, Freddy. It was the best I could think of after you were
attacked. When you mentioned that the footpads spoke
Russian, I suspected that you were targeted because of
your interest in Sophia. I thought Prince Kirov was behind
it, of course.''

"You kenned wrong, guvnor. I put out feelers with
some friends that ken wot goes on with that group. It was
the Frenchie that put them up to it," said Will calmly.

Both gentlemen stared at him in amazement. "Surely
you are mistaken," said Sir Frederick. At Will's emphatic
shake of the head, he flushed with anger. "Why, that
scurvy blackguard. Why would he have done it?"

"I think because he wants Sophia for himself," said
Lord John with quiet, sudden certainty. He moved restlessly. "We must do something, Freddy. We cannot allow
her to remain in the same house with that one. Even Kirov
may not suspect a threat from that direction."

Sir Frederick soothed him. "Prince Kirov will hardly

hand the count an opportunity to harm Sophia, John. And I promise you that Will and I between us will work something out." He shot a quick glance at Will, who nodded and flexed his big hands.

Lord John fell back on his pillow, suddenly exhausted. "All right, then. But I want to know everything that goes on." He paused, then said irritably, "Damn Kirov for his devilish marksmanship. I could almost admire him for it if I had not been the target."

Sir Frederick laughed. He and Will left then to talk over the situation and to meet with the two Bow Street Runners assigned to the case. Sir Frederick wanted to be sure that every movement to and from Prince Kirov's town house was monitored. He knew it was almost too much to hope for, but perhaps they would be fortunate enough to catch Prince Kirov in the act of moving Sophia Wyndham on her return journey to Russia.

18

WHEN PRINCE Mikhail Kirov and his companions had returned to his town house, he gave orders that Sophia was to be escorted to a second-story room. He entrusted Fedor with the key to Sophia's room, which caused the Comte de Chaleur to raise his brows in disbelief. As Sophia was led off by Fedor and a couple of servants, Prince Kirov threw himself onto a sofa. "I am dead on my feet from this hole in my shoulder. Send for a doctor, good Comte," he said, examining his bloodied coat with a grimace of self-pity.

The count did not deign to answer, but his eyes flamed for a bare second at being addressed as though he were a flunky. He looked at a footman and snapped his fingers. The footman, who understood that he was to attend to the matter, bowed and left the room.

Prince Kirov recovered sufficiently from his despondency to pour himself a cognac and offered another glass to the Comte de Chaleur. "Come, my dear friend. We must drink to our success today. My cousin is safely with us and the pesky Englishman is dead," he said with an expansive grin.

De Chaleur accepted the cognac with a bow. The gentlemen lifted their glasses. Prince Kirov finished his drink with a flourish. He tossed the wineglass into the fireplace, where it shattered, then he threw back his head, laughing loudly.

The count smiled slightly as he watched the prince over the rim of his wineglass. "Barbarian," he breathed contemptuously. He watched Prince Kirov pour himself another drink in a new glass and toss it down. He knew that Prince Kirov would be well on his way to drunkenness by the time the doctor arrived.

* * *

The bedroom door was closed. As Sophia heard the key turn in the lock, she stamped her foot. She was at once very angry and afraid.

"How dare Misha treat me like a parcel to be retrieved at his will," she exclaimed furiously. But Sophia knew that really she had herself to blame for her predicament. It had been sheer folly to go to Whiting Green alone and unprotected. She should have guessed that something of this sort could happen. Yet even in hindsight Sophia knew deep in her heart that she would not have acted differently. Her own safety had never occurred to her. She had been desperate to stop the duel. But she had failed and even now Lord John's life hung by a thread. This was what made her so afraid. Lord John could die and she would never know it. Her eyes filled and Sophia shook her head hard. She would not cry, not now.

The Comte de Chaleur . . . how she detested that man! With bitter regret Sophia thought over how expertly he had manipulated her. He had deliberately informed her of the duel, knowing that she would attempt to stop it and that she would be too late because he had told her the wrong hour. Then the count had only to point out her vulnerability and Prince Kirov had done the rest. Her cousin was naturally pleased to have her in his power so that he could take her back to Russia. He would undoubtedly reward the count handsomely. On the thought Sophia felt bile rise in her throat.

Sophia swept a glance about her. She could not just wait tamely until her cousin decided it was time to leave London. She had to escape. She had to go to Lord John. She was totally impervious to the pleasant proportions of the bedroom or its attractive furnishings. It was only a prison to her. Her eyes fell on a second door, half-hidden by the draperies of the four-poster bed, that she had not previously noticed. She ran to it, hoping that it would lead to a way of escape. But the door opened onto a charming sitting room with a small fireplace. Sophia did not bother to enter after a swift glance around the sitting room informed her that there was not another exit.

Sophia turned back into the bedroom with a frown. The door that led to the hall was securely locked from the outside, but there had to be another way out of the apartment. She went to one of the windows and lifted aside a velvet drape. The bedroom faced out from the back of the house and overlooked an overgrown garden. The garden was enclosed by a brick wall, but Sophia could make out in one corner of it a small door that must surely let onto the street. It flashed into her mind that she could climb down from her window and make good her escape through the garden's outer door. But when she looked down at the dizzying distance to the ground, Sophia felt her stomach twist and knew escape in that direction was impossible.

The fear that she had kept at bay was suddenly overwhelming. She had tried to ignore the images that her active imagination had conjured of Lord John lying dead, his face ashen and forever still. Sophia's eyes filled suddenly and she whirled away from the window, threw herself across the wide bed, and burst into tears. She never knew how long it was before she fell asleep, her tears still wet on her cheeks.

A knock on the door awakened her. Sleepily Sophia glanced around. Instantly recalling where she was, she sat up. She dashed her hand across her face, unwilling to let show any trace of her bout of self-pity. She would not give her cousin the satisfaction.

Sophia stood up and smoothed her rumpled skirt as she heard the key rattle in the lock. Pride stiffened her spine. As the door opened, she said frostily, "What do you want here, Misha?" But it was not Prince Kirov who entered. The dwarf, Fedor, bowed to her. Behind him stood a footman with a covered tray. Behind them in the hall there was a large Russian manservant. Prince Kirov was not in sight, and Sophia was suddenly bitterly disappointed.

"Where is Prince Kirov, Fedor?" she asked sharply.

"The master sends his regrets, mademoiselle, but he is detained by business," said Fedor expressionlessly. He waved the footman with the tray into the room.

Sophia vaguely noticed the footman's frank stare as he passed her to go into the sitting room. "Ridiculous! Misha is never involved in business. Fedor, tell Misha that I demand to see him immediately,'' she said.

The footman returned from the sitting room without the tray. He left the bedroom. Fedor took hold of the door-knob. "I shall do as you request, mistress." He closed the door.

Sophia rushed to the door. "Fedor!" She heard the grate of a key in the lock, but even so she urgently twisted the doorknob. "Fedor! Listen to me. I wish to see Misha!" There was no answer.

Sophia rested briefly against the unyielding door. Then she turned and went to the washstand to pour water from the pitcher into the basin. Her hands trembled as she put down the pitcher. She thought she would be better able to face whatever happened after freshening her appearance. Sophia looked at her cloak and crumpled gown, but there was nothing much she could do with them. She splashed her hot face and hands and dried off on the washstand towel. She smoothed her hair as best she could. Then she went into the sitting room to inspect the luncheon tray that the footman had left. She was determined to have all her wits about her when next she saw her cousin.

Sophia heard nothing from Prince Kirov that afternoon. Her dinner was brought on a new tray, the old one taken away. Fedor maintained silence and would answer nothing to her questions or appeals. So it went for two days. Sophia saw no one but Fedor and the footman who brought her meals and lit her evening fire. She was deter-mined not to give up on her demands to see Prince Kirov, but her spirits flagged little by little. She whiled away the hours staring out across the garden, at the rain and watery sunlight.

On the third day, when Sophia was ready to scream from the boredom and loneliness of her days, she decided it was time to try different tactics with Fedor. She had always treated him with the respect due another individual, but perhaps that was the wrong way to deal with the dwarf. Perhaps he answered better to arrogance. Perhaps he would be nettled into speech if she addressed him in English, which he understood only imperfectly.

When the door opened, Sophia did not bother to look away from the window. "How honored I am by your company, Fedor," she said with heavy sarcasm.

The chambermaid who had entered gaped at her tone. "I 'ave but brought your luncheon, miss."

Sophia whirled to stare at the chambermaid. She ran to the door and yanked it open. She stopped abruptly on the threshold at sight of the tall Russian servant who waited outside. Fedor was there also. His slight smile was sad. "I am sorry, mademoiselle," he said.

"I understand, Fedor. It is Misha's wish," said Sophia quietly. She stepped back into the room and gently closed the door.

When she turned back to the chambermaid, the girl was eyeing her shrewdly. " 'Tis true what Jem said, then. You were brought here and made a prisoner."

"Yes," said Sophia.

The chambermaid pitched her voice a shade louder. "I'll just put the tray on the table in the sitting room, miss. It'll be ever so much cosier." With a jerk of her head, the chambermaid indicated for Sophia to follow her.

"Very well." Sophia trailed after the chambermaid. She wondered what the girl had to say to her, for it was clear that she was bursting to speak.

The chambermaid set the tray down with a solid clunk that rattled the dishes. Then, standing with her hands on her hips, she stared at Sophia appraisingly. "It's said you were brought here at crack of day, kicking up a dust at the master something terrible."

Sophia colored slightly. "That is true. Prince Kirov abducted me and I was very angry with him. I still am."

"And you are set just now to fly into him again." The girl nodded her head in understanding, then her eyes narrowed. "Does the master want to ravish you, then?"

Sophia was surprised into laughter. "Misha ravish me? Oh, no, he merely wants me to marry a Russian prince of disgusting habits." She saw by the chambermaid's expression that she needed to explain a little better. "My aunt, who is Prince Kirov's mother, contracted me to wed a very wealthy, powerful man to further her ambitions.

But I escaped to England. I am now living with my English relations, Charles and Matilda Wyndham, on Charles Street. Prince Kirov came to London to persuade me to return to Russia. I refused, but he did not accept my decision."

"But why shouldn't he, miss?" asked the chambermaid. "Ye're English."

"I was helped out of Russia by an English gentleman. For Prince Kirov it is a matter of pride," said Sophia. She paused a moment because of the sudden constriction in her throat. "Prince Kirov shot the English gentleman. I do not know if his lordship lives. That is why I want so desperately to leave this house."

She saw that the chambermaid had emptied the tray of its dishes and was now preparing to depart. Sophia put out her hand in appeal. "I beg of you, do not go so soon."

"I must, miss. The little man is a clever one. He'll guess we talked if I stay even a moment longer, and he'll not let me come again." The chambermaid bobbed her a curtsy. "I will try to help you, miss, I truly shall." With that the chambermaid hurried back through the bedroom and knocked on the door. Sophia followed, but slowly. The chambermaid was let out and did not glance back. The dwarf looked at Sophia for a long moment.

Sophia instinctively drew herself up. She said coolly, "Fedor, pray inform Misha that I require an audience of him. It is degrading to be locked away, without even conversation to lighten the dullness of my days."

The dwarf bowed and closed the door.

Sophia hoped that she had laid to rest any suspicions that he may have had about the serving woman. She wanted desperately to talk to the young chambermaid again. For the first time in days Sophia felt some hope for her situation. She turned toward the sitting room and with a lighter heart went in to her solitary luncheon.

Sophia was to be disappointed in her expectations of renewing her conversation with the chambermaid. When next the serving woman was allowed into the room, she was accompanied by the dwarf. The chambermaid hardly glanced at Sophia as she collected the luncheon dishes. Sophia studiously ignored her presence, focusing instead on Fedor. "Good afternoon, Fedor. To what do I owe your visit?" she asked affably, a trace of irony in her voice.

Fedor smiled and made a slight bow. "I have come with the master's regrets, mademoiselle. He is still weakened by the doctor's cupping of his wound and remains abed this afternoon."

Faint alarm tinged Sophia's expression. "I did not know. You did not tell me that he had asked for a doctor! Is Misha all right, Fedor?"

"*Da*. The master suffers only a little." The dwarf hesitated and his glance was sly, meaningful. "His head bothers him more than his wound, which is nothing."

Sophia understood immediately. She knew Prince Kirov's penchant for getting himself roaringly drunk. "Good. You may tell him that I am glad he feels wretched," she said with satisfaction.

Fedor grinned. He had always felt a liking for his master's kinswoman. He knew that she held Prince Kirov in true affection, and in addition she had always treated Fedor himself with respect. The dwarf was fierce in his need to be looked upon as a man like any other. Nothing could gain his enmity quicker than to be casually discounted because of his lack of stature. "The master has given his permission for you to visit the library or the gardens as you wish, mademoiselle," said Fedor.

Sophia glanced at the key that he held. "Since I am locked into my rooms, I assume that I shall not be allowed even this small freedom without escort." Fedor bowed in answer. Sophia's color rose, but she said calmly enough, "I suppose it is better than remaining here with nothing to occupy me. The library it shall be, Fedor."

As Sophia was led through the house by Fedor and the ever-present Russian servant, she used the opportunity to memorize something of the way the various rooms were situated, hoping that the information would in some way aid her later.

Sophia was ushered into the library. She stopped dead.
She stared at the gentleman who already occupied the
library. Fedor curiously looked up at her face, sensing
strong emotion.

The Comte de Chaleur turned from his contemplation of
the fire in the grate, having heard the swish of skirts. He
smiled at her. Sophia saw that he did not intend to come
forward to greet her or even to bow. Her slanted eyes
narrowed at his disrespect.

"Mademoiselle Wyndham, how utterly charming that
you join me," said de Chaleur.

"Is it? I find it quite the contrary," said Sophia.

The count did approach her then and took her hand. "It
is understood that you are angry, *naturallement*. But it is
the fortunes of fate. Prince Kirov was determined to have
you, whatever the price, even at the risk of giving offense
to you."

Sophia pulled free her hand. "And what price did you
receive, Comte? I am certain that it must be a handsome
sum that you require for your assistance in such matters,"
she said scathingly.

Anger flickered in his black eyes. "I do not wish to
quarrel with you, mademoiselle. Come, let us make ourselves comfortable by the fire so that we may talk." He
looked down at Fedor, who stood behind Sophia. "Be-
gone, insect," he said in French. He returned his glance to
Sophia and did not see the angry glitter in the dwarf's eyes.

"Fedor remains at my request, monsieur," said Sophia
coldly, also in French, disliking his tone.

The count shrugged. "As you wish, of course." He
gestured for her to precede him and thereafter ignored the
dwarf. The count noticed with amusement that Sophia
walked past the settee, choosing instead to seat herself in a
wingback chair. He took the settee.

Sophia disregarded de Chaleur for an instant. Fedor had
followed her to stand beside her chair. She deliberately
addressed him in French so that the count understood her.
"Fedor, pray choose two or three volumes for me. I shall
not wish to stay overlong." The dwarf's face was expressionless. He bowed and turned to the nearest shelf.

The count was rather surprised that the Russian woman could lay claim to a civilized tongue and, further, that the dwarf understood her. When he heard the request she made to the dwarf, he laughed in outright disbelief. "I am astonished, mademoiselle, that you allow ignorance to serve you in such a way." He waved toward Fedor, who was reading titles.

"Unlike English or French servants, Fedor is a man of education," Sophia said with dangerous quiet.

The count stared at her, taking note at last of the glittering expression in her exotically slanted eyes. He said softly, "I sense that you dislike me, mademoiselle."

"Rather it is myself and Misha that I dislike. We have permitted ourselves to be gulled by a man of small principles," said Sophia.

Fedor paused in his task to glance at them.

The count shrugged, unaffected by her insult. "You are a political innocent, Mademoiselle Wyndham. I made it possible for you to attend the duel. Is that not what you wished?"

Sophia's voice shook. "You informed me that the time of the duel was a half-hour later. You meant for me to be too late to stop it. I was in time only for my own abduction. And you meant for Misha and Lord John to fight and perhaps both to die." She stopped, taking a deep breath to control herself. It was difficult with de Chaleur sitting opposite, mocking her with his thin smile. She said, "You have the cunning of a rabid fox, monsieur. You betrayed me. I know that you must someday turn on my cousin. What harmful lies do you weave for Prince Kirov, monsieur?"

The count crossed elegant ankles. "I am astonished, mademoiselle. Prince Kirov abducted you, not I. But still you speak with concern for him. Mademoiselle Wyndham, be warned. Loyalty is a wasted emotion. It gains one nothing." The expression in his eyes was bitter as he recalled his disillusionment when the monarchy was restored. He had rejoiced and returned to France from long years of exile, certain that his lands and position would at last be returned to him. But it did not happen,

and thus he was reduced once more to living by his wits.
He was galled by the scarcely concealed scorn that he
sensed in those he associated with, whose pedigrees could
never match his own illustrious line but whose fortunes far
outstripped his reduced circumstances.

"Comte de Chaleur, I bid you good day," said Sophia
with distant civility. She rose and signaled Fedor, who held
several volumes. She and the dwarf left the library.

The count stared after her, his thoughts still so tinged
with bitterness that he interpreted into her erect carriage a
contemptuous disdain for all that he was bred to be. In
that moment Sophia Wyndham embodied the full sum of
slight and insult that he had borne since attaching himself
to English society.

When Sophia was safely outside the library she said,
"Fedor, pray do not again show me into a room alone with
that odious gentleman. I wish nothing to do with the
count."

"He is my master's friend," said Fedor noncommittally.

"Misha is a fool about people. He sees nothing but what
he wishes to in those he likes. You must be his cunning in
this instance, Fedor. He will not listen to me," said
Sophia. She shivered. "But enough of the count. Pray take
me into the garden, Fedor. I should like to walk in the sun-
shine today."

The dwarf made a courtly gesture with his hand and then
preceded Sophia down the hall. He had been given much to
turn over in his keen mind, not the least of which was the
count's self-avowed lack of loyalty.

Sophia spent the afternoon exploring the garden. Sometimes she spoke to Fedor. Once as she turned about a
grand circuit of the grounds, she asked him to leave her.
The dwarf honored her request and withdrew, taking the
bodyguard with him. Sophia enjoyed the illusion of freedom as she walked. When she reached the wall in the
farthest corner of the garden, she glanced about her to see
that the overgrown shrubbery and trees hid her from view.
Satisfied, Sophia stepped swiftly over to the door set into
the wall that she had seen earlier from her bedroom

window. As she had thought, the door was locked against trespassers. Its bolt was rusted, but when Sophia worked at it gently, she could feel it give way in its slot. She turned away then, her heart pounding in excitement. She would need only several moments alone from her constant shadows to escape. Sophia was confident that once she had slipped out of the garden into the next street, she would be able to hail a cab and direct it to her aunt and uncle's address. She planned to take several pound notes from her reticule to be secreted in her dress pocket when she returned to her room. Whenever she next visited the garden, she would then be prepared.

It occurred to her that it would not be wise to have Fedor find her near the door when he came to look for her. Sophia walked swiftly down one of the paths until she found a suitable bench. She sat down to wait.

Several minutes elapsed. Sophia had actually begun to enjoy the sun and the buzz of bees when Fedor and the bodyguard burst onto the path. Sophia jumped, genuinely startled. "Why, Fedor! You gave me such a start."

The dwarf bowed. "Forgive me, mistress. When you did not reappear I became concerned for you."

"I forgot the time, Fedor. I was watching the clouds go by and thinking how wonderful it would be to be so free of cares. Besides, whatever could happen to me here?" said Sophia. She rose and looked around her as though in regret. She memorized the spot. "I suppose you have come to tell me that I must return indoors."

"*Da*, mistress. The master has asked that you join him at dinner beginning this evening," said Fedor.

"Indeed. I shall be very happy to join him. I have a few things I wish to say to Misha," Sophia said. She turned down the path and, accompanied by Fedor and the constant bodyguard, returned to the house.

19

WHEN SOPHIA had been escorted to her room, she found a chambermaid putting clothes into the wardrobe. Upon Sophia's inquiry, Fedor told her that Prince Kirov had ordered the housekeeper to purchase some gowns, undergarments, and toiletries. The chambermaid that Sophia had spoken to before was overseeing the filling of a large tub. The last copper pot was emptied of the steaming water, and the servant who had brought it left, followed by the chambermaid's recommendation to step lively. Fedor closed the door. Sophia heard the key turn once more in the lock. She was alone with the friendly chambermaid. "I see that you are required to share my company," she said.

" 'Tis no great thing, miss. I will call for more hot water for the rinsing if it be needed," said the chambermaid. She glanced at the door and beckoned for Sophia to come closer. She hissed, "The big one will be directly outside, miss. We must speak soft, belike."

"I shall enjoy a hot bath. Pray move the screen a trifle more to the side. I believe there is a draft," said Sophia in a normal tone. Her mind was working swiftly and she whispered, "I know that someone is always outside the door, but are the passages free?"

"Aye, miss. No one but the upstairs maid to worry about. The little man sticks close to the master unless he is needed to bring the key," said the chambermaid, under cover of dragging the screen over the carpet.

"I had forgotten Fedor," said Sophia. "He always seems to have the key." She paused in her undressing. "I cannot exchange clothes with you, then."

The chambermaid was startled. "What, miss? Oh, I could never!"

174

Sophia saw that the chambermaid was not as staunch or adventuresome an ally as she had hoped. She sighed. "No, I suppose not. It was only a thought. I shall have to think of something else."

"Yes, miss," said the chambermaid, relieved.

When Sophia had finished her bath and dressed in one of the gowns that she found in the wardrobe, she was escorted downstairs to the dining room. Prince Kirov awaited her and greeted her with a touch of restraint, as though he were not quite certain of her reaction. Sophia did not make it easier on him. She returned his greeting coldly. The Comte de Chaleur joined them and Sophia pointedly turned her shoulder on him. Prince Kirov was left with the burden of the conversation. When dinner was over and Sophia rose from the table, ready to be escorted back to her room, she left Prince Kirov glumly staring at his wine.

Once more in her room, she said to herself, "And that, dear Misha, is just the beginning. I shall make you so miserable that you will gladly see me free. At least, that is my hope."

Thereafter, Sophia's days took on more meaning. She was allowed to join Prince Kirov and the count for meals. Each time Sophia saw her cousin, she posed the same question about being given her freedom, and each time he denied it, she became cold as ice. Prince Kirov began to dread meals. He felt that he could not relegate Sophia to solitary meals in her room once again because it was a point of pride to him. He also could not show that she was wearing on him so thoroughly.

Sophia used her times outside the bedroom to observe and note the doings of the household. She paid particular attention to the servants visible. She did not believe that the English servants were as likely to do Prince Kirov's bidding as were his Russian bodyguards, but still she could trust none of them to truly aid her. Even the chambermaid who had expressed herself willing had no intention of actually placing herself at risk for Sophia's sake. Thereafter it took but a few days for Sophia to reluctantly decide

that there was no way that she could physically escape the
town house. She was too closely guarded. Even her
thought of slipping through the door in the garden wall
was beyond her ability, since Fedor never seemed to leave
her alone long enough to take advantage of it.

Sophia thought over her problem. One day while in her
sitting room with one of the books that Fedor had gotten
for her, she tore out the white flyleaf. Sophia found a pen
and wrote a short note. She then folded the paper into a
small twist and slipped it into her pocket. When next she
saw the chambermaid, she persuaded the girl to agree to
carry the note to the Wyndham address. "My uncle and
aunt are generous and will certainly reward you handsomely," she said hopefully.

"I will do it, miss," said the chambermaid.

Sophia was nervous at dinner that evening. She could
not help wondering if the chambermaid had been able to
slip away on her errand. The Comte de Chaleur commented on her unusual restlessness and laughed when
Sophia shot a dagger glance at him.

"Indeed, cousin, I, too, have noticed," said Prince
Kirov.

"It is nothing but a foolish headache. I shall be better
for a little more wine," Sophia said.

Prince Kirov regarded her thoughtfully. Sophia
pretended not to notice. He snapped his fingers and Fedor
went to him. Prince Kirov bent to whisper in his ear. The
dwarf bowed and left the dining room. Prince Kirov
reached for the half-full wine bottle and his goblet and rose
from the table. "Let us go to the drawing rom. Sophia,
you will join us this evening as my guest," he said with a
broad smile.

"I am honored, Misha," said Sophia with a trace of
irony.

With an elaborate show of courtesy Prince Kirov stood
aside for Sophia to precede him, then followed. De
Chaleur brought up the rear.

Sophia entered the drawing room and suddenly stopped
short, the color draining from her face. She stared,

appalled, at the chambermaid, who appeared small between the two Russian manservants flanking her. The chambermaid was attired in her cloak and bonnet, obviously preparing to go out. Her face was terrified. Fedor took her reticule and opened it. He brought out a small twist of paper.

Prince Kirov seated himself, placing his goblet and the wine bottle on a stand next to his chair. "Comte, pray do the honors and read that little paper."

The count took the twist and undid it. He glanced at it and his eyes gleamed. "It is a note to mademoiselle's uncle, Monsieur Charles Wyndham."

"As I knew it to be." Prince Kirov looked gravely at Sophia. "I know you well, little cousin. There was a reason for you to be nervous. I asked Fedor to bring me the last servant that you saw today. If it had been but a few moments more, this little bird would have already flown."

Sophia stared at her cousin defiantly. "You cannot say that you are disappointed, Misha. I know that if you were held against your will you would have attempted the same."

"True. But I cannot allow you to go unpunished," said Prince Kirov. His hand shot out to close around Sophia's wrist and he yanked her to him. "It was a most childish trick, Sophia, and so you shall be treated like a child," he said, and turned her over his knee to deliver a sound spanking.

For two seconds Sophia was too astonished to react. Then humiliation boiled up within her. She cried out and struck at him futilely.

The count leaned against the mantel at once disdainful and fascinated by the scene.

The chambermaid watched aghast.

Sophia was at last released to the custody of one of the large Russian servants. Humiliation flushed her face. Her fists were clenched. "I shall never forgive you, Misha," she choked.

Prince Kirov stared at her coldly. "That, cousin, is of supreme indifference to me. You! Return her to her room." As Sophia was led stumbling from the room, he turned hard eyes on the shrinking chambermaid. "As for you, you are dismissed this instant. Fedor, put her out onto the street. Perhaps the chill of night will teach her the folly of her ways."

"But my things . . . And I 'ave back wages owed!" Prince Kirov did not acknowledge the chambermaid's shrill protests as she was taken from the room. A few moments later the chambermaid's pleadings were cut off by the banging of the front door.

"What a thoroughly enchanting evening. I am hugely entertained," said the count.

Prince Kirov gave him a baleful look and then reached for his bottle of wine. But he did not remain with de Chaleur for many more minutes. Instead, he left the count to his own company and sought out the privacy of his rooms. The happenings of the evening had upset him.

Sophia was in a towering rage. She was angrier than she had ever been in her life. Restlessly she paced the bedroom. After a while her eyes were drawn to the gathering twilight outside the open window. She threw open the window and tossed back her head to breathe deeply of the night air. Unbidden came the thought that the air was freer than she. She stared down into the depths of dark shrubbery. Her eyes narrowed, giving her abruptly the look of a slant-eyed feline. "I shall do it," she said tightly.

Sophia swung about and went over to the four-poster bed. Ruthlessly she stripped off the linen sheets and knotted the corners until she had a long unwieldy rope. Sophia tied one end of the rope of sheets to a bedpost and yanked on it with all her weight to be certain it would hold. Then she donned her cloak.

Sophia threw the rough rope out of the window. She looked out. The end of the rope swung lazily several feet above the ground, but Sophia thought the remaining distance was not too great. She climbed onto the windowsill and swung one leg over. With a deep breath and holding tightly to her improvised rope, she swung out her other leg.

With the rope clamped tight between her thighs, Sophia began a cautious descent. Her weight dragged on her shoulders and hands. Sweat beaded on her face and she bit her lip. The rope spun as she descended and she held on helplessly, breathing fear with great shallow gulps of air. She refused to look down to check on her progress, but as the minutes passed and she did not fall, she was encouraged that she might yet gain the safety of firm ground.

In his second-story apartment Prince Kirov stood at his window contemplating the evening sky. It was his favorite hour of the day in London. When the fashionable quarter of the city was lighted with the new gaslights, the resulting glow reflected to the sky and reminded him of the midnight sun of Russia.

A movement caught his eye and he leaned closer to his window, frowning. The movement resolved itself into a wildly spiraling figure against the face of the house. With astonishment he watched as the figure descended with painful slowness some odd sort of rope. He realized at once that it was Sophia, but astonishment and disbelief held him spellbound, rooted to the floor.

Suddenly the rope parted and he watched in horror as she fell. "Sophia!" He lunged out of his apartment and down the private stairs that let onto the garden. Within minutes he had reached the grounds and run over to the small huddled figure on the graveled walkway.

Sophia looked around as she heard his hard, rapid approach. Tears streaked her face and she protectively clasped an ankle.

Prince Kirov dropped to one knee beside her. "Little cousin, Sophia, are you all right? I thought you had killed yourself."

"It is my ankle only, Misha. I have stupidly twisted it." Sophia threw up her chin. "If it had not been for that, you would not still have me at your mercy."

"Oh, Sophia. Do you hate me so much, then?" asked Prince Kirov with a groan. He dropped his head into his hands, plunging into sudden despair.

Sophia regarded him, unmoved. She knew that his mercurial emotions were real and profoundly felt, and it gave her a sense of satisfaction that he suffer. "I do not hate you, Misha. But you have taken me from the people I love. Indeed, you even tried to kill Lord John. I am so very angry with you."

He looked up, his expression searching and somber. "You are angry enough to risk death," he stated. She nodded, returning his gaze steadily. Prince Kirov sighed. "Come, Sophia. I shall help you go in. I wish almost that Prince Tarkovich would eat himself to death. You are too bold a woman to be sacrificed to that one. My mother should have done better for you."

Sophia accepted her cousin's hand and allowed him to support her into the house.

The Comte de Chaleur was still sitting in the drawing room, contemplating the fire over the rim of a wineglass. He looked up in surprise when Prince Kirov and Sophia came in through the door from the garden. His brows rose higher as he realized that Sophia limped and was leaning heavily on her cousin's arm.

Prince Kirov saw his curious glance. He said briefly, "My cousin twisted her ankle during our walk. Pray be so good as to pull the bell for a servant to assist her to her room, Comte."

The count rose from his chair to comply with the prince's request. Sophia sank into a chair. She averted her face determinedly from the two men's gaze. The three waited in silence until the footman came in. Sophia accepted the footman's help and started from the room on his arm.

"Good night, Sophia, and rest well," said Prince Kirov. The count echoed his sentiments.

Sophia did not reply, only inclined her head with an ironic expression in her eyes.

When she had gone, Prince Kirov went to the decanter to pour a glass of wine. He tossed it back and then stood fiddling with his empty glass, a frown between his heavy brows.

De Chaleur shot him a comprehending glance as he once more seated himself. "Mademoiselle Wyndham is not resigned to her fate," he said.

Prince Kirov rounded on him and his expression mirrored his frustration. "My cousin remains fiercely opposed to me. Even I, who thought to know her so well, am surprised by her continued obstincy." There was grudging respect in his voice.

The count steepled his fingers. "Perhaps it would be best for all concerned if mademoiselle did not remain in England. Her obstinacy must of necessity erode once the journey to Russia is actually begun. And too, I wonder if her English friends may not make a foolhardy attempt to retrieve her."

"Yes, you are right. Sir Frederick Hawkesworth is a loyal man. He will naturally go to the Wyndhams," said Prince Kirov slowly. Actually he was not particularly concerned about what Sir Frederick might do. But it was not for the Comte de Chaleur to know of Sophia's attempted escape, or of his own certainty that she would try again. And perhaps on her next attempt she would be badly injured. He did not want to take that chance. Prince Kirov made a mental note to personally collect the rope of sheets abandoned in the garden and to give them to Fedor, who could be trusted to dispose of them discreetly. "You are undoubtably correct, Comte. Sophia will be safer out of England."

"Allow me to make a suggestion, Prince Kirov. I know that your social obligations tie you to London for a few weeks yet. However, my own engagements are of the slightest moment and may be canceled with little trouble. I could therefore personally escort Mademoiselle Sophia to the Continent and wait for you at the château," said the count suavely.

Prince Kirov sensed an unusual tenseness in the Comte de Chaleur's voice, but he paid little heed to it as he thought over the suggestion. He abruptly nodded. "Good. It is a good plan. You will leave in the morning with my cousin. Tonight the housekeeper will pack those articles Sophia will require on the journey. I hope that your engagements can be taken care of this evening, Comte?''

The Comte de Chaleur inclined his head. An easy smile curved his thin lips. The strange tenseness that Prince Kirov had earlier noted was gone. "Indeed, my lord. I foresee no problem. I am but happy to be of some small service to you."

Prince Kirov nodded. "I shall wish you good night then, Comte." The wound in his shoulder pained him and he shrugged irritably. "This house is too small for me. I will be glad to leave it." He turned and left the room through the door to the garden.

De Chaleur looked after him with a grimace. He would never understand the Russian's taste for the open air. In the count's estimation, for all his royal blood Prince Mikhail Kirov was little better than a barbarian.

The count did not know that Prince Kirov himself swept up linen sheets from the walkway and took the awkward bundle back to his own apartment to be given to his discreet personal servant, Fedor.

20

THE PENNILESS chambermaid spent a miserable, fearful night huddled in a deep doorway. She had no place to go and no references. What friends she had were fellow domestics like herself, and though they were good-enough sorts, they could not be expected to endanger their own positions by aiding someone sunk in disgrace. Just before first light the chambermaid rose stiffly and made an attempt to smooth her crumpled skirts. She straightened her bonnet and then marched off toward Charles Street. She had a keen memory for names and places. She would see this Master Wyndham, she would. And if she had a bit of luck, the gentleman might even be so kind as to give her a reference so that she could find work in a proper English household. There would be no more service with foreigners for her, she thought with a sniff.

The porter at the Wyndham town house did not welcome the chambermaid and tried to close the door on her, but she was a determined young woman with a hearty set of lungs. It was but a few moments before her strident demands to see Master Wyndham brought Charles himself onto the scene.

"Here, now, what is this?" he asked.

"I've come about Miss Sophia, sir," said the chambermaid. Charles motioned sharply for her to be allowed inside. The chambermaid shot the porter a triumphant look as she stepped past him into the hall.

"Now, young woman, what is it you have to say?" asked Charles.

The chambermaid told her story hurriedly. He asked a few sharp questions to test her truthfulness. By the time she had finished, Charles' face had taken on a purple hue.

He swung around, roaring that a constable be found and brought to him immediately. The porter left the house on the run to do so.

Matilda came hurriedly into the hall. "Whatever is the matter, Charles?"

"Prince Kirov has our Sophia locked up in his house, the bloody bastard! I shall have his rotten heart for it," said Charles.

"Charles!" Matilda was shocked by his immoderate language. "But how can you know for certain? Remember what Sir Frederick told us. We must have proof—"

"This young woman saw our Sophia and talked with her. Tilda, she witnessed Sophia being beaten by Kirov," said Charles. There were tears in his eyes.

"Aye, 'tis true. Begging your pardon, Mistress, but I was dismissed for trying to bring a note from Miss Sophia to the master here. That was why the prince beat Miss Sophia, for writing the note," said the chambermaid.

"Oh, my Lord." Matilda looked at her husband. "Charles, what do you mean to do?"

His brown eyes were hard and cold. "I shall bring Sophia home."

An hour later, outside Prince Kirov's town house, Will was the interested observer of an altercation. A short stocky gentleman had arrived with a constable in tow and demanded to speak with Prince Kirov. After a short wait Prince Kirov himself appeared at the door, arrogance in every inch of his bearing. Will was fascinated to overhear bits and parts of the argument. It was out of the corner of his eye that he first noticed a carriage departing from the far side of the prince's town house.

Will swung about, suddenly alert. When he saw a pale feminine face at the carriage window and recognized the mounted horseman riding behind, he swore. He ran after the carriage as fast as his legs would carry him, but he lost it in the wakening London streets. He stood a moment, chest heaving, then turned and raced back the way he had come. He had to alert Sir Frederick and the guvnor.

* * *

Sir Frederick stepped around for his daily visit with his irritable invalid friend. To satisfy the curious, he had put it about town with Richard Richardson's aid that Lord John had been laid up a few days with a putrid throat. He was therefore dismayed to find visitors in Lord John's sitting room. Sir Frederick quickly recovered and advanced to greet Caroline Richardson. "Caroline, you appear ravishing as ever." He shot a dagger glance at her husband, who stood beside her. Richard merely shrugged.

Caroline accepted Sir Frederick's kiss on her softly powdered cheek. "I came to see for myself how my brother is, Freddy. But he only growled like a bear at me and refused to answer a single question, so I waited to see you. And do not attempt to fob me off, Freddy."

"I am insulted, Caroline. How can you think I would do so? Of course you are concerned for John. But take my word for it, he has merely contracted a fever and a putrid throat. It is of no consequence, really. John is bound to be up and about soon," said Sir Frederick with a confident air.

"Stuff and nonsense, Freddy. I know all about the duel. Richard cannot keep a secret from me for long, as he well knows. I had it all out of him first thing this morning," said Caroline.

"I also told you there was no cause for alarm and what John's reaction would be to your mother-henning," said Richard with a certain measure of satisfaction. "As you saw for yourself, John is making a splendid recovery."

"Indeed. And has he also recovered his scattered wits? John has carried this quixotic business too far, and so would Miss Wyndham have told him if he had not gone off half-cocked," said Caroline witheringly. "I have never known John to do anything so foolish. Fighting a duel! You, at least, should have stopped him, Freddy."

Sir Frederick found himself on the defensive. "John had little choice, Caroline. The matter was forced on him and his honor was at stake."

"Of course John had a choice," said Caroline impatiently. "He could have—have talked to that horrid Prince Kirov."

The gentlemen shared a look of mutual understanding. There was no point in attempting to explain the finer points of a gentleman's code of honor to the ladies. They never fully understood it.

Richard took Caroline's arm. "Now that you have satisfied yourself about John and given poor Freddy a raking-over, Caroline, let's be off."

She pinkened, at once contrite, and gave Sir Frederick her hand and a warm apology. He took it in good spirit and waved them out. Then, after announcing himself with a negligent knock on the door, he went into the bedroom.

Lord John sat in a wingback chair near the fireplace, an open book on his knees. He wore a scowl. "If Caroline is with you, Freddy, I—"

"Be at ease, John. They have just this moment left," said Sir Frederick. He hitched himself onto the corner of an occasional table and proceeded to swing his booted foot.

"Thank God for that," said Lord John, his expression lightening. "I thought she would drive me mad with her exclamations and scolding. Caroline actually demanded that I go home with her so that she could nurse me, until Richard put his foot down. He told her that I was not a puling babe in need of gruel and tucking in at night. And he was in the right of it. That is exactly what Caroline would have done."

Sir Frederick laughed. "At least you were up and about when Caroline and Richard dropped by, or I suspect that you might not have escaped so easily. How is the wound?"

Lord John gingerly flexed his shoulder. "It complains still, but I am able to ignore it. I don't know what was in that sawbone's concoction, but it is doing the trick."

"Knitbone," said Sir Frederick promptly. He saw the speculative expression on his friend's face and grinned. "I have not turned quack just yet, John. Will suggested the herb to the good doctor, who expressed astonishment that he had not thought of it himself. It seems that Will's sister is a bit of a dabbler in herbal remedies. She always recommended knitbone to Will after his worst bouts."

"Will is a very useful fellow," observed Lord John, gingerly flexing his shoulder.

"Quite," agreed Sir Frederick.

All of a sudden the very person they were discussing burst into the room, his chest heaving. He spoke in explosive gasps. "Guvnor! The Frenchie . . . 'e 'as taken the miss . . . a carriage." He told what he had observed.

Lord John threw aside his book and leapt to his feet. He spoke to Sir Frederick in a tight voice. "The count will be acting under Kirov's orders. My guess is that they are pointed toward Dover. Kirov more than likely has a yacht waiting there."

Sir Frederick nodded, already moving toward the door. "Will and I will set forth immediately. We shall send word to you when we have freed Sophia." Will nodded staunchly.

"On the contrary, Freddy. I ride with you," Lord John said. He was shrugging into a coat, grunting at the twinges in his chest and shoulder.

"You cannot be serious, John. Why, you are still weak as a cat. I should like to know how you expect to hold up under the brutal pace I mean to set," said Sir Frederick explosively.

"Be damned to you, Freddy," said Lord John. He took a sheathed sword out of the wardrobe. He smiled when he saw his friend's expression. "I promise you that I shall be in good-enough form when we catch up with them. You shan't have to worry that I will collapse at a crucial moment."

"That is the stupidest assurance you have ever uttered," said Sir Frederick in disgust.

Lord John laughed. "Quite. However, I am determined to go. I will allow nothing to stop me."

Sir Frederick recognized the implacability in his friend's tone and accepted the inevitable. "I would wager a monkey that your sister would come close to it," he said.

"Caroline!" Lord John laughed and agreed. He was putting clean shirts and breeches in a portmanteau. "I had meant to send a note around to Richard immediately to let him know what is happening, so that he can cover for us here, but perhaps it would be best to have it delivered in an hour or two, when we shall have left.''

"Richard is not the only person that we must notify, John," said Sir Frederick somberly.

Lord John paused in his packing. "You are thinking of Charles and Matilda Wyndham, of course."

"I gave them my word, John," said Sir Frederick.

"Then let us plan to meet downstairs in a few minutes, Freddy. That will give you time to pen your note to the Wyndhams while I arrange for a team of four," said Lord John.

Sir Frederick nodded. "Oh, John, take your walking stick. I intend to carry the heavier blade you have there and save you from the temptation of trying to use it while in your weakened state." Lord John grimaced at him, but nodded. Sir Frederick left the bedroom.

Lord John looked at Will. "I hope you intend to join us, Will. We'll have need of your abilities before this is done."

The big man flexed his broad calloused hands. A small smile touched his face. "There be no need to fash yerself, guvnor. Oi'll be squaring up beside ye." He touched his forelock in casual salute and left to make his own preparations.

Lord John grinned. He felt a keen sense of relief that at last something was happening.

Sir Frederick did not enjoy his call on the Wyndhams. Charles Wyndham expressed eager determination to join the younger gentlemen on their journey. Sir Frederick was forced to exert all of his diplomatic powers to persuade him otherwise, privately thinking that the older man would not be able to keep up the pace and subsequently become a handicap when they finally caught up with the count.

Charles argued strenuously and told Sir Frederick of his abortive visit to Prince Kirov's town house early that morning. "The fellow at last deigned to allow the constable to search the house, saying that he had nothing to hide. But the constable found Sophia's handkerchief, with her initials plain in the corner," said Charles. He snorted. "Kirov told a tale then, believe me. He said that Sophia had gone to him, greatly confused over the state of her heart, and asked him not to acknowledge her presence to anyone so that she could reflect undisturbed. Then Sophia is supposed to have decided to take a repairing lease somewhere. Kirov said that he respected her privacy enough not to inquire into her plans. Have you ever heard such a Banbury tale?"

Sir Frederick was frowning. "If Prince Kirov became so cooperative and allowed a search, it was because he knew that the count had gotten Sophia safe away. However, since the handkerchief was found, he must know that he is still very much under suspicion. I doubt if he will leave London immediately. He must be confident of meeting the count, with Miss Wyndham, at a prearranged location. All of which means that we must find de Chaleur and Miss Wyndham before Prince Kirov arrives with his blasted entourage." He looked up at Charles Wyndham. "I am sorry, sir, but the possible danger is such that I really must ask you to remain here in London."

"Certainly not, Sir Frederick. Charles and I both intend to go with you. Sophia is our niece and it is our duty," said Matilda firmly.

Charles took her elbow. "Hush, Tilda. Pray give over a moment. There is some merit in Sir Frederick's argument." He ignored his spouse's idignant gasp and turned to their visitor. "We shall do as you ask, Sir Frederick. For the moment, we shall do better to remain here and let you young gentlemen hotfoot it after our dear Sophia and that blackguard the Comte de Chaleur."

Relieved, Sir Frederick quickly took his leave. Matilda fumed in silence until the door closed behind Sir Frederick. She rounded on her husband. "How could you, Charles? We cannot simply wait, safe in England!"

"Quite. We wait only for Prince Kirov's departure from London, Tilda. I'll wager that the Comte de Chaleur gives our spirited young gentlemen a fine chase. But the prince will lead us directly to Sophia. And when we find her, there shall be an account settled," said Charles, his eyes hard.

"Oh, my dear," said Matilda. Her hand briefly covered her mouth in surprise. She suddenly reached up to kiss him. "You are a fine man, Charles. I shall begin the packing at once."

"Very well, my dear. I believe I shall just stroll over to the club for a few moments, if you do not mind," said Charles calmly.

Matilda assured him that she did not yet require his assistance. She was totally unsuspecting of what he meant to do.

Charles directed his steps to a certain address. When he inquired after the master of the house, there was a brief delay before he was let in.

Prince Kirov awaited his visitor in the sitting room. He did not offer a seat to him. "You have once more wasted your time, Mr. Wyndham," he said coldly. "As I told you before, Sophia is not with me."

"I have not come to inquire Sophia's whereabouts, sir. I am well aware of your answer to that. On the contrary, I have come on your account, Prince Kirov," said Charles.

Prince Kirov was startled. "On my account? What do you mean?"

"I have come to give you fair warning, sir. If Sophia is harmed in any way and I discover that it is at your hand, I shall myself split your gizzard." Charles Wyndham smiled, and for that instant his warrior ancestors looked coldly through his eyes. "Good day to you, sir." He bowed, then thrust open the sitting-room door and left.

Prince Kirov listened to Charles Wyndham's swift footsteps cross the hall. The front door crashed as he departed. Prince Kirov had always had contempt for the English, learned from his mother. He was therefore amazed and awed by the loyalty of Sophia's English countrymen. He raised a heavy brow at the ever-present Fedor, who stood silently beside him. "I respect that one, Fedor. He speaks with a man's heart."

Fedor did not answer. He was unhappy with the turn of

events. He did not trust the count and he was anxious about Mistress Sophia being alone with him. That was the reason he had slipped her the little present before she was taken to the carriage. It was hardly enough but it was all he could do until the master decided to follow them.

21

THE COMTE de Chaleur and Sophia stopped at an inn in Dover for dinner before going on board the yacht.

The count made several attempts at conversation, but Sophia was in no mood for the polite amenities. She could only think of the Russian attendants guarding the doors. Hidden inside her cloak, she again touched the sheathed dagger that Fedor had given her. It was like a talisman. She was not completely helpless.

Finally the Comte de Chaleur leaned back in his chair. Slowly he swirled the red wine in his goblet. He said, "Miss Wyndham, this determined silence ill becomes you. I have long admired your vivacity and warmth of manner toward others. It was this that first drew me to you and brought me to an appreciation of your considerable beauty."

"Indeed. I suppose I must be complimented," said Sophia coldly. Except for the count, she would not now be a prisoner. Instead, she could have been at Lord John's bedside, tending his needs. Sophia's throat tightened. She still did not know for certain that Lord John had survived his wound. But she refused to think that he had not.

"I am a man capable of passionate emotion, mademoiselle. I feel deeply and I act instantly on my instincts. We go aboard soon. All the world shall recede in reality, leaving only we two. We shall have only these baboons to watch over us. I think then we shall come to know one another very well," said de Chaleur.

Sophia stared at him with startled suspicion. "I do not know what you mean, monsieur."

The count laughed softly. "You are coy. Come now, mademoiselle. The Englishman taught more than mere dalliance to you. *N'est-ce-pas*?"

Sophia flushed. She said angrily, "I find you offensive, Comte!"

"Ah, but I flatter myself that you shall feel quite differently before the coast of France appears," said the count. He smiled and there was a hot light in his eyes as he gazed on Sophia's lovely face, now flushed with rose. "I am a most desirable lover, as you shall find, mademoiselle."

Enraged, Sophia picked up her plate and threw it at him. The count tried to duck, too late. She had the satisfaction of hearing a cry of mingled surprise and pain as hot gravies splashed him. He batted the meat and vegetables from his coat while Sophia watched. She did not flinch when he leapt out of his chair to come around the table after her. Her voice stopped him. "Misha expects to find me whole and in good health, Comte. I do not think he would be pleased if I were harmed," she said in Russian for the servants' benefit.

The count stopped short, breathing heavily. His dark eyes went from her to the Russian servants posted in the room. They watched him with suspicion, hands near their belt knives. The count's sword hand clenched once, then relaxed. He bowed to Sophia. "I must honor Prince Kirov's wishes," he said in labored Russian. Then he switched to English. "But I promise to you that I shall not soon forget the insult you have done to me."

"I believe that you were the first to offer insult, monsieur," said Sophia coolly. Her heart thumped painfully in her breast, but she would rather die than allow her agitation to be apparent to de Chaleur.

The count returned to his chair and broodingly stared into his wine. But before long he smiled again. "Do you wonder how I shall get you aboard the ship without a scene, mademoiselle?"

Sophia was taken aback. She had that moment been planning to appeal to the crowd on the quay for help. The count brought a knife into sight and moved it so that the blade glittered. "Thus, mademoiselle. If you begin to make an outcry, I shall press this home. Then I shall say that you have fainted and carry you aboard.''

"How shall you explain my death to Prince Kirov, monsieur?'' Sophia challenged.

De Chaleur shrugged. "When we have sailed I shall throw your body into the sea. I shall say that you threw yourself overboard in irrational despair and drowned. The prince will believe me.''

Sophia went cold. She believed that he would do as he said and the sailors, if asked, would swear that he told the truth, for of course none would run the risk of being accused of participation in a murder. Sophia decided that she would put off her escape attempt awhile longer. Perhaps she would be luckier in France.

Within the hour the tide turned. The count and Sophia boarded the small ship. Sophia was unsurprised when she was escorted to a small cabin and locked in. She crossed to the narrow bunk and sat down with a sigh. She stared at the toes of her kid boots and watched the roll of the boat. She felt the beginnings of unease in her middle and quickly closed her eyes against the sight of movement. But within moments Sophia was definitely queasy. She lay back on the bunk and resigned herself. Bravely she told herself that crossing the English Channel would take only a few hours. On that worthwhile thought her stomach heaved and she reached frantically for the basin beside the bunk.

The small ship had slipped free of the English coast when the Comte de Chaleur finally made his way below to the cabin. He took the key from his pocket and fitted it into the lock. He smiled as he imagined how the metallic click must affect the young woman within. He opened the door and stepped inside. "It is I, mademoiselle,'' he said silkily, and stopped short.

In seconds he had retreated, cursing, back into the passageway companionway. He relocked the cabin door and then stared at it with a black scowl. Almost he could believe that the woman had become seasick just to thwart him. "We shall wait, then, mademoiselle,'' he muttered, and turned on his heels to return to the upper deck where he could breathe.

* * *

Sophia's first impression of the Château de Balon was one of quiet beauty. The carriage traveled the road between an avenue of stately trees that suddenly gave way to an open park. In the midst of the green expanse rose the château, gleaming white in the late-morning sun and encircled by a moat.

Sophia let down the window as the carriage passed through the park and clattered across a stone bridge set over the moat. She looked down at the still, dark water. A breeze ruffled the water's surface and sunlight sparked the waves.

The massive stone walls of the château, covered here and there with the green tracery of vines, rose to cut off the sky. The château's tall windows were divided into small squares framed in white. Slate-roofed rounded towers at either corner softened the three-story building's rectangular facade.

From the courtyard twin flights of graceful steps rose up and outward, then folded back like wings to meet to form a balcony at the main entrance on the second story. Sheltered in the balcony's deep shadow and flanked by the double flight of steps was a door fastened with a rust-crusted bolt.

The carriage stopped and the count opened the door. He stood aside to allow Sophia to descend. The gravel crunched briefly under her boots, then she and the count were walking up the rise of stone steps set out in a saw-tooth pattern that linked the courtyard to the carriageway.

"I doubt the countess is in residence at present. But no matter. I am known by her servants. We shall be well-cared-for," said the Comte de Chaleur.

"The countess?"

"The château belongs to the Comtesse de Tourne. *Naturallement*, milady is delighted when at any time Prince Kirov and his party avail themselves of her generous hospitality." De Chaleur paused, and his tone was insinuating. "Prince Kirov is a favored guest."

Sophia pretended not to understand the count's meaning

and did not speak to him again as they walked up one set of the graceful steps. They were let into the château's formal hall by a grave porter attired in red-and-white livery.

A stately butler appeared to inquire their business. The Comte de Chaleur held a short conversation with the butler while Sophia took in her surroundings. The hall was of grand proportions. At one end was a huge stone fireplace, and off to the side was a wide staircase that rose to an intermediate landing with a wide, inviting window before it continued upward to the third story. Heavy beams supported the ceiling, and frescoed murals of heroic knights covered the walls. Sophia wandered to an inlaid table and ran her fingers across the silken surface. She wondered what future this magnificent, proud place held for her.

The count dismissed the butler with a curt word. When he approached Sophia, she saw that a deep frown was etched between his dark brows. "I am informed that the countess is at home."

"This annoys you, Comte?" asked Sophia, quick to sense his irritation.

His eyes narrowed slightly. "You are surprisingly observant, Miss Wyndham. The footman will show us to our rooms so that we may refresh ourselves. Then we shall meet once more for luncheon."

Sophia inclined her head and followed a footman up the wide staircase. Her initial favorable impression of the château was shaken when she walked into the bedroom given to her. She stopped dead at the sight of the magnificently furnished chamber. Mantel and ceiling paintings of religious subjects were framed by gilded moldings and vied with similar paintings on the door and wainscoting. Every remaining inch of wall space was hidden behind tapestries. The heavily carved wardrobe and tapestry-covered chairs were almost swallowed by the opulence. But the crowning glory of the room was a vast canopied bed hung about with fine silver and gilt embroidery.

Sophia stared at the shimmering bed in disbelief. Finding her voice, she turned to the footman. "*Pardon*, but surely there has been a mistake in bringing me here. This is obviously a chamber for a royal guest."

The footman shrugged and a sly expression crossed his face. "The Comte de Chaleur requested this particular room for your ladyship. It adjoins his own." The man nodded significantly at a large painting on the wall opposite the bed. Sophia realized with shock that the painting actually camouflaged a door panel, cunningly set to blend with the wainscoting.

Sophia's blood suddenly coursed hot through her veins. So the count meant to entertain himself during this stay at the château, did he? Her eyes glittered when she looked at the footman. "The painting offends me. Cover it at once with that wardrobe." Sophia pointed at the heavy wardrobe beside the disguised door. The footman was startled. She held his glance with hers. He bowed, then put a shoulder to the wardrobe.

Sophia watched as the wardrobe was slowly pushed in front of the door, effectively blocking it. She thanked the winded footman and asked him for the key to the room's outer door. The footman located the key for her and was at last allowed to bow himself from the chamber.

Sophia tapped the large old-fashioned key across her palm as she thoughtfully studied the chamber's furnishings for a suitable hiding place. A decorative set on an occasional table caught her eye. But as she lifted the urn to slide the key underneath, it occurred to her that de Chaleur could easily request the chambermaid to find the key for him. Sophia abruptly changed her mind about the urn. She would carry the key with her at all times. She slid the key deep into the pocket of her dress, thinking that when a clean gown had no pocket she would carry a shawl and knot the key in a corner of the shawl.

Sophia poured water from a pitcher into the washbowl and splashed her hands and face to cool herself and wash off the travel dust. She was smoothing her hair when there was a soft knock on the bedroom door. At Sophia's call, a footman entered. "*Excusez-moi*, mademoiselle. Luncheon is served."

Sophia turned away from the washstand mirror and indicated her readiness. She followed the footman downstairs, reflecting that she was starved. She had not eaten since the ship had left England.

The footman led Sophia across the grand hall and opened a plank door. With a bow he stepped aside for Sophia. She stepped into the large dining room. On its wall hung turquoise and gold tapestries. A massive table dominated the center of the flagged stone floor and a sideboard stood to one side. Tall brass candlesticks and a centerpiece of freshly cut red and white roses graced the table. There was only one person in the room. Sophia's lips tightened.

The Comte de Chaleur stood with his back to a tall window. His figure was silhouetted in the bright sunlight and Sophia could not make out the expression on his face. She walked gracefully forward and acknowledged him with a mocking curtsy. "Monsieur le Comte, do we dine alone, then?" she asked, glancing toward the table. To her surprise and delight, she discovered three place settings. The footman and butler waited to serve them.

"Unfortunately not, Miss Wyndham," said the count in English. He moved away from the window to offer her a chair. Sophia saw then the naked fire in his dark eyes and was glad to be able to turn her face away.

When Sophia was seated, she thanked him coolly. The count's fingers brushed her slender neck as he straightened, and Sophia had difficulty suppressing a shudder.

The count seated himself opposite Sophia so that he could study her delicately boned face. "The countess is habitually tardy, so we shall begin without her," he said, and snapped his fingers for the servants to begin serving.

The dining-room door opened. A woman with striking features, black hair and eyes entered. She was gowned in a silver dress cut low to reveal a well-proportioned rounded bosom. Rubies accented her petit earlobes and a magnifi-

cent necklace of rubies and diamonds slipped out of sight
between her full breasts. Her attire made Sophia stare. The
woman's dark brows arched delicately as she looked at the
Comte de Chaleur, who rose hastily to his feet. He bowed
over her fingers. "You are *magnifique*, madame."

"*Bien sûr*," said the Comtesse de Tourne, satisfied. She
glanced swiftly about, utterly ignoring Sophia. "Misha is
not with you?"

"Prince Kirov follows, madame." The countess pouted
and practically flounced into the chair that de Chaleur held
for her. The count gestured toward Sophia. "Allow me to
make known Mademoiselle Sophia Wyndham, who is
Prince Kirov's cousin."

Interest at last lighted the countess's sloe eyes. She said
swiftly in Russian, "You are fortunate in your relations,
mademoiselle."

Sophia inclined her head noncommittally and replied in
Russian. "But how is it that you speak Russian and so
well, madame?"

"Ah, so you are indeed Russian! I thought for an instant
it was but a poor joke of the Comte de Chaleur's," exclaimed the countess, delighted. "He has a very bad sense
of humor, that one." She sent a sly glance toward the
count, whom she disliked. "I was exiled for years in Russia
until Napoleon Bonaparte was no more. Then I returned
home and all was restored to me, unlike the poor count.
His hopes were trodden to dust, you understand. Some
were more fortunate than others in Bonaparte's defeat."

The count, whose command of Russian was not great,
was nevertheless able to follow the countess's remarks and
his face darkened.

The countess turned her bare shoulder on him and
prepared to devote herself to Sophia. "But now tell me
about Misha. He is a great favorite of mine. You must
have many stories of him."

Sophia realized instantly that she had discovered a
means of establishing a friendly footing with the countess.
"Indeed I do, Madame la Comtesse. I lived with my aunt,
Misha's mother, for several years."

The countess nearly purred with satisfaction. "I am called Marie by my friends. And it is certain that we will be friends, dear Sophia, *n'est-ce-pas*?"

"I do hope so," said Sophia quietly. She could not help but hope that perhaps the countess could be persuaded to help her to return to England. Thereafter, through the truly delicious luncheon, Sophia exerted herself to at once satisfy and further pique the countess's curiosity about Prince Kirov, which proved insatiable.

The countess invited Sophia to walk with her in the gardens after luncheon. She confided that she loved flowers. "I adore roses, the deep blood-red ones, best of all. They have such beauty and grace. Yet they are imbued with mystery and will sharply prick if not handled with care," said the countess.

"That may be said as well of some women, Madame la Comtesse," said the count, breaking the silence that had fallen over him since the countess's snub.

The Comtesse de Tourne smiled sweetly but continued to only address Sophia. "We shall take our leave now, dear Sophia, so the count may enjoy his wine. It is a very fine vintage." Delicately she forbore to point out that the count had already drunk several goblets of her excellent wine.

As the ladies rose from the table, de Chaleur sardonically saluted them with his goblet. The countess deigned not to see him and swept from the dining room with Sophia in her wake.

22

THE LADIES left the shelter of the château and entered the formal gardens. The countess's light voice was a pleasant accompaniment to Sophia's thoughts. Sophia walked slowly, allowing her eyes to take in the beauty surrounding her. The trim beds dazzled the eye with color and were offset by deep-green hedges clipped to resemble elephants and lions and other animals. Cool white statuary was placed here and there, as were stone benches. The still moat bounded with gardens, its surface ruffled by the warm breeze that blew gently against Sophia's skirt. Beyond the girdle of dark water stretched a far expanse of smooth green lawn that ended abruptly against stands of tall silvery birches. Sophia stared at the trees, made small by the distance. She knew that the road lay hidden there beneath the birches. It was the road that led home to England. She sighed.

The Comtesse de Tourne was secure in her own importance, but gradually it had dawned on her that her guest was not quiet merely out of respect. "You are pensive, Sophia," she said. Her clever eyes were on Sophia's face as she graciously indicated a stone bench. "Sit with me, *ma petite*." When Sophia was seated, she said without preamble, "Now, you must tell me why you are unhappy."

Sophia stared at her in astonishment. She had not believed herself so transparent.

The countess smiled. "I have surprised you, Sophia. But I am one who senses what is not said. For this moment I am Marie, your friend. You must confide in me."

Sophia felt a rush of hope. "I shall, and with all my heart confide in you, madame." She plunged at once into

her tale and related why she had gone to England. She told
how her aunt and uncle had received her into their home as
their own daughter. Sophia spoke of all that she missed in
her new life, omitting only her feelings for Lord John.
Anger flashed in her eyes when she told how Prince Kirov
was forcing her to return to St. Petersburg. She drew a
breath, then placed a pleading hand on the countess's arm.
"Pray help me, madame. I am desperate."

The countess laughed. "My dear, I can think of nothing
finer than to be in Misha's power. He is so virile a man, so
incredibly beautiful. *Non*, Sophia. I shall not endanger my
friendship with Misha for you. You must do your duty and
marry this prince who was chosen for you."

"But I do not love him. Surely you of all people must
understand, madame, for you are a woman of passion who
commands the admiration of men," said Sophia, instinctively employing flattery.

"This is true," said the countess, nodding. She leaned
over to pat Sophia's tense fingers, and her smile was kinder
than before. "*Ma petite*, let me tell you something. I, too,
married at the wishes of my family. The count was a good
man, but very dull." She shrugged. "I had lovers, of
course, but I fulfilled my duty and I lived in comfort. Now
the count is dead and I am free to choose the course of my
life. And I still live in comfort. Do you understand me, *ma
petite*? Do your duty, child, for there is something to be
said for comfort."

Sophia lowered her eyes to her hands. "Perhaps we are
too different, madame. I do not wish a dull husband and
many lovers. I wish for only one man."

The Comtesse de Tourne raised her thin brows in
surprise, then she smiled. "Ah, I begin to understand. You
have already a lover, *n'est-ce-pas*?"

Sophia's color rose. "No, madame, I have no lover. But
it is true that I am in love."

"And he wishes to marry you, this man?" asked the
countess.

"I do not know," said Sophia unhappily. Then, as the
countess laughed, she said fiercely, "But how am I to ever
know if I am forced to marry another?"

"Who is this man?" asked the countess. "Is he an in-eligible *parti*, perhaps?"

"He is an English lord," said Sophia proudly. "You will forgive me when I do not confide his name, madame."

The countess sighed and smiled wearily. "Such youthful passion. I envy you. It has been a long time since I felt so strongly for any one man."

"Madame, can you help me? I would be forever in your debt," said Sophia.

"Of course, *ma petite*. Who am I to stand silent before true love?"

Sophia's eyes sparkled. "Thank you, madame."

"When Prince Kirov arrives, I shall speak to him at once. Perhaps I may persuade him to release you and perhaps not," said the countess.

Sophia's spirits plummeted. She knew the outcome of such a discussion. "Madame, I had hoped for a carriage or perhaps a horse."

The countess looked at her in surprise. "You wish me to betray Misha, in effect? I am affronted, Mademoiselle Sophia. Misha is a very close, valued friend. He would be oh-so-very-angry with me." She shivered, though not at all in apprehension. "Almost, it would be worth it. Misha is so very beautiful when he is angry. But *non*, I shall speak with him only. And with that, mademoiselle, you must be content."

Sophia rose and curtsied. "Then I shall say good day, madame."

The countess inclined her head, amused by Sophia's desperate dignity.

Sophia held high her head as she exited the garden. She would not allow herself to show the disheartenment she felt, and hoped that she could reach her room before she burst into a passion of tears.

After her stormy weeping Sophia fell into a deep sleep. The happenings of the past several days had taken their emotional and physical toll. She did not waken until a chambermaid knocked at the door some three hours later to rouse her and help her to dress for dinner.

When Sophia walked downstairs she felt much

refreshed. The countess had chosen not to aid her, but that was certainly no reason to give up all hope. Sophia had decided that she must familiarize herself with the household's schedule and the grounds of the château. There must be a stables, and even though Sophia was shy and a little fearful around horses, she thought she should be able to mount one of the great creatures and ride it to freedom. At least she hoped that she could. But she had to act quickly while there was only the Comte de Chaleur to stop her. Once Prince Kirov and his party arrived, Sophia knew that she would be too closely watched to make such a simple plan successful.

Sophia entered the drawing room to discover that the countess had not yet come down. De Chaleur was the only one in the drawing room. She had no wish to be alone with him and turned to go. The count was not a man to be put off so tamely. He stepped in front of her, barring her passage to the door. "Do not run away just yet, Miss Wyndham. We have much to discuss between us," he said.

"I can't think what it could be about," said Sophia with deliberate disdain.

He reached out and drew a finger down her jawline. Sophia drew back sharply. He laughed, low and confident. "I know you will recall a certain conversation in England, my lady. It is past time to—"

Suddenly there was a commotion in the main hall. A great voice was raised in command and Sophia recognized it with disbelief. "Misha!" She slipped past the count, who was left with a tight-pinched angry expression. His fingers clenched once, twice. Then his expression smoothed to blandness and he, too, went into the main hall to greet Prince Kirov and his entourage.

Sophia flew into the main hall. She stared at her cousin in consternation. "Misha!"

Prince Kirov caught up her hands and carried them to his heart. "You are no longer angry with me, little Sophia?" he asked hopefully.

Sophia freed her hands. Her cousin's early arrival dashed any hope that she had of escaping by using one of the countess's horses. Her frustration and anger were reflected in her voice. "On the contrary. I am furious with you, Misha."

Prince Kirov shook his head. He espied de Chaleur and strode over to clap the slighter man on the shoulder. The count winced under the friendly blow. "My good Comte de Chaleur! I must thank you for providing safe-conduct for my precious cousin."

"You arrive several days sooner than anticipated, your highness," said the count, disdaining to comment on Prince Kirov's approbation.

Prince Kirov waved his hand airily in dismissal. "I am a hearty fellow. A bite of meat and a sip of wine and I recovered quickly from the cupping."

"How felicitous," murmured the count blandly. The expression in his dark eyes was impenetrable, but Sophia was certain she detected a flicker of temper that was quickly hidden.

"Prince Mikhail Kirov."

Prince Kirov turned quickly, and met the countess's gaze. She came down the stairs and stopped when she was level with the tall Russian. The countess was arresting in a deep-blue gown of low décolletage. Pearls encircled her slender throat before falling between her full breasts. Her dark-brown amber eyes were luminous, her raven hair twined in a profusion of curls about her well-shaped head.

Admiration for her loveliness lit Prince Kirov's eyes. He went forward to take her slender hand and to sweep a deep bow to her. "Comtesse, it is a great pleasure to see you again," he said softly.

"I, too, am happy to renew our acquaintance, Prince Kirov," said the countess. She allowed him to draw her down the last few stairs until she stood beside him.

Prince Kirov raised her fingers to his lips for a lingering kiss. He said softly in his mother tongue. "In Russia it was Misha. Have you forgotten so soon, my dove?"

The Comtesse de Tourne smiled faintly. Lightly she squeezed his fingers before withdrawing her hand from his clasp. She gave a slight shake of her head. There was warmth in her eyes as her gaze fell on Sophia. "I and your cousin, Miss Wyndham, have become as sisters, Prince

Kirov. We have spent together many hours in talk.''

Prince Kirov glanced toward Sophia, his brows raised.
''I am delighed, of course. But what could you find so
stimulating to talk about?''

''We spoke of love, *naturallement*,'' said the countess,
slanting a look at the prince's face. A certain warmth was
kindled in his eyes and she was satisfied. ''But enough of
talk. Prince Kirov must surely be famished, and so we go
to the dining hall.''

The Comte de Chaleur had been listening with a faint
twist to his lips. Now he interceded. ''Forgive my dis-
inclination to join the happy party, madame. I supped
earlier and planned to ride afterward.'' He bowed to them
all and walked swiftly away.

''I do not miss de Chaleur's company,'' murmured the
countess.

Prince Kirov offered an arm to each lady. He ad-
monished the countess. ''That is uncharitable of you, my
lady. He is my friend.''

The countess shrugged her indifference as he seated
them in the dining hall.

After Prince Kirov had satisfied his most ravenous
feelings, he turned to Sophia. ''So, cousin, you have
enjoyed the countess's hospitality.''

''Madame la Comtesse is a gracious hostess,'' said
Sophia. Her cousin's eyes slid away to the countess.
Sophia was quick to sense the unmistakable warmth in the
meeting of their gazes. She paused, then said, ''I thought I
glimpsed the library earlier. If you should not mind it,
Misha, I should like to retire early to my room with a good
book. I know that you and the countess have much to talk
about as old friends.'' She was already rising from the
table as she spoke.

''Of course you may go, Sophia. I do not wish to intrude
on your pleasures,'' said Prince Kirov in an understanding
voice.

Sophia curtsied. As she left the dining hall she received a
dazzling smile from the countess, who promptly forgot
Sophia's existence the instant she stepped through the
door.

23

THE NEXT morning at the breakfast table Prince Kirov mentioned that the countess had pleaded Sophia's case with him. "You should not have brought the countess into our private family affairs, little Sophie," said Prince Kirov. "Though charming, she is not a discreet person." He glanced at Sophia and spoke in Russian rather than English. "She was very affected that you go to a loveless marriage. She says that you confided in her about your lover, an English lord. Do you deny that you told her this?"

Sophia colored, acutely aware of the Comte de Chaleur's presence. She did not know how well he understood Russian, but probably it was enough for him to follow Prince Kirov's words. She said proudly, "I admit that I am in love, Misha, and if I could claim him in truth my lover, I would do that too."

Prince Kirov nodded. Almost imperceptively tension relaxed in his shoulders. "Good, cousin. You have not been dishonored then. This English lord was perhaps more of a gentleman than I thought."

"He is alive, Misha," said Sophia fiercely. "Do not dare to speak of him as though he is dead."

Prince Kirov shrugged. "Perhaps you are right, little one. But it matters not. You are destined for another. Family honor must come before the whims of a young female. In time the Englishman's memory will dim."

"Never," exclaimed Sophia, her eyes flashing. She leaned toward Prince Kirov and said passionately, "My heart is in England, Misha. How can you be so cruel as to tear me apart this way? If you take me back to Russia, I shall die, Misha. I know that I shall."

Prince Kirov rose and came around the table to press her shoulder. "You are so young, Sophia. Naturally you are overwrought to realize the end of your first romance. Believe me, I remember well the misery. But once you are again with your Russian family and friends, you will come to feel differently."

Sophia caught his hand and looked up at him with tears in her blue-gray eyes. "Please, Misha, I beg you . . ."

Prince Kirov's expression did not change, but his eyes wavered. He would not admit even to himself how deeply her distress moved him. But he knew his duty and hers. "We leave after breakfast tomorrow for Poland," he said abruptly. Turning on his heel, he gestured to de Chaleur to accompany him and exited the breakfast room.

The count followed at a slower pace, his eyes thoughtful as Sophia bowed her head on her arms on the table. He had understood enough of the swift exchange in passionate Russian to know that the girl was desperate to escape the enforced journey to St. Petersburg. He decided quickly what needed to be done. It was fortunate that he had made the habit of riding alone. His ride that morning would be excuse enough for the errand he must run before he approached the girl later after dinner.

The Comtesse de Tourne preferred coffee to be served in the drawing room and each evening she and her guests repaired there after dinner was concluded. The drawing room was furnished in the grand manner. It was all rich wood paneling, gilt-framed portraits, and Oriental porcelain mounted in gilt bronze. The armchairs were covered in gold, red, and green petit point. A Persian rug covered the stone flags and brocade drapes accented the inset windows.

That evening in the drawing room, the count approached Sophia, who morosely stared out the window at the setting sun that glistened across the dark waters of the moat. "Mademoiselle, I could not but overhear much of your earlier conversation with Prince Kirov. I wish to convey to you my regrets that I was, in effect, an instrument of your undoing," he said in a low tone, keeping his eyes on Prince Kirov and the countess, who laughed together across the room.

Sophia presented to him a cold expression. "Truly you astound me, Comte de Chaleur. I had not thought you to be a gentleman of such fine feelings." She made to withdraw from him.

The count inclined his head, a faint smile on his lips. "I am sensible enough of your plight, mademoiselle, that I offer you my aid." Sophia checked at his words and looked back over her shoulder at him with suspicion. The count smiled more broadly. "I interest you, then, mademoiselle?"

"For the moment only, monsieur," said Sophia.

De Chaleur laughed outright. Prince Kirov curiously glanced their way. He had only rarely heard the count's laughter, but then Sophia could be an amusing little thing when she wished.

The count half-turned to the window and pointed out the sunset. "See, it will be a beautiful, clear night, mademoiselle. A traveler could move swiftly on the roads on such a night."

He was now in partial silhouette, a sinister figure that caused Sophia's heart to beat a little faster in apprehension. "What are you saying, Comte?" she asked quietly.

The count no longer smiled. His hard eyes were watchful. "Only that I will aid you to escape the château, mademoiselle. For a price, naturally."

Sophia stared at him. "What price, monsieur?"

His eyes suddenly flared with a glittering light visible even in the shadows. He allowed his gaze to drop to her bare shoulders and the deep décolletage of her gown. His slow, burning glance lingered on the pulse that beat at the base of her throat, and then rose to her soft lips.

Sophia's skin felt scorched by the intensity of his gaze and she shivered. She had no doubt at all what it was that he wanted of her. She hesitated, sensing the irrevocableness of her decision.

"My price is not of importance now, mademoiselle, for there is little time to speak. I have arranged for a carriage tonight, in only a few hours' time," said the count.

Sophia was startled and dismayed. "But it is too soon! No, I cannot. You must give me time to decide, monsieur," she said.

"Prince Kirov leaves for Poland tomorrow. It is tonight or not at all, mademoiselle," the count said dispassionately.

Sophia stared down at the moat, trying to think, to decide. The Comte de Chaleur frightened her in a way no one else had ever done. She knew without the shadow of a doubt that the price he would demand for his aid would be to become his mistress. The very thought frightened and repelled her. But to go with her cousin into Poland was equally unthinkable. Once across that border, her chances of returning to England would dim almost to nothing. Sophia looked up at the gentleman waiting for her answer. "Very well, monsieur. I accept your offer."

He nodded, satisfied and pleased. "I will come to your room after midnight. Bring only what you can comfortably carry in one hand, mademoiselle, for we must be swift. I will have a carriage awaiting us at the bottom of the front steps."

Sophia nodded her understanding and moved away from him without a word. He watched her go with a faint smile.

Sophia's thoughts were uneasy. She did not trust the count, but his offer was the only alternative that had presented itself. The countess had been of no use at all, for Prince Kirov had not been persuaded to change his mind. Sophia doubted that the countess had overly exerted herself on her behalf, besides.

Sophia had thought of one escape plan after another, only to discard each as improbable of success. The stables were too well guarded, the servants too well trained, she herself too well watched. No, the count's offer was her only chance now. But Sophia was determined that the price she paid would be far lower than that the count intended to receive. And somehow she would free herself of him, too, when his usefulness was at an end. Sophia firmly squelched the trembling doubts in her mind.

The evening seemed at once to crawl and to speed. Sophia watched the clock move with agonizing slowness, but at last Prince Kirov allowed that it was time to retire to their beds. The count had already excused himself some minutes earlier. Prince Kirov sent a meaningful glance toward the Countess. She inclined her head slightly, faintly smiling. Prince Kirov gallantly escorted both ladies upstairs. His good night to Sophia was hearty and he then continued down the hall with the countess to her room.

Sophia took to her room with mixed feelings. She was relieved to be away from the others, but anticipation of de Chaleur's appearance kept her tense. Quickly she locked the door. The chambermaid had left a burning candle for her on the night table and Sophia picked it up. Then she opened her wardrobe and by candlelight looked to see what she could possibly carry with her. Sophia decided quickly on two muslin frocks, a shawl, her nightclothes, a clean pair of stockings and underclothing, and her toothbrush and toothpowder and hairbrush. She would wear her woolen cloak over her gown. She changed from evening dress to a plain gown that was more serviceable for travel. Everything else she packed tightly in a bandeau box and knotted its strings. She sat down on her bed to wait, too tense to nap for the hour or so remaining before the count was supposed to come for her.

At last there was a scratching at her door. Sophia blew out the candle and went swiftly to the door. "Who is it?" she asked softly.

"It is I, mademoiselle."

Sophia turned the key in the lock and for a horrible instant she wondered if the count had set an elaborate ruse to gain access to her bedroom. That particular apprehension vanished at sight of de Chaleur, dark-cloaked and booted with a rapier at his side. He was staring down the hall. When the door creaked open he turned his head. His expression was grim, but there was a burning light in his

eyes. Sophia realized incredulously that the count was
reveling in this desperate venture. He held out an
imperious black-gloved hand to her.

Quickly Sophia slipped through the bedroom door. She
fumbled with her bandeau box deliberately to give her the
excuse not to accept his clasp. The count smiled thinly, but
did not make an issue of her ploy. He beckoned her to
follow him and together they went swiftly down the hall.
Most of the candles had been snuffed, but here and there a
solitary taper in an iron bracket offered pools of flickering
illumination so that they had no difficulty in making out
the way.

De Chaleur and Sophia passed the countess's rooms.
They had hardly gone five steps down when behind them
the countess's door opened. They spun about. Attired in a
dressing gown, his blond hair mussed, Prince Kirov stared
at them. The startled, bewildered expression in his eyes
suddenly sharpened as he took in their traveling cloaks.
His voice was still sleep-roughened. "Guards, to me!"

With a muttered oath de Chaleur freed his sword and
lunged. His swift attack was sudden and deadly. Sophia
screamed. Prince Kirov twisted to one side, but too late.
The gleaming silver blade slashed into his side like a
burning viper. He bit back a cry and fell heavily against the
stone wall. Prince Kirov struggled upright. Rage burned
pain-bright in his blue eyes. "Traitor!" he roared. He
threw himself at the count, his one object to get inside the
sword and place his powerful hands around the Frenchman's neck.

De Chaleur smiled and raised his blade. His cold intent
snapped Sophia from her horrified paralysis. "No!" She
threw herself at him, grabbing his arm. With all her weight
she dragged his aim off center. Cursing, the count threw
her off. He sidestepped Prince Kirov's rush and viciously
slapped the flat edge of the sword against the side of his
opponent's head. Fresh blood suddenly matted Prince
Kirov's golden hair. He hit the stone floor to lay still,
breathing hoarsely.

"Misha!" Sophie started to go to him, but she was flung

back by the count. He held her struggling in an inflexible grip while he slowly drew back the rapier to administer the death blow. "Barbarian," he breathed in contempt.

Alarmed shouts in Russian and French drawing nearer penetrated his concentration. The count's head snapped around, the sword still poised. He cursed softly as he heard the sound of many running boots coming from the main staircase. Swiftly he turned, his cloak swirling about his lean figure. He had kept his steely grip about Sophia, but she renewed her struggle. "No, I shall not go! Misha! I must see if you have killed Misha!"

De Chaleur whipped her against the stone wall, once. While she was still stunned, he forced her, stumbling and unresisting, quickly back the way they had come. He dragged Sophia into a little-used servants' passageway seconds before the guards burst onto the scene to discover Prince Kirov lying unconscious, crumpled in a pool of his own blood.

The count held her pressed against the rough stone wall and the point of his sword pricked her throat. Sophia gasped. "Unless you wish to die, mademoiselle, do not utter a sound," he breathed hoarsely.

Sophia was mute, her head pounding. She pressed as close to the cold stone wall as she could, away from the punishing sword point and the count's heavy presence.

They were each silent, listening to the harsh shouts of Russian guards and heavy thudding of running boots. The noise faded slightly and the count jerked Sophia away from the wall. "We go now, milady," he said softly. Sophia hung back and he recognized her hesitation with a laugh. "My sweet lady, you have little choice. What do you think the guards will suspect if you appear from this deserted quarter far from your rooms? I shall tell you. The barbarians will split you on their swords if they find you anywhere outside of your rooms."

Sophia had to admit there was truth in what he said. The Russian guards, naturally suspicious and made upset by the attack on their master, could well find in her a scapegoat. Not very happily she allowed the count to lead her

swiftly down the narrow irregular stone passageway.
Under the vaulted roof, small slits of windows let in arcs of
moonlight and clammy night air. Sculptured stone heads
clothed in wimples seemed to express pitying laughter at
her plight.

They ran swiftly down the spiral stairs, the count always
with his sword held before him, his free hand tight on
Sophia's wrist. Sophia could hardly keep up as she
stumbled along behind him, her skirts and cloak in the
way. Ahead of her the count looked like a dark bat, his
black cloak swirling out from his shoulders, his footfalls
soft and lithe.

At last they reached the bottom of the spiral chair. With
a sharp blow of his sword de Chaleur broke the rusted lock
on the heavy plank door. Sophia was astonished when the
door opened with the whisper of well-oiled springs.

Again he read her thoughts and his teeth flashed in a
grin. "I naturally plan ahead, milady. A little oil does
wonders, does it not?" he asked, and then urged her out.

The night breeze swept Sophia's cloak around her. She
was able to take a steadying breath as the count paused
briefly, his sword at the ready, his eyes glittering as he
swept a glance about them. The terrace was deserted. He
started swiftly across the flagstones, pulling Sophia with
him. She saw that a carriage waited for them in the deep
shadows cast by the château's height. As they reached the
terrace steps, a shout split the black night as a sentry
caught sight of their fleeing figures.

The count's fingers tighened like steel wires around
Sophia's wrist and he ruthlessly pulled her along at a faster
pace. They flew down the stone steps set out in a sawtooth
pattern.

Sophia stumbled on the last step. Crying out, she fell to
the graveled carriageway. Her wrist was jerked free of the
count's grip by the momentum of her fall, and she landed
on her palms and knees.

"*Mon Dieu!*" The count cast a quick look up at the
entrance doors where guards flowed out and thundered
down the twin stairs with the rococo arabesque iron hand-

rails. He stooped to catch Sophia around the waist, then
practically hauled her across the carriageway to the coach,
a string of curses breaking like a torrent from his lips. A
manservant had the door open. The count tossed Sophia
into the carriage and slammed the door. "Whip up the
horses, imbecile! Do you wish to die?" he shouted as he
sprang up onto the box beside his accomplice. The manservant did as he was bid, just as anxious to escape the
roaring Russians who were now but steps away from the
vehicle.

The count stood poised with his sword, balanced easily
despite the rocking of the carriage, but the Russian guardsmen were too late. One snatched at the unlit lantern on the
outside back of the coach, but his uncertain grip was
tossed off by the coach's gathering speed.

24

THE COACH clattered across the stone bridge over the still moat and the château was quickly left behind. The Comte de Chaleur settled down on the box and for the moment cradled his glittering blade across his knees. He threw back his head and laughed. The coachman glanced sideways at his master, at the unholy expression on his narrow face and the wicked blade, shimmering like a snake in the moonlight. He surreptitiously crossed himself.

Inside the coach Sophia caught the sound of the count's laughter. She shivered. The man was a veritable devil. She had never known a man so ruthless, so callous. She could still feel the point of his sword against her throat and the burning of the wound where it had drawn blood. Her palms stung where the gravel had scraped them raw in her fall, and her ribs felt bruised where he had clamped her to him as he lifted her from the ground. Even now she felt the same astonishment at his extraordinary strength. The count was a small man, barely topping her own short inches, and yet he had tossed her up into the carriage with as little effort as if she were a sack of meal. Sophia had heard that swordsmen were immensely strong and now she knew it to be true. She shuddered again. She knew now that she could not win a physical struggle against his steely strength. For her to escape the count would take cunning and fortitude. Her lively imagination conjured up horrific visions of the punishment she could expect from such a ruthless man if she failed in her attempt. She had no doubt that he would make certain that there would not be a second opportunity.

Sophia shook her head. "Stop it at once," she exclaimed aloud, aware that her fear was working against her and paralyzing her will. She must plan and weigh her possible opportunities. For instance, they could not keep up such breakneck speed for long before the horses gave out, which meant that they must stop soon at a posting house. There must be a moment then, while the horses were changed. Sophia thought also of simply jumping out of the flying coach. But she was desperate, not mad, and the probability of breaking a leg or even her neck in her leap for freedom was more of a risk than she admittedly wanted to accept. And she did not think the count, when he stopped to retrieve her, would be altogether sympathetic to any injuries she might sustain.

For courage she touched the small blade, given to her by Fedor, that was hidden inside her sleeve. De Chaleur knew nothing of it, of course. Sophia did not know if she could actually stab a man, but she was willing to let the count be the object of her first lesson. Her almond-shaped eyes narrowed, giving her a very un-English look. She had seen poor Misha fall to the count's sword, to lay motionless in a pool of his own blood. If it ever came down to a question of her honor or ending the count's life, Sophia believed that she would try to strike him down. The strength of her own determination somewhat cheered her. Sophia curled up on the coach seat and prepared to nap until it was time to decide the course of her future.

Back at the château, Fedor badgered and bullied the guardsmen into laying their master in bed. He himself made the master comfortable and treated the head and chest wounds. He was pleased with the clean edges of the chest wound. The count at least was not a butcher. His sword had entered with neat precision and had exited without unnecessary tearing of the flesh. There had been much blood, of course, but the master was a big man. He could afford to lose an amount that would of a certainty kill a lesser, smaller man.

Fedor on the whole was well-pleased. His master, though unnaturally pale and breathing with abnormal heaviness, would live. The dwarf had sent two of the

Cossacks to follow the trail of the coach to its destination, but to do only that. Fedor knew his master well. Prince Kirov would want to punish the traitorous Frenchman himself.

After attending to his master, the dwarf silently entered the countess's bedroom. As he had expected, she had earlier taken her usual dose of laudanum and so had not been roused by the commotion. With infinite care, the dwarf measured out an additional dose from the laudanum bottle on the bedside table and administered it gently to the countess, who instinctively swallowed when her nose was pinched.

Fedor did not know how high her tolerance for laudanum was, but he wanted to be certain that she would be asleep longer than was her custom. His master would need time and quiet to make his decisions, and Fedor knew well the countess's probable hysteria when she learned of the murderous attack that had taken place just a space of feet from her bedroom door. If she chanced not to waken from the extra laudanum . . . Fedor shrugged philosophically. None would question the good lady's demise and believe only that she had taken an accidental overdose. By then her Russian lover and his entourage would be well away.

When Prince Kirov awakened, his throat was parched and his lips cracked from thirst. He croaked for water. Immediately his head was raised and a cool draft entered his mouth, bringing life to his being as the liquid found its way down. He opened his eyes and saw the dwarf's wise face. "Faithful Fedor," he sighed.

"Yes, my prince," said Fedor soothingly.

Prince Kirov's ribs hurt abominably and he puzzled over it until he remembered the count's sword striking with the speed of a snake. "Traitor! Devil's spawn!" he shouted, attempting to sit up. He quickly decided that was not the most intelligent move and collapsed again on the pillows. He glanced at the dwarf, who was unperturbed by his master's apparent ravings. "Fedor, where is the Comte de Chaleur?" he asked with deceptive mildness. Only his eyes and his clenched fingers on the coverlet betrayed the rage that consumed him.

"He is gone, lord, and the Lady Sophia with him," said Fedor.

Prince Kirov ruminated over that information. "My cousin, Sophia, screamed when the count attacked me, Fedor," he said, throwing a grave glance at the dwarf.

Fedor bowed his head in acknowledgement. He decided quickly how to couch his information to best please his master and also because Sophia had always shown Fedor the respect due him. "The lady was not anxious to make the count's escape easier, lord. She was seen to fall to the ground and refuse to rise, and the count was forced to lay hands on her and throw her into the coach."

Prince Kirov slapped the blankets. "I knew that it must be so! My cousin has a loyal heart, Fedor. She would not willingly betray me to my enemy. We are of one blood, after all." He had forgotten that he had once considered Sophia's character weakened by her English heritage.

"Yes, lord," said Fedor, his expression noncommittal. His private opinion was that females were naught but trouble of one sort or another. The countess was one sort and Sophia was proving to be another.

"We must find little Sophia, Fedor. She will try to be brave, but she will tremble until she is safe again with me," said Prince Kirov. His features hardened and a hot light sprang into his eyes. "And we must certainly find the good count, Fedor. I want very much to kill him."

"Yes, lord," said Fedor calmly. "I have sent Cossacks after the count, but only to follow and see where he goes."

"Very good, Fedor." Prince Kirov grinned wolfishly at the dwarf. He knew well Fedor's desire for respect. "The count disdained to see you, my faithful one. Before I kill him I shall tell him that it was you who sniffed him out for me."

Fedor unconsciously caressed the hilt of his small dagger and his grave face creased into a surprisingly youthful smile. "I shall look forward to the day, lord."

Prince Kirov nodded, suddenly exhausted. He fingered

the bandage around his head. He had an excruciating headache that threatened to blind him. "I shall rest until the Cossacks return, Fedor. Bring them to me no matter what the hour." The dwarf bowed, backing to the door. Prince Kirov yawned and burrowed further under the blankets. He suddenly bolted up again and hissed with pain from his thoughtless move. He pressed a hand against his sore ribs. "Fedor, the countess—"

The dwarf surprised his master with a rumbling chuckle. "Madame la Comtesse did not stir during the attack, lord, and sleeps still."

Prince Kirov's expression registered astonishment. "I knew that she took a sleeping potion before I left her, but—" He stared at the dwarf's suddenly bland expression. He said slowly and with evident admiration, "My Fedor, how happy I am that you love me. You are an arch conspirator."

"Yes, lord." Fedor bowed once more and quietly left his master alone to rest.

Prince Kirov did not sleep at once, however. He stared broodingly at the velvet bed hangings, his expression introspective. A fleeting grin briefly lighted his face as he recalled the pleasant interlude with the so-fair countess from which he had been returning to his own bed when he surprised the Comte de Chaleur. In his mind he reviewed the count's treachery. The count had tried to kill him, an unarmed man. He had hardly been able to defend himself, being still half-asleep. He had been barely conscious after the attack, his vision wavering, darkening, but he had sensed that Sophia somehow deflected the de Chaleur's blade from entering him for a last lethal time. Her screams and pleas yet rang in his ears. Prince Kirov sighed. Sophia had proven herself brave and noble. She had defied the devil's spawn in an attempt to save him. He dismissed the fact of her travel dress. The count had momentarily seduced her with his viper's tongue. It only mattered that Sophia had answered the call of their shared blood when necessary. Prince Kirov's heart swelled and emotion threatened to overwhelm him.

"I shall make everything up to you, little Sophia. I swear

it," he vowed passionately. He thought a moment and shrugged. Perhaps he would even intervene on Sophia's behalf with his mother. It would be interesting to assert himself as head of the Kirov family. When his father had died, he had been content to allow his mother free reign in her ambitions. Perhaps his indulgence of her wishes had been a mistake.

A white-hot light flared in Prince Kirov's eyes. As for the Comte de Chaleur . . . One fist clenched slowly on the coverlet. De Chaleur was a traitorous dog and so must die. The Cossacks would soon run the count to the ground, and then he, Mikhail Kirov, would personally deal with him. Prince Kirov reflected on that future meeting with great satisfaction.

His brows suddenly gathered in a frown. He had forgotten Sophia. The Comte de Chaleur would almost certainly make her his mistress. It distressed Prince Kirov that he could not rush immediately to her aid, but he was in no condition to deal with de Chaleur as honor demanded. Yet, if he did not go, Sophia would be at the devilish Frenchman's mercy for days. Prince Kirov brooded blackly over his dilemma.

Suddenly the bedroom door crashed open. Startled, Prince Kirov looked up. He recognized the two Englishmen who stood in the doorway. Lord John held Fedor in a painful wrestler's hold, his arms twisted behind his back. The dwarf's eyes were black with helpless rage. The other Englishman shoved a frightened footman into the room. The servant stumbled, then regained his balance and scurried to the far reaches of the bedroom.

Sir Frederick dusted his hands together. "Awfully sorry to arrive without notice, Prince Kirov. The man there opened the door and he was persuaded to guide us," he said calmly.

"Of course." Prince Kirov studied them narrowly and read easily the wary set of their stance. "May I ask how you found me?"

"Your style of travel is somewhat flamboyant, Prince Kirov. You were remembered," said Sir Frederick blandly.

Prince Kirov nodded, rather pleased that he had made

such an impression on the French peasants. But it was also
something to keep in mind if he ever wished to go unnoticed.

"You do not appear particularly startled to see us, my
lord." Lord John's tone was challenging, his eyes hard.

"Why should I? I would do the same. I salute you. We
are more alike than I thought," said Prince Kirov calmly.

"The devil," Sir Frederick said, shaking his head with
disgust.

"We have come for Miss Wyndham," said Lord John
curtly.

Prince Kirov nodded affably. "Naturally. But first will
you not let go my poor Fedor? It pains me to see him
treated thus."

Lord John did not shift his grip. "Not before we have
his word that he will keep that damnable dagger sheathed.
He is a little too quick with it for my comfort."

Prince Kirov threw back his head and laughed. He
waved at the dwarf, saying in Russian, "Fedor, the English
lord respects your prowess too much to free you. Shall I
give my word of honor that he has nothing to fear from
you?"

The dwarf's expression relaxed and a reluctant smile
tugged at his lips. "Yes, my lord. I shall not harm
them . . . unless they attack your person."

Prince Kirov glanced at Lord John. He held out his
hands, palms up. "You have heard. I give you my word of
honor that Fedor will be at peace."

Lord John released the dwarf, who immediately took up
his place at his master's bedside. "And now for business,
Prince Kirov. I want Miss Sophia Wyndham."

"She is not here," said Prince Kirov, who had been
thinking furiously and now came to a quick decision.

"Damn your eyes!" Lord John took a furious step
toward him.

The dwarf's dagger appeared from nowhere. Prince
Kirov gently lowered the dwarf's taut arm. "No, Fedor.
Understandably Lord John is upset. I would be also in his
shoes." He looked up at Lord John and said flatly, "The

Comte de Chaleur kidnapped my cousin only a few hours ago."

The Englishmen stared at him, appalled and only half-believing. "And you stood by while he waltzed out with her," Sir Frederick said derisively.

Prince Kirov's eyes flared with anger. With one large hand he dramatically threw back the coverlet. The thick bandaging that covered his ribs was bloodstained. "This is how easily I allowed that viper's son to go, my lord. Unarmed, I stopped his saber with my body and my head. And while I bled my life's blood on the stones, I heard my cousin's screams and pleas for mercy. Yes, my lord, to my shame I allowed the count to take her!" Prince Kirov's voice suddenly broke. With the back of one hand he dashed tears from his eyes.

Sir Frederick was embarrassed by his blunder. "I do apologize, my lord. I had no idea—"

Lord John interrupted him. He was white-faced. Prince Kirov was struck by the haunted look that had entered the man's eyes. He realized that the Englishman had a proper respect for Sophia's perilous position. "We must go after them, Freddy. There is no time to be lost." Sir Frederick nodded, his face settling into an expression of determination.

Prince Kirov stopped them with a pleased chuckle. They glanced back at him, startled. "Fedor sent my Cossacks after them some time ago, gentlemen. They have orders to follow only until the count reaches his destination before sending a report back to me." He narrowed his eyes, which suddenly glittered. "I wished to deal with de Chaleur personally. I am certain you understand."

"But you are in no condition for a fight, man," exclaimed Sir Frederick. "He will have the advantage over you for weeks yet."

"And by then it will be too late for Sophia," said Lord John quietly, his watchful eyes on the giant lying in bed.

"Yes." Prince Kirov met his gaze squarely. He spoke slowly, deliberately in Russian. "You are the lesser of two evils, my lord. At least I know you for an honorable man

who will not harm Sophia. And so I make you the proxy of
my own honor, Lord John. When the report comes on the
count, Fedor shall go with you to see that justice is done.''
The dwarf drew in his breath in sharp surprise and stared
at his master. Prince Kirov raised his brows and waited.
Finally the dwarf gave a slow nod as he accepted the
necessity for leaving his master's side.

"I shall find him," said Lord John. His expression was
grim. Abruptly it struck Sir Frederick that his friend
appeared uncommonly dangerous these days.

"Good. Then, while we await word, you and Sir
Frederick must be made comfortable. Perhaps wine and a
meal?'' Prince Kirov spoke in French and now glanced at
the footman still crouched on the far side of the room. Interpreting correctly his duty, the footman edged past the
mad, crazy English and hurried out of the room. "Fedor,
pray show our friends to the dining hall. And then perhaps
you should inquire after the countess's health." He looked
meaningfully at the dwarf, who bowed his understanding.

"The countess?" asked Sir Frederick alertly. "One
supposes that she is exceedingly beautiful?"

"The Comtesse de Tourne is exceedingly beautiful, yes.
And she is also a most warm and hospitable lady," said
Prince Kirov blandly.

"There, John! We've another beautiful damsel to
introduce into our tale. And I suppose the Comte de
Chaleur must assume the role of dragon now that Prince
Kirov is laid up," said Sir Frederick cheerfully.

"Quite so, Freddy," Lord John said. He grinned as
Prince Kirov's brows rose in astonishment. "His lordship
speaks fancifully but correctly, Prince Kirov. If necessary,
I meant to kill you to free Miss Wyndham."

Prince Kirov contemplated him for a moment. "It is
strange how fate twists. I believed that I had slain you in
England. Now you will avenge my honor."

"Not yours, Prince Kirov. But possibly Miss
Wyndham's. You and I have yet a score to settle," said
Lord John pointedly.

Prince Kirov nodded. "You are right. We may yet meet
again as enemies. I regret only that I shall not see the count

die. Good health and good hunting to you, my lord.'' He settled himself among his pillows, preparing to sleep.

Lord John nodded. He turned to follow the dwarf from the room. Sir Frederick was at his side and said in a furious whisper, " 'Pon my word, John. You've as much tendency to bloodlust as does that Russian fool. What possessed you to throw down the gauntlet like that?''

"The devil,'' said Lord John with grim humor. He nodded at Will, who stood waiting for them in the hall.

Lord John and Sir Frederick had time for a satisfying meal and a short rest before the fire. They held wineglasses as they spoke together softly. Will was content to sit away from the fire, his back to the wall where he could watch the door. He did not altogether trust the foreign-speaking company that they found themselves with. The report came soon, brought by a Cossack of few words. Upon the Cossack's arrival the Englishmen adjourned to Prince Kirov's room to hear things for themselves. The Comte de Chaleur and Sophia had been followed to an inn where they stopped apparently for the night. The Cossack horseman was waiting for further instructions.

Prince Kirov made plain his wishes. Fedor fingered the hilt of his dagger. The Cossack glanced expressionlessly at the three Englishmen and said gutturally, "Come, we shall get you horses.''

Within minutes the small party of five was mounted and departed, to Sir Frederick's infinite regret, before the Comtesse de Tourne awakened to discover her newest guests.

Behind at the château, Prince Kirov contemplated his bed hangings. He was unable to return to sleep, having too much to think on. A few hours later he had even more to think about. A missive sealed with wax that bore the imprint of his family crest was brought to him with his breakfast tray. Prince Kirov seized it and impatiently waved away the footman. From the day that he had left Russia he had naturally kept a continuous messenger line open to St. Petersburg so that his whereabouts were always known. Apparently now there was news that had to be sent to him.

He broke the seal of the envelope and spread open the single sheet that was inside, wondering what his mother now had on her devious mind. Prince Kirov read with gathering irritation that a diplomatic protest had been conveyed by the British ambassador to the czar regarding Sophia's abduction. Princess Elizaveta suggested that he delay his return to Russia for the moment, as the czar was not pleased. He was in the midst of negotiating a far-reaching alliance that required England's cooperation and he did not desire a political scandal. In short, the Kirov family's standing with the czar was jeopardized. Sophia Wyndham had become a liability. Princess Elizaveta wrote bluntly that Sophia must be gotten off the family's hands as quickly as possible.

Prince Kirov muttered darkly to himself. His eye was caught by a postscript and he read that Sophia's intended husband, Prince Tarkovich, had died choking on a bon-bon. Prince Kirov grimaced in disgust. "I can well believe it. Tarkovich deserved to die. He was a glutton," said Prince Kirov aloud.

He lowered the missive and stared unblinkingly into space, turning events over in his mind. Sophia must be gotten rid of in order to salvage the family's honor in the czar's eyes. She had accomplished that already by going off with the Comte de Chaleur. Prince Kirov thought that if he were a heartless man, he would now leave Sophia to her fate. But he had made a vow and even sent the English-men after her.

Prince Kirov bolted upright in his bed, hardly noticing the flashes of pain from his wounds. Of course, the Englishman was the answer. Lord John Stokes must marry Sophia to save her from ruin and incidentally erase the Kirov's family responsibility toward her. If Lord John refused, then Misha felt it would be his duty to kill him for the insult to Sophia. But he could not ensure the success of his brainstorm by lying abed at the château. He must follow the Englishmen and see with his own eyes that Sophia was properly provided for.

With a fleeting regret, Prince Kirov thought of the

beautiful countess and shrugged. A man's honor was a harsh taskmaster. He shouted for his servants and gave orders to prepare for travel. Prince Kirov got out of bed and stood up, swaying. He decided that without doubt Sophia had become more trouble than she was worth. He shook himself and resolutely ignored his injuries. He went downstairs to get into his waiting carriage.

25

WITH A START Sophia awakened to the sound of voices. Instantly alert, she realized that the carriage was no longer moving and the voices came from just outside the window. Cautiously she peered out.

Sophia saw that the count was addressing a short round man dressed in the garb of an innkeeper. Overshadowing them was the dark outline of the inn silhouetted by the first faint signs of dawn. The innkeeper was nodding in reply to the count's question. "*Oui*, monsieur. We are but a small village. Mine is the only inn, as you can see."

"Do you have much traffic in this place? Are there points of interest for the traveler?" asked the count.

The innkeeper sighed. "Alas, no, monsieur. There is only this one highway. Very few travelers stop in our poor village. Why should they? We have only the convent, two miles farther on, and who wishes to stop to stare at high walls of stone, eh? No, we are a poor, forgotten village." The innkeeper's voice was forlorn, resigned.

The count did not sound at all disappointed by the innkeeper's gloomy description. "Nevertheless, my friend, your village is of interest. My cousin and I shall wish to stay at your establishment for several days. We desire quiet, you understand. My cousin is of a nervous disposition and begged me to bring her into the country for her health."

"So! Then we have much to offer you, monsieur." There was now excitement in the innkeeper's voice and Sophia nearly laughed at the obvious upturn in his disposition.

Soon the count and Sophia were established in a parlor that connected separate bedrooms. The innkeeper's wife was a voluble woman who kept up a constant stream of chatter as she went about making up a fire and directing a sleepy chambermaid to lay out fresh linens for the guests. "It is chill in these early-morning hours, *n'est-ce-pas*? You'll want a bit of fire in your rooms as well and when you rise, the sitting room will already be as cozy as you please. Shout for breakfast when you are ready and I shall see to it that you have it still hot from the kitchen. Will you be wanting a cup of chocolate in your bed, mademoiselle? I can send the girl up to you immediately you waken."

Sophia smiled and was about to reply when the count interposed, saying smoothly, "My cousin dislikes strangers about her and particularly in the morning, madame. I will call you when she wishes for a chambermaid to attend her toilet. She will prefer to have her chocolate here in the sitting room with myself."

The innkeeper's wife regarded him with visible astonishment and then eyed Sophia somewhat askance. "I understand, monsieur. It shall be as you wish, monsieur."

The innkeeper's wife was not a stupid woman and recognized her dismissal. She bowed and left the room, closing the sitting room firmly behind her. And as she told her husband, "They are a strange couple, Henri. The gentleman speaks for her and yet she does not care for it. I saw it in her eyes. She does not like this cousin of hers."

"You see too much that is not there, Yvette. The mademoiselle is but high-strung. I told you what the monsieur said," said Henri placidly as he figured up what profit his guests' stay could mean.

His wife stubbornly shook her head. "They are not as they should be. There will be trouble for us."

"Enough of your shadows, woman," said Henri with unusual force.

His wife subsided, shrugging.

Upstairs the strange couple faced each other with the length of the room between them. Inside her cloak Sophia fingered the hilt of the small dagger that Fedor had given her and that she had kept, as she thought, for this moment. "And what now, monsieur?" she asked quietly even though her heart pounded.

"We now retire, mademoiselle," said de Chaleur. He saw her eyes narrow and waved a negligent hand. "Do not misunderstand me, mademoiselle. I am a nobleman. The payment of your debt will not be as ignoble as you suspect. We shall be several days in this spot. Even though Prince Kirov is a stubborn, persistent man, he will not quickly find us here in this secluded village."

"Then you do not believe he is dead?" asked Sophia quickly.

The count laughed softly. "*Non*, mademoiselle. I did not have the time to make certain of him. The prince will undoubtedly come to us eventually."

Sophia hid the coldness that stole over her at his casual statement of murderous intent. "Then you must see immediately to further travel arrangements, for I do not wish to remain within my cousin's reach," she said.

"You are impatient, Miss Wyndham, and so you cannot see the realities. Prince Kirov will pursue us even to England's shores. I do not care to be hunted like a craven animal. *Non*, I prefer to stand my ground, here in this place, and negotiate with him," said the count.

"Misha will never compromise," said Sophia, her eyes half-alight with something akin to pride in her cousin.

"So I think also. Before his arrival, therefore, we will come to a mutual understanding."

"What shape do you anticipate this understanding to take, monsieur?"

The count smiled. His eyes glittered with a hot light. "This village has its priest like any other. I will request him to attend us here at the inn. When Prince Kirov discovers us at last, we shall be husband and wife, mademoiselle."

Sophia stared at him. "And if I refuse?"

The count's eyes grew cold even though he still smiled. "Then you will have become my mistress, Miss Wyndham."

There was a short silence as Sophia digested the enormity of her situation. She did not believe for a moment that the count offered her a true marriage. He was too mercenary to tie himself legally to a penniless woman.

However, if she were to believe that the count had married her, she would naturally be much less inclined to protest whatever monetary arrangements he was able to make with her cousin. And Sophia had no doubts that the count meant to have out of Prince Kirov a substantial dowry. Later, when it was much too late, she would discover that the banns were false or the priest a charlatan. Sophia was almost relieved by the thought. She could not imagine a worse fate than to be forever legally bound to the murderous monster who watched her so calmly. But it was equally unthinkable to be forced to become his mistress. "You have given the matter much thought, monsieur. I must beg your indulgence for time to order my own thoughts. But now, I find that I am extremely fatigued, monsieur," she said.

The Comte bowed. "I wish you good night then, mademoiselle. I trust a few hours' reflection will bring you to see the wisdom of my proposal."

Sophia curtsied. "You will forgive me if I do not give you my hand, monsieur," she said woodenly.

"We have several days in which to become better acquainted," agreed the count. He did not miss the flash of anger in her eyes and he enjoyed the evidence of her high spirit. It suited him to grant her a few hours, for she would in the end come to him. And her humiliation would make his victory all the sweeter.

Without another word Sophia turned and entered the bedroom allotted to her by the innkeeper's wife. She closed the door and deliberately shot the bolt home. She knew that the count would be waiting for the grating sound, but when she heard his soft laugh, she was unprepared for her own reaction. A moment later she heard his door close.

Sophia raised her hands up to her face. She was shaking with rage. She swung around to glance about the small room by the light of the fire, and her eyes were drawn to the shuttered window. The Comte de Chaleur thought that he had her neatly trapped, but he would learn differently, she thought.

Sophia went to the small window and unlatched the

shutter. She tried to push it open, but the wooden frame was swollen tight and gave only an inch or two. Sophia looked around for something to use as a wedge. She espied the heavy iron poker next to the fireplace and snatched it up. Quickly she put the poker through the small opening and threw her weight against the lever. Sophia staggered as the shutter gave way with a sudden squeal of wood. Catching herself against the wall, she stood tensely for a moment, her heart pounding while she waited to learn if the count had heard. But she did not hear his door open.

Sophia turned again to the window, now anxious to be gone before an early riser outside saw the open shutter. She belted up her skirts to free her legs before she dragged a chair up under the window and climbed onto the sill. From her vantage point she looked around. She was on the second story and overlooked the far side of the inn yard through the branches of a massive gnarled oak tree. Across the yard was the deserted road and beyond that a copse of trees. If she could gain the trees, Sophia thought she could escape the notice of anyone who might be stirring in the inn. But time was shortening quickly, Sophia thought as she cast a glance at the lightening sky. Dawn was almost on her and the village would soon waken.

Sophia took a deep breath and reached out to grasp the branch nearest her. With her heart in her mouth she placed her foot on another branch lower down and transferred her weight to it, simultaneously letting go of the window-sill. The branches dipped wildly. For a nightmarish moment she felt again the sensation of falling from the rope outside Prince Kirov's town house. But this time she did not fall. The branches stopped swaying and Sophia loosened her death grip. Carefully, slowly, she began to work her way toward the inside of the old tree. When she reached the trunk, she sobbed in relief and leaned against it to feel its rough support. But when she heard a cock crow in the distance, she roused herself. Time was swiftly running out.

Sophia began the climb down.

Several minutes later she stood on the ground beneath

the old tree. She was scratched and bruised, her dress and cloak were ripped in several places, and she was dripping with perspiration. But she was very proud of herself. She glanced quickly around and then sped across the road to the copse of trees, just as the sun sent its first rays across the village.

Half an hour later a strange figure emerged from the protective cover of the trees that lined one side of the road, while on the other lay green fields. The disheveled woman trudged to the bell hanging beside the gate set in the white-washed walls of the convent. She pulled on the bell with urgency.

When the gate's shutter was opened, the young woman said, "I desire sanctuary, Sister. Pray allow me to enter."

Surprise crossed the nun's face. The shutter closed and the gate opened. Sophia cast a last glance down the road. A farmhand on a horsecart of hay was passing by the convent and peered at her. Without hesitation Sophia entered the convent. The gate closed behind her, shutting out the farmhand's curiosity.

Sophia was shown immediately to the abbess, an older woman whose gray eyes were serene and wise with her years.

"Well, child? I am told that you have requested sanctuary of us. Can you tell me why?"

The abbess's voice was kind, and struck a chord deep within Sophia's bruised spirit. She burst into passionate tears and flung herself at the abbess's knees. The nun gently stroked her hair, understanding that the tears were a long-overdue release.

When at last the storm was past, Sophia hiccupped a few times and tried to make light of it. "Forgive me, ma'am. I do not normally cry upon first acquaintance."

"There is nothing to forgive, child. Clearly you are sorely grieved in spirit. It is natural that your unhappiness find open expression," said the abbess. She drew Sophia to a chair beside her own. "Now, child, it is time that I hear your story."

Sophia nodded. She recounted all that had taken place

from the moment she had met Lord John to her escape from the Comte de Chaleur. During the recital the abbess did not comment but her eyes widened more than once at the extraordinary tale that her guest unfolded. "Surely you must understand why I desire sanctuary, ma'am. The count is a frightening man and determined in his actions. I do not know where else to turn," said Sophia. She looked anxiously at the abbess.

The abbess nodded. "I grant you sanctuary, child. This evil man shall not harm you while you are within our walls. As for your future, we must send to your aunt and uncle. Two of our sisters travel often to the market in the next village. There is also a mail coach that makes a regular stop there. You shall write letters to the British embassy in Paris to be forwarded to your family. The sisters will be certain that they go on the mail coach."

Sophia felt a tremendous relief. Her eyes misted. "I thank you with all my heart, ma'am."

The abbess rang a tiny silver bell and a nun appeared at the study door. "You will go with Sister Maria now, child. She will show you where you might rest and bring breakfast to you. We will talk again later."

Sophia rose and curtsied. She started to follow the smiling nun who waited for her when the abbess's voice stopped her.

"Sophia, do not concern yourself over that man, the count. It will not occur to him for some time that you are with us. And when he does come, I shall meet with him," said the abbess.

Sophia curtsied once more, her smile a mute thank-you, and followed the nun from the room.

But the abbess was wrong. De Chaleur knew before noon that Sophia had taken refuge at the convent. When Sophia did not come out of her room for breakfast when it was announced, he assumed at first that she was pouting. But after two hours there was still no sound from her room and he became suspicious. He forced the protesting land-lord and a waiter to break down Sophia's stout door, only to discover that she was gone. The count flew into a violent

rage, vowing to slice her into small pieces for her imperti-
nence. The innkeeper remembered his wife's words and
crossed himself at the wild look in the monsieur's black
eyes.

The count roused the village, and both it and the
immediate environs were searched without success. But a
certain farmhand, who had been on the road outside the
convent just after dawn, recalled the strange woman who
had rung the bell at the convent's outer gate. The count
was duly informed. He smiled coldly, called for his horse,
and within seconds had galloped down the road toward the
convent.

De Chaleur furiously rang the bell and was granted
admittance to the abbess. He arrogantly demanded that
Sophia be brought to him on the instant. The abbess
declined, saying that Sophia had the right to choose
sanctuary. He realized that he had set her back up with his
arrogance, so he set his teeth in the face of her calm and set
about ingratiating himself with her. "Mademoiselle is not
well, *ma mère*. She is incapable of choosing what is in her
best interests."

"Then it all the better that mademoiselle should remain
for a time with us, Monsieur le Comte. The peace of our
lives is in itself healing," said the abbess.

The Comte de Chaleur sat back seemingly at his ease.
But the abbess noted the tense air about his person. He
appeared to her like a steel coil set to spring. "Abbess,
your charity is gracious. But I must make you aware that
mademosielle's affliction is unfortunately of a somewhat
violent nature. For your own safety and that of the good
sisters I must insist that she be restored to my protection."

"You are saying that mademoiselle is stricken with a
sickness of mind and heart?" asked the abbess.

The count inclined his head, certain that he had swayed
her at last.

"It is truly noble of you to wish to shoulder such a
responsibility, monsieur," said the abbess. "However, as a
gentleman of the world you are less equipped to handle
spiritual disease, whereas we have much experience. *Non*,

more than ever I believe mademoiselle needs what only we may offer.'' She rang her bell and a nun appeared as the abbess stood up. ''Good day to you, monsieur.''

The count stared at her. His first impulse was to throttle Sophia's whereabouts out of the old woman, but he hesitated before the strength in her clear eyes. His religious upbringing had been a strict one and he was discovering to his fury that it inhibited him. At last he said softly, ''You have not seen the last of me, Abbess.''

''As you wish, monsieur,'' said the abbess calmly. The waiting nun gently called the count and he turned on his heel to follow her out.

The abbess stared at the closed door as she laid a light finger on the crucifix about her neck. She shook her head with regret over what she had seen in the Comte de Chaleur's eyes.

26

THE COMTE de Chaleur returned to the inn in a black temper. With an abrupt order for wine he retired to his suite of rooms. For an entire day he remained brooding within his rooms, leaving the inn only once to ride around the area encompassing the convent as he searched for a way to gain secret entrance. The innkeeper and those in the village who chanced to encounter him that afternoon gave him a wide berth, for there was a murderous look in his eyes. The innkeeper, though not an overly brave man, was yet a compassionate one and took it upon himself to serve the count rather than subject his waiters to the gentleman's uncertain temper. It was his private penance for brushing aside his good wife's intuition.

The innkeeper despaired of ever being rid of the count when two travel-stained gentlemen and a band of foreign-looking horsemen arrived at the inn to inquire of a certain couple who might have passed that way.

Upon the innkeeper's voluble assurance that they had indeed, and his listing of his grievances, the gentlemen and a rough-looking individual dismounted. They strode into the inn to disappear upstairs in the direction of the Comte de Chaleur's rooms. The other horsemen remained in their saddles. Their expressionless faces and their fierce attire hinted to the innkeeper that his troubles were not yet over. He retreated to the kitchens and lamented to his wife, "Surely God is punishing me for desiring more than I had, Yvette!"

The count was brooding before the fire, wine bottle near to hand, when his door crashed open against the wall. He leapt up, his hand going instinctively to the rapier at his side. His eyes narrowed in startled recognition as Lord John and Sir Frederick entered the room. He did not know the big man who followed them, nor was he particularly curious about him.

Sir Frederick kicked shut the door but the count ignored his action. Instead he fixed his eyes on Lord John. "So. I had thought I had seen your death, monsieur."

"As you see, I am not so easily done in," said Lord John in a hard voice.

De Chaleur's black eyes glittered with a strange light. "So much the better, milord. I have wanted to kill you for a long, long time for your impertinent interference between myself and Mademoiselle Wyndham."

"The abduction of unwilling ladies is a cad's game, Comte, and one that you seem particularly fond of," said Lord John grimly. "Where is Miss Wyndham?"

The Comte de Chaleur shrugged. He nodded toward the closed bedroom door. His smile was malicious. "Not every lady is unwilling, nor as virtuous as you seem to suppose. Indeed, our dear Mademoiselle Wyndham has developed a certain taste for . . . games."

With a smothered oath, Lord John started forward but found himself caught back by a viselike grip on his shoulder. He said angrily, "Let be, Freddy. I'll not stand by for more of his insinuations."

Sir Frederick spoke urgently. "John, listen to me. Look at his eyes. He's mad. He is panting for the chance to spit you on that sword of his, whether or not you are armed."

Lord John did not take his eyes off the Comte de Chaleur, who smiled ever so gently at him. "Then give me your sword, Freddy. I'll meet him, now." Without looking, he handed his walking stick to Will, who accepted it awkwardly.

"John, you are not yet up to snuff," began Sir Frederick.

"Damn your eyes, Freddy! Give me that sword," grated Lord John.

Reluctantly Sir Frederick loosed his sword, which was heavier and longer than the blade hidden in Lord John's walking stick, and handed it over.

"You are so eager to die, then, milord?" asked de Chaleur. He slid his own blade from its scabbard and arced

the thin flexible steel with his hand. The rapier flashed
silver in the afternoon light as he suddenly slashed it
toward the carpet. "Mademoiselle shall be disturbed to
discover blood staining the carpet."

Lord John involuntarily glanced toward the closed bedroom door. It struck him odd that there had been no sound
from behind the door since his and Sir Frederick's
entrance. In that instant the Comte de Chaleur attacked.

Lord John's reaction was instinctive. He threw up his
blade to counter the count's body thrust. Steel rung against
steel.

The count laughed softly. He eased back, disengaging.
"You surprise me, milord. Somehow I had not expected
such speed of you." He shifted easily, alert for an opening.

Lord John circled with him. His heart pounded with the
flood of adrenaline in his veins. He knew that he had
narrowly escaped death in that single moment of inattention.
He would not allow his thoughts to wander again. "Perhaps I
intuitively expected your lack of honor, Comte. It is, after all,
gentlemen who salute with the blade."

The count shrugged in contempt. "You speak of codes
devised by cowards who must prepare themselves to face
cold steel. I am not so weak." He leapt and his sword
slashed viciously toward his enemy.

Lord John parried; then, whiplike, his blade wrapped
itself around his opponent's weapon. But the count disengaged with a flick of his wrist and jumped back. Lord
John smiled tightly at the flash of astonishment that
crossed de Chaleur's face. "I had excellent fencing
masters, monsieur. Perhaps the outcome shall not be as
simple as you expect."

The count's face darkened. "Perhaps, milord." He
closed the distance between them once more.

Sir Frederick could not remove his gaze from the lunging
fighters. "Will, break down that door and find Miss
Wyndham," he said.

The big man nodded and went to do as he was bid. He
looked in both bedrooms and reemerged to shake his head
at Sir Frederick's inquiry. "She bain't be 'ere," Will said,
troubled.

The air hissed with the flashing, darting blades. Steel
rang with staccato swiftness. The swordsmen lunged and
disengaged in a flowing, grotesque dance. The flurry of
blows was so fierce that Sir Frederick could no longer
make out the separate blades. The opponents' harsh
breathing filled the chamber. They thrust aside chairs and
overturned the table in their frenzy. With the crash of the
table the innkeeper and sundry others came on the run.

The innkeeper paled at sight of the combatants and
protested shrilly. Will and Sir Frederick forcibly thrust him
out of the room. Sir Frederick turned the key in the lock.
The innkeeper pleaded and beat on the door, threatening
to call for the local *gendarme*. Sir Frederick shouted at him
to do just that, and the crowd noise on the far side of the
door subsided.

A clatter brought Sir Frederick around. He saw that the
count had managed to knock Lord John's blade from his
hand and stepped back, the wild light in his eyes
triumphant. Lord John staggered back, one hand clamped
against his shoulder where the half-healed bullet wound
had been reopened.

"Now, milord. It is time." The count lunged at the dis-
armed man who braced himself to meet him.

An explosion filled the chamber. The Comte de Chaleur
staggered, then fell headlong. His sword fell from nerve-
less fingers. Lord John stared at him, then up at Sir
Frederick, who was calmly repocketing a smoking pistol.
Lord John's voice was a dry whisper. "That was terribly
unsporting of you, Freddy."

"I couldn't very well allow you to be murdered, John.
Sophia would never forgive me," said Sir Frederick
reasonably, going over to help him upright.

Lord John grinned. "You make the devil of a guardian
angel, Freddy. Have I thanked you yet?"

"No, but then I imagine your conscience will prod you
to it one day," said Sir Frederick. He examined Lord
John's shoulder and tied it off with his handkerchief.
"You'll do, John."

Will returned the walking stick to Lord John, who
thanked him. Then he asked, "How is Sophia?"

Will and Sir Frederick exchanged a quick glance. Sir Frederick hesitated. "She isn't here, John," he said reluctantly.

Lord John stared at him, appalled.

A ghost of a laugh drifted to them and as one they turned to find the Comte de Chaleur's malicious gaze upon them. His face was a ghastly white and death sat hard on his expression, yet he smiled.

"Damn your eyes, de Chaleur. Where is she?" said Lord John softly.

"The convent, milord." He saw the shock on their faces. The malice flared brighter in his eyes. He thought he knew how to exact his revenge. "I tired of her . . . quickly."

"You lie, de Chaleur." There was a white line drawn about Lord John's mouth.

The count gathered his strength for a last laugh. "I pity you, milord. You are a romantic fool." He sagged then and life slowly left his glazing eyes.

The two men stared down at the dead man a moment longer, mixed emotions warring within them. "If he were alive, I would cheerfully throttle him to death," said Lord John.

"Aye, he was a true villan," Sir Frederick said.

Lord John looked at his friend. "I hope fervently that he lied, Freddy." There was anguish in his eyes.

"We had best be about it, then," Sir Frederick said, removing the key from his waistcoat pocket and unlocking the door. The gentlemen started through, then paused at sight of the motley gathering of guests and inn employees in the hall. The innkeeper, who was in the forefront, craned his neck so that he could see past Lord John's shoulder. When he glimpsed the count's body, a strange look of relief crossed his face. He said faintly, "The monsieur . . . he is dead?"

Sir Frederick glanced swiftly toward Lord John, who had stiffened. "I shot him and I cannot regret his demise overmuch. The Comte de Chaleur forced a duel on his lordship here, who was known by the late count to be recovering from a grave accident."

The innkeeper nodded and there were murmurs among the crowd. "I believe it, milord. The monsieur was of a temper most formidable. He was a madman, that one. I am happy that you survived, milord."

Two of the waiters went into the room and matter-of-factly took hold of the count's body to carry it out.

"Can you direct us to the convent?" Lord John asked, anxious to be off.

"Ah, you have come for the madwoman," said the innkeeper, understanding at last.

"I beg your pardon?" asked Lord John, startled.

"The young mademoiselle who was with that one. My good wife, Yvette, swore that the mademoiselle did not like her so-called cousin. The monsieur said that the mademoiselle needed quiet because she suffered a disorder of the nerves. But my Yvette did not believe him. She was right," said the innkeeper with simple pride in his spouse.

"What happened to the mademoiselle?" asked Lord John impatiently.

"That is an odd thing, milord. This very morning the terrible monsieur ordered that her door be smashed open but she was gone, with the open shutter to tell the tale. The monsieur was wild then," said the innkeeper with an expressive shudder.

"I can well imagine," Lord John said dryly.

"*Oui*, and he shouted for the whole village to be searched and all questioned. Then Pierre, a good lad but slow, you understand, said he had seen a madwoman, her dress torn and twigs in her hair, outside the convent. The monsieur leapt on his black horse and was away in a cloud of dust. But he came back without the mademoiselle and in a rage most terrible," said the innkeeper.

"I do believe that the count may have lied once more, Freddy," said Lord John. He strode away down the hall.

Sir Frederick sighed in resignation and followed after him, Will bringing up the rear.

When Lord John and Sir Frederick walked outside, followed by Will, they found that Fedor and the Cossacks were waiting for them still. The dwarf appraised the Englishmen with a swift glance and nodded in satisfaction that they were unhurt. "It is well. We have seen the count's body. Now we return to my master with our report."

Sir Frederick exchanged a swift glance with Lord John, then said, "But are you not curious about Miss Wyndham?"

Fedor's expression was fleetingly amused. "I have no instructions regarding the lady. Good-bye, milords." With a sharp word to the Cossacks, he wheeled his mount and led off the horsemen at a swift canter.

The villagers who stood about watched them go, murmuring.

"Well, what do you make of that?" asked Sir Frederick, stupified. "I thought Prince Kirov wanted to take Sophia back."

"Undoubtedly he does, but he neglected to express it to his obedient lieutenant. Fedor has made us a present of time, Freddy. Let us use it well," said Lord John. He mounted his horse, wincing a little at the twinge of pain in his shoulder.

Beside him, Will climbed awkwardly into his own saddle. He did not care much for riding, but he was game enough to keep pace with the guvnor.

"Do you know, John, I no longer envy those knight-fellows their glorious quests and their brave deeds," said Sir Frederick as he also mounted.

"Why is that, Freddy?" asked Lord John, glancing at him curiously as they started off.

"If a knight's quest was anything like our recent adventures, he missed the comforts of life." Sir Frederick sighed mournfully. "What I wouldn't give for a hearty dinner, a fine bottle of claret, and a soft bed."

Lord John laughed and spurred his mount. "Come along, Freddy. We'll soon have Sophia safe and then you'll feel altogether differently."

"Too true, for then we shall have Prince Kirov and his fiendish Cossacks in pursuit," said Sir Frederick. Lord John only grinned and Freddy had a sudden moment of insight. "By Jove! I do believe you are enjoying this romp!"

"A little," admitted Lord John.

"You are stark staring mad," said Sir Frederick with finality.

The three horsemen arrived at the convent. Will suggested that he hold the horses while Lord John and Sir Frederick went inside. The gentlemen were shown to a small room, and the abbess was informed that Mademoiselle Sophia had visitors. The abbess remembered what the count had said and she asked the nun who brought the message what these visitors looked like. The two gentlemen were described as one being a tall, fair man and the other as shorter and dark-haired. The abbess was satisfied then that the count had indeed returned and had brought with him the tall cousin that Sophia had spoken of.

Without granting an interview to the gentlemen, the abbess sent word that Sophia was not receiving guests that day. Lord John and Sir Frederick looked at each other in astonishment. They had no choice but to leave the convent without being able to speak to Sophia.

The abbess later told Sophia of her visitors. Sophia was also certain that the gentlemen were Prince Kirov and the Comte de Chaleur, though it puzzled her greatly that Prince Kirov should have made his peace so easily with the man who had betrayed him. Sophia gratefully thanked the abbess, who told her also that her letters to the British embassy and her relatives had been sent on their way. Sophia had only to remain where she was, safe within the confines of the convent, and wait for the Wyndhams to arrive.

Lord John and Sir Frederick were both astonished and disturbed by their rebuff at the convent. For several days thereafter they made the daily pilgrimage to inquire if Sophia would accept visitors, but each time the answer was the same, gentle and final.

"We are getting nowhere with this, John. We have been kicking our heels for days," said Sir Frederick in frustration.

"Yes, I know. I don't know why Sophia is not receiving visitors, but it must have something to do with her treatment at the count's hands," said Lord John, at last voicing the thought that had haunted him. His jaw tightened. "I must see her, Freddy, and let her know that we are still her friends, that we care for her despite whatever may have happened."

"Perhaps Sophia simply has a touch of a cold, John," said Sir Frederick unconvincingly.

"I hope it is nothing worse than that," said Lord John grimly. He could not help but wonder what the Comte de Chaleur might have done to Sophia.

Sir Frederick sighed and stood up to stretch with bone-popping satisfaction. "There's nothing for it, then. I'll go to the British embassy in Paris and send word off immediately by diplomatic packet to the Wyndhams. The letter will get to them faster that way than by regular post. They at least might have a chance in getting past that blasted receiving room. I will be back as soon as I am able."

Lord John stood in his turn and pressed his friend's shoulder. "Thank you, Freddy. And you understand why I cannot myself leave?"

Sir Frederick nodded. He flashed a quick grin. "Pray keep a level head about you when that Russian arrives. He's not a bad sort, only more hotheaded than he ought to be. But you'll be safe enough with Will beside you, I'll warrant."

"Indeed, and so do I," said Lord John dryly, and glanced into the public taproom at Will, who had begun to pick up a few words of French and had quickly established friendship with a big Frenchman due to his arm-wrestling expertise.

Sir Frederick laughed as they walked out of the inn. He called for his horse. "You know, I was a bit cast down when it dawned on me that Sophia had eyes for no one but you. But since then it has been forcibly borne in on me that a fickle heart in love is much more comfortable than one steadfast and true."

Lord John laughed. He raised his hand in farewell as Sir Frederick mounted. But before Freddy had wheeled his horse and left the inn yard, a dust-covered coach swept through the narrow gate and rolled up to the inn. The coach window was let down and a gentleman put out his head. "Pardon me, but could you tell me if this . . . 'Pon my word, it is Lord John and Sir Frederick. My Lord!"

27

LORD JOHN was startled to hear his name called. He was even more astonished to recognize the gentleman in the coach. "Mr. Wyndham, sir! Freddy, look who is here." He strode over to open the coach door.

Sir Frederick stared a moment, then grinned. He dismounted and called for a stablehand to take his horse back to the stables. He walked over to the coach as Charles Wyndham helped Matilda down. "What a stroke of luck. I shan't have to miss my dinner, after all," he said.

Lord John grinned. He addressed the Wyndhams. "It is a rare pleasure to see you both. But how did you know where to come? Freddy was but this moment going to ride to the British embassy so that we could send word by diplomatic packet. We neither of us thought you would be in France."

"Quite. I distinctly recall that you were remaining in London," said Sir Frederick sternly.

Matilda slipped her hand into Sir Frederick's arm. "Pray do not scold us too much, Sir Frederick. We waited in London as long as we could."

"Aye. We waited until that Kirov fellow decided it was time to leave England. Then we followed his trail in hopes that he would lead us to Sophia. And now the hunt is nearly over," said Charles with grim satisfaction.

Lord John exchanged a glance with Sir Frederick. "Let us go into the inn. I shall ask the innkeeper to bring us refreshment." The Wyndhams agreed that this was a fine idea. The group was ensconced comfortably in a private parlor and were brought small finger sandwiches with lemonades to drink.

Lord John leaned back in his chair. "Now, tell us how

you happened to come to this village. I am very curious to discover how you knew that Sophia is here."

"Then you have seen her?" Matilda asked quickly.

Lord John shook his head. "Miss Wyndham took refuge in the nunnery and has refused our attempts to visit with her."

Matilda was astonished. "But how odd. You are her dearest friends."

"You must remember that the poor girl has been through a great deal, Tilda. She is probably still hysterical over her escape from that cur, the Comte de Chaleur," said charles. "That is one blackguard that I wish to get my hands on."

"You need not concern yourself with the count. Sir Frederick and I settled accounts with him several days ago," said Lord John quietly. He met Charles Wyndham's astonished glance.

The older man nodded, a faint smile on his lips.

"But how do you know about de Chaleur?" asked Sir Frederick.

Charles smiled at Sir Frederick's astonishment. "When Tilda and I ran Kirov to ground at the château, we realized that we could not ourselves rescue Sophia. So naturally we went to the British embassy, where there was a letter for us from Sophia. A day later and we would have missed it completely as it was due to go to London in the first packet."

"Sophia explained everything about the count," said Matilda. She smiled at Lord John and Sir Frederick with tears in her eyes. "I know that when Sophia realizes how much you have done on her behalf, she will be very grateful. For myself and Charles, I can truthfully say that we are overwhelmed by your kindness in aiding her." The gentlemen bowed, acknowledging her gratitude. Matilda turned to Charles and laid her fingers on his sleeve. "My dear, I should like to go see Sophia now."

"Of course. We shall go immediately," Charles said. The Wyndhams rose. Charles addressed Lord John and Sir Frederick. "Tilda has the right of it, gentlemen. We stand in your debt."

"It has been an extraordinary adventure. I doubt if I shall ever embark on another so blithely," said Sir Frederick, raising a laugh from the company.

"Sir, if you and Mrs. Wyndham do not object, I should like to accompany you to the convent," said Lord John.

"Of course. We would not have it any other way," said Charles.

The party went downstairs to the inn yard. Lord John collected Will from the taproom while Sir Frederick called for their horses.

The Wyndhams reentered their carriage for the short trip to the convent while the three horsemen rode alongside. When the party reached the gate at the convent, Charles announced their names to the nun who answered the bell, and requested that they be allowed to see Miss Wyndham. The nun's eyes widened. She immediately showed the visitors inside and courteously asked the visitors to wait, while she left the room.

"This has been the sticking point for us," said Sir Frederick.

Lord John looked at him.

It was but a few moments later when the nun returned and requested the party to follow her. The hall the visitors crossed was quiet and echoed with their footsteps. At the far end of the hall the nun opened a door and gestured for the Wyndhams and the three Englishmen to enter. They did so and found the abbess awaiting them, Sophia at her side.

Lord John took a hasty step forward. Sir Frederick blocked his way. "Not now, John," he said quietly.

Sophia and Matilda rushed to embrace each other, exclaiming tearfully. When they at last parted, Sophia threw herself into her uncle's waiting arms. "Oh, Uncle Charles!"

He smoothed her hair. "There, my dear. It is all over. We shall take you home."

Sophia straightened, but held on to his lapel. "Oh, how thankful I am that you and my aunt have come," she said, dashing away glad tears.

"Of course we came. We love you a great deal, dear Sophia," said Matilda tenderly.

Charles agreed in a voice gruff with emotion.

"And who might you gentlemen be?" asked the abbess, looking at the three men who had hung back from the reunion. Two of the gentlemen looked suspiciously like those who had been described to her as the men who had earlier attempted to visit the mademoiselle.

Sophia turned, curious. For the first time she noticed Lord John and Sir Frederick. "Oh!" She flew across the room to meet them, laughing and crying. "Oh, Freddy!" She held out her hands to him, but he ignored them and caught her up in a friendly embrace.

"We are too good friends to stand on ceremony, Sophia," he said, and kissed her roundly.

Sophia emerged laughing from Sir Frederick's embrace. Her eyes sparkled with life. She turned at last to the gentleman who stood by so quietly and watched her with a curiously intent gaze. "Lord John," she said, almost shyly.

Lord John took the hand that she offered him, but drew her up close to his chest. He did not care any longer that there were others in the room. His blue eyes were warm. "We, too, should not stand on ceremony any longer, Sophia," he said softly.

Sophia colored, completely enthralled by the intensity of his gaze. She waited breathlessly as Lord John slowly bent his head to find her soft lips. Willingly she lifted her face to meet him.

Her aunt and uncle exchanged a quick glance. "Well, Tilda, it appears that we shall be having a wedding," said Charles.

The abbess was a little shocked. It astonished her that the English could express passion in so public a manner and that the mademoiselle's relations were so blasé. Slightly flustered, she turned to Sir Frederick. "I must apologize, sir. I realized but moments ago that it was you and this other gentleman who in days past attempted to see Mademoiselle Wyndham. I had assumed from the des-

criptions given to me that you were the men that
mademoiselle had fled from.''

Sir Frederick was somewhat offended. "My dear
ma'am! I assure you that I and Lord John do not bear the
slightest resemblance to Prince Kirov and the Comte de
Chaleur,'' he said.

The abbess laughed. When she spoke, her voice was
gentle. "As I told you, the gentlemen were described to me
in only a vague way. I did not expect mademoiselle to have
the friendship of two such gallant heroes.'' Sir Frederick
was mollified by the abbess's flattery. The abbess turned to
the Wyndhams in an invitation. "May I offer you all
refreshment? We have an excellent wine from our own
humble vineyard.''

Matilda cast an indulgent eye on her niece, who still
stood within the circle of Lord John's arms, her golden
head now resting on his broad shoulder. "What a wonderful notion. If we may just repair to another room?''

The abbess took her meaning, and with a glance at Lord
John and Mademoiselle Wyndham, she agreed. But before
she could lead the way out of the room, the door was
thrust open. Prince Kirov strode in, one arm in a sling. He
was followed by Fedor and a few of his men.

A young nun ran behind the prince and she hurried to
the abbess's side. "Mother, forgive me. I did try to stop
them,'' she said, greatly upset.

The abbess laid a protective arm about her shoulders.
"It is all right, Sister Jeanne,'' she said. She looked sternly
at the huge man who dominated the room. She knew now
what Sir Frederick had said was true. No one could have
mistaken this giant's identity.

"Misha!'' Sophia was incredibly happy to see that he
had not been killed by the count, but then she remembered
why he had followed her. The welcoming light went out of
her eyes. "I shall not go with you, Misha.''

Charles Wyndham stepped in front of Sophia,
effectively blocking her from view. "I shall not stand idly
by and allow my niece to be abducted once more,'' he said
shortly. He opened his coat to reveal the butt of a pistol

and he laid his hand on it. There was a hard look in his eyes.

"Uncle Charles," exclaimed Sophia, stepping around him.

Her aunt caught hold of her arm and firmly pulled her back. "There is nothing more that can be said, Sophia," said Matilda urgently.

Lord John and Sir Frederick ranged themselves beside Charles Wyndham. Will took up a stance close by and flexed his hands. He studied the Russians with a knowing eye and chose his man. Lord John twisted the top of his walking stick and released the hidden sword, tossing aside the hollow stick. Sir Frederick brought his pistol out of his pocket.

The young nun began to sob and fell to her knees, clutching at the abbess's habit. The abbess laid hold of the crucifix about her neck and spoke urgently to the nun. "Pray as you have never prayed before, Sister Jeanne."

The tense tableau was suspended for several moments. Prince Kirov stared into the eyes of each of the men who faced him and read their union and steady purpose. He threw back his head and laughed.

"The fellow has a queer sense of humor," said Sir Frederick feelingly.

"Stand firm, sir. It is a trick," said Charles Wyndham.

Lord John did not say anything, but waited, his eyes narrowed on Prince Kirov and those with him.

Prince Kirov directed a flourishing bow to the abbess and the young nun beside her. "Forgive me if I have frightened you or given you cause for offense. I vow by all that is holy that you shall not have cause to regret this day," he said with a grave smile.

After a moment's hesitation, the abbess nodded wary acceptance.

Prince Kirov again turned his gaze on the Englishmen. He waved his hand at them. "Put away your weapons, gentlemen. I have no desire for bloodletting. Sophia is free to do as she wishes. It is no longer necessary that she return to Russia."

Charles Wyndham and Sir Frederick stared at him in suspicious disbelief.

"Why have you changed your mind?" asked Lord John shortly.

Prince Kirov looked at him. There was amusement in his eyes. "I received word that Sophia's intended is dead. The honor of the family is satisfied. My little cousin is free to do as she wishes."

Sophia slowly came forward to stand between Lord John and her uncle. "Prince Tarkovich is dead? But how can that be?"

"The prince choked on a bonbon," said Prince Kirov.

Sir Frederick whooped with laughter. He put away his pistol. "That story is just ludicrous enough for me to believe it," he said.

Matilda joined her husband. He looked down at her. "I am at once relieved and disappointed, Tilda. Isn't that odd?"

"Never mind, Charles," she said.

"Misha, I want you to know that I still intend to remain in England, despite Prince Tarkovich's death," said Sophia sternly.

"I understand, Sophia. My heart bleeds in sympathy for you. What does Russia hold for you now? But you have found a new home with your English kindred and I give you permission to remain with them," said Prince Kirov graciously.

"You are too good," said Sophia, irony in her voice. She did not dare meet Lord John's eyes. She knew that he would be sharing her amusement and she feared that she would not be able to suppress her laughter once she looked at him.

"There is only one thing that I must scold you for, Sophia," said Prince Kirov. She raised her brows inquiringly and he shook his head. "A diplomatic protest was lodged with the czar by your English friends. Surely there was no need to bother him with our family disagreement, Sophia."

"By Jove, it worked," said Sir Frederick, absurdly pleased.

Prince Kirov turned to Lord John. "Fedor told me that you met with the Comte de Chaleur. I regret his death."

"I trust that it will not interfere in establishing a friendly relationship between us," Lord John said.

Prince Kirov shrugged. "Of course not. I only wished to reach him first. You understand, milord."

"Of course," said Lord John. There was the barest quiver in his voice. Sophia heard it and she laughed at him. Lord John struggled a half-second, then he also laughed.

Still laughing, Sophia held out her hand to her cousin. "I shall miss you, Misha. Even though you tried so hard to ruin my life."

"I am not done yet, little cousin," said Prince Kirov.

Sophia stared up at him, suspiciously wondering what he could possibly mean. With great ceremony Prince Kirov placed her hand in Lord John's. Sophia blushed fiercely.

"I entrust my cousin Sophia to your care, milord. Be warned that she will lead you a pretty dance. I suspect that she will be the better for a beating now and then," said Prince Kirov gravely.

Sophia did not know where to look.

Lord John glanced down at her averted face. He felt her fingers tremble in his hand and smiled tenderly. When he looked up to meet Prince Kirov's gaze, he said with equal gravity, "I am touched by your trust, Prince Kirov. You may certainly rely upon me to keep a close rein upon Miss Wyndham."

Sir Frederick clapped Prince Kirov on the shoulder. "Well done, Prince Kirov! You will come to the nuptials, I trust. It will be a fabulous affair, I swear."

"Freddy!" exclaimed Sophia, painfully embarrassed. She was keenly aware of Lord John's hand on hers and she could feel his intense gaze on her face even though she would not meet his eyes. Her protest was lost amid the well wishes of her aunt and uncle.

"I will unfortunately not be returning to England. There are matters in Russia that I must attend to," said Prince Kirov, his thoughts centered on his mother. He had decided that it was past time to take an active role in the affairs of the Kirov family. Since his father's death his

mother had directed all and she had very nearly led the
family to disaster with this business over his cousin Sophia.

"That is a pity. We must explore this problem to the
fullest, Prince Kirov. I know that the Wyndhams will have
something to say about it. Abbess, is there a room where
we might together hold our discussion?" said Sir
Frederick.

The abbess acknowledged that there was another
chamber. Within seconds Sir Frederick had led everyone
from the receiving room and gently closed the door,
leaving Sophia and Lord John alone.

Lord John still retained her hand. He brought her
fingers to his lips. "It appears that another marriage is
being arranged for you, Miss Wyndham," he said.

"Is it?" said Sophia softly, her breath suspended as she
looked up into his blue eyes.

"I offer myself as your bridegroom. It seems to be
somewhat expected of me," said Lord John with a half-
smile.

Sophia felt the light go out of her heart. She had thought
he meant to declare his love for her. She had waited and
hoped for him to do so for so long. It was a bitter pill for
her to realize that he was guided still by his gentleman's
code. His sense of honor had initially led him to step aside
when he believed Sir Frederick was serious about her. Now
he offered her marriage, not for love but because it was
expected that he do the decent thing by her.

Sophia freed her hand from his and turned away so that
she would not have to meet his eyes. "Nonsense, my lord. I
realize that any number of people must by now be aware of
my disappearance. My reputation is naturally ruined and
can only be salvaged by a quick marriage. But you have no
obligation to me," she said quietly. She took a breath and
forced a smile to her lips as she turned. "Indeed, I can
return to Russia with Misha and it will not matter what is
said in London. Perhaps I will visit England again one
day."

Lord John stared at her, appalled by what she was
saying. She had actually taken his teasing in earnest. He
realized that she had gone through too much to recognize

his true intent. Sophia curtsied to him and began to walk away. It came to Lord John in a flash that if she was allowed to walk out of the room, he would lose her forever. He moved swiftly.

Sophia gasped as Lord John caught her up hard in his arms. Then his mouth descended on hers and he kissed her hungrily. All thoughts winged out of her mind and she could feel only the demands of his lips. When Lord John at last allowed her to emerge from his embrace, Sophia was no longer in doubt of his passion for her. She buried her head against his shoulder, and her fingers clutched his lapel. "Oh, John."

Lord John held her away from him so that he could smile into her eyes. "You are sometimes very foolish, Sophia. I love you with a passion as great as life itself."

"Are you certain, John? Do you really wish to marry me?" asked Sophia tremulously.

"I would not have twice almost gotten myself killed dueling over you or chased you halfway across Europe if I intended to let you marry anyone else," said Lord John.

"I suppose that is true," said Sophia. She sighed happily as she settled once more against his shoulder. Then she raised her head again as a thought occurred to her. "But what of my reputation? You know what will be said. Your career surely cannot stand for such scandal, my lord."

"We shall be respectably married at the British embassy in Paris, where, by the by, I have been appointed. As for my career, I believe marriage will but sharpen my diplomatic skills," said Lord John. His eyes laughed at her.

"How do you mean, my lord?" asked Sophia, eyeing him suspiciously.

He caught her up so suddenly that she gasped. His breath warmed her upturned face. "Dearest Sophia, diplomacy is but the subtlest form of seduction," he said.

"John!" She tried to loose herself but found that he could be quite ruthless when he chose.

Lord John imprisoned her chin with one hand and once more took possession of her mouth. Sophia slid her arms around his neck and happily acceded to the demands of his lips.

COMING IN APRIL 1988

Vanessa Gray
Lady of Property

Dawn Lindsey
A Proper Proposal

Ellen Fitzgerald
Julia's Portion

The New Super Regency by
Mary Balogh
Secrets of the Heart

 SIGNET REGENCY ROMANCE